PRAISE FOR
ARE YOU STILL THERE

"An intriguing mix of a whodunit and social commentary on the tragic and all-too-common problems of bullying and teen suicide."—*Kirkus Reviews*

"The pacing moves quickly...Reluctant readers will stay with this one as they try to figure out who really planted the bomb." —*School Library Journal*

"Scheerger establishes an authentic high-school environment in which, despite the fact that student bullying is understood, nothing concrete has been achieved to curb it, and plenty of bystanders look on helplessly. Gripping and timely."—*Booklist*

"This is an interesting premise with a gripping, edge-of-your-seat ending."—*VOYA*

Are You Still There

SARAH LYNN SCHEERGER

Albert Whitman & Company
Chicago, Illinois

For my parents, Nancy and Larry—
thank you for always being there.

Library of Congress Cataloging-in-Publication
data is on file with the publisher.

Text copyright © 2015 by Sarah Lynn Scheerger
Hardcover edition published in 2015 by Albert Whitman & Company
Paperback edition published in 2016 by Albert Whitman & Company
ISBN 978-0-8075-0438-3

Printed in the United States of America
10 9 8 7 6 5 4 3 2 1 LB 20 19 18 17 16

Design by Jordan Kost
Cover images © Dawn D. Hanna/Getty Images, Shutterstock.com

For more information about Albert Whitman & Company,
visit our web site at www.albertwhitman.com.

Stranger's Manifesto
Entry 1

I am a speck of dust
Invisible to the naked eye—
Unless the sun glances against me just so
And you see for a moment
That I am one of many.
Flecks. Floaters. Dust parachutes.
Dirt in the air.
Do you know
That you are bumping into me?
That you are surrounded by me?
That you are breathing me?
And then you are contaminated.
Infected by what is me.
We are not so different,
You and I.
You just don't know it
Yet.

1

EARLY OCTOBER

Barefoot, I step onto the cold toilet seat in the girls' bathroom and it doesn't even gross me out. I'd shoved my clunky sandals in my backpack an hour ago when this whole thing started. I knew I might have to hide. And if I had to hide, I couldn't make a sound. My life depended on it.

Somebody is coming.

I hold on to the side of the stall to brace myself and try not to breathe. Well, try not to breathe loudly. *Don't panic*, I tell myself. *It's probably just a drill*. Maybe the resource officer is running around checking that all the teachers locked their doors, according to protocol. Maybe Principal Bowen's voice will come back on the loudspeaker and tell us the lockdown has been lifted. That this was just a drill, and we all passed it with flying colors.

Even me. The idiot who picked the wrong time to pee. That's why I'm stuck in this bathroom instead of hiding under a desk like everyone else at Central High. I can still hear the echo of Principal Bowen's words, "Students, if you're not already in a classroom at this time, do not attempt to return to one. You will be putting yourself at risk of harm. Stay put and take cover." But exactly how do you take cover in a public bathroom?

Just a drill, just a drill, just a drill, I promise myself. But drills last fifteen minutes, max. They rush us through the protocol so that we can get back to the important business of solving quadratic equations and dissecting fetal pigs. It's been way more than fifteen minutes. I've been hiding in the girls' bathroom for over an hour.

I hear them again. Shushing footsteps against the concrete. Like someone's trying to sneak up on me. Since the whole world has been flipped to mute, the shushing seems loud. My heart beats in my ears. Pulsing, thudding, pumping…echoing through my body. We used to make fun of my sister, Chloe, for saying strange things like that when she was little. "My elbow's hungry," she'd say. "My nose is afraid." "My pinky toe wants a turn."

Only now the thoughts of Chloe grip me and make the pulsing, thudding, pumping of my heart stop so suddenly that the blood pools in my veins. Because I know Chloe's stuck somewhere on campus right now too. Hiding.

If she's still alive.

* * *

I pee in my pants. Just a little. Not enough to soak through my jeans. But still. I haven't done that since elementary. The shushing footsteps pass me by, move on down the hall, and I relax for a moment. Big mistake. Because that's when I pee.

How ironic that here I am, standing in the girls' bathroom, hiding out, and here, of all places, I pee in my pants. I've been holding it since I got here. Because I got all freaked out about peeing. Like it'd make too much noise.

It's been boring. I won't lie. My legs ache and my mouth is desert dry. All I can do is think, so it's driving me crazy. Because I know how this plays out. I've watched the news. I've debated gun control laws in AP government. Some crazy kid with a revenge agenda plows down fifteen innocent students.

But *I'm* not supposed to be on this end of it. I've already sent in my early action application to my top-five colleges and everything. I'm the kind of kid that's supposed to be going somewhere in this world. Not the kind of kid to die in a bathroom stall.

Shushing steps. Many of them. They're in the bathroom now. I can hear them breathing. They can hear me breathing. It is then that I realize something that sucks more than anything has ever sucked in the history of my seventeen years of life. *This is not a drill. And I'm gonna die. On a grimy public bathroom floor.*

The door to the bathroom stall slams inward. If I had not been standing on the toilet seat, it probably would have broken my nose. I grip the walls, paralyzed, and stare at the three cops pointing guns in my face.

They haul me off the toilet and pat me down, but I think they can tell right away that I'm not who they're looking for. Maybe my tear-streaked face and blackout-worthy hyperventilation gives me away.

"Come with me," the bald-headed cop whispers, grabbing onto my arm. "Don't speak. Just walk quietly. We're still in a lockdown situation."

I walk with him because, come on, what am I going to do? Argue? He has my arm gripped so tightly that my fingers are losing circulation. He is ushering me toward an evacuation point and I think he's more nervous than I am. I wonder if he knows who my dad is. Most cops do.

This is the real deal. No drill for sure. The air feels thin, like we've somehow gained hundreds of feet in altitude and I can't get enough oxygen in my brain.

The bright Southern California sunlight blinds me with rays, and I squint. The campus is so quiet it has that eerie ghost-town feel. Maybe it's the stress, but the corners of the buildings blur as I pass them, as if they're all part of a painting and the artist is smearing the edges.

I hope I don't pass out.

* * *

We all gather on the far end of the football field. Clustering like frightened refugees, huddling together for warmth because even though this October day is seventy-five degrees and clear, my bones are cold.

My ears are malfunctioning. Everything I hear is blunted, far away. Like I'm underwater. *Bomb found on campus after anonymous tip. Bomb has been disarmed successfully. Police will conduct a thorough investigation. Safety precaution. Everyone will be released to guardians. One by one. Procedure will take hours. Be patient. Stay calm.*

Everyone is milling about, stunned. I've gone to school with some of these kids since elementary, but in this moment I only care about one. I scan the crowds, searching for the purple streak in my sister's thick, black hair. She's got the kind of hair that tangles easily, so she only brushes it when she first gets out of the shower and it's all conditioned up. She's been wanting to cut it for at least a year, but Mom says short hair will make her face look too full, so Chloe settled for dying it black. Mom was not happy.

Back before the hair dyeing, people used to call us Irish twins. Thick, wavy red hair, green eyes with hazel flecks. People call Chloe's natural color "strawberry," but that makes no sense if you really think about it. Strawberries are truly red. Her hair is more the color of freckles. So Mom got all pissy when she dyed

4

it black. The purple streak was just icing on the cake. How so totally Chloe. Same as sticking out her tongue with a big fat "Screw You" pierced through it.

Chloe's shirt finds me before her face does. All black, but with little-kid rounded yellow letters. *Pooh is my homeboy.* As much as I'd tried to talk her out of it when I first saw her ordering that shirt on the Internet, for a moment I love Pooh. And Piglet and Tigger and everyone else in the Hundred Acre Wood.

Her face is red. That dark-dark mascara and eyeliner combo has smeared down into the hollows of her eyes, making her look like a Halloween character back from the dead. I run like I'm in a movie—all slow motion and hair flapping behind me—and bear-hug her, and she squeezes me back and buries her face in my neck.

"Gabi," she whispers, her breath smelling like red licorice, "I thought I'd never see you again."

I try not to cry and then I'm crying anyway, holding on to her like she might turn to sand and slip through my fingers.

And then it comes to me. I don't think we've hugged like this since we were little girls.

2

Mom's chin goes all taut when she's tense. She's thin anyway, but when she juts her chin forward, her skin has to stretch further and her whole face looks tight. Like an ad for plastic surgery gone wrong.

Chloe and I have parked ourselves at the kitchen table, eating grapes. "We're okay, Mom. Relax. It's over," Chloe tells her and pops a couple grapes in her mouth. She never washed off the black makeup, so I can't look straight into her eyes.

Mom sits perched on the edge of the kitchen chair, looking like a nervous little bluebird. "Dad won't be home until late tonight. They've called him out to the school to help with the investigation." She clasps her hands together and flexes and un-flexes her fingers. I'm tempted to reach over and place my hands on hers to make her stop, but I don't.

"Okay, so Dad might get blown to smithereens, but he's not around much anyway, so we won't really notice." Chloe gets this ridiculous half-smirk on her face like she thinks she's hilarious. I kick her under the table. Mom's hands flex. Un-flex.

"The whole thing's probably just a hoax, Mom. Some stupid freshman on a dare," I tell her, pulling a grape off the vine.

"Hey, hey!" Chloe complains. "Don't knock freshman. Frosh rock."

"Sorry. I forgot your boyfriend is a freshman," I tease.

She throws a grape at me. It bounces off my shoulder. Mom's not supposed to know Chloe has this thing for a little stoner boy... He's actually her age but he got held back a grade. Quality dating material. She always picks winners.

"Oh. Uh, just kidding." I mouth "sorry" to her when Mom isn't looking.

Mom stands, her chin still stretched tight. "It's late. I guess you'd better get dressed for clinic, Gab." Flex. Un-flex.

Clinic. The low-fee medical clinic, my volunteer opportunity because it looks good for college apps. My stomach drops fast and hard. Don't I deserve the day off?

"Uh. I don't think my head's in the game today, Mom. I'd rather just stay home with you guys." *Plus*, I want to scream, *I've already submitted my top-five early action apps*. Mom wants me to get into Georgetown University in the worst way. She had a brief stint there herself, but she dropped out junior year to marry my dad. I have no idea why she didn't just finish her units in California when they moved here.

Not being conceited or anything, but my chances of getting in (to at least one of my top-five schools) are pretty high, what with my four AP classes, my rocking GPA and SAT scores, my place on the cross-country team, and my dizzying array of life-broadening volunteer experiences. Just saying.

Mom nods too fast, like she is disappointed but doesn't want me to know. "Oh. Okay. Can they manage without you?"

"Yeah," I say slowly, my stomach dropping again but knowing I will go. Because it's the "right thing" to do. Good little Gabi Mallory, always does the right thing. Dependable. Responsible.

Disciplined. Boring, yes, and social life submerged in the toilet...but destined for success, preferably at an elite East Coast school. *Yuck.*

Mom nods again, and I can see her breathe a tiny sigh of relief. She's seriously got this internal master plan for me, and if I don't follow the Perfect and Elite-University-Destined Daughter rule book to a *T*, she thinks the world will crumble into dust.

I look at Chloe and set my grapes on the table. The black mess under her eyes is ugly but intriguing. She looks like a model for some kind of creepy artistic magazine.

"Oh, stay home. Rebel a little!" Chloe advises, her smirk back full force. "It'll make your boobs grow."

"Very funny."

* * *

I survive a four-hour shift at the clinic. Then I run on the treadmill (while listening to an audiotape of my AP government textbook) for fifty minutes. *Good girl, Gabi.*

I'm toweling my hair dry from my post-run shower when my cell vibrates on my dresser. I peek. Gabi, are you there? It's my bestie and study buddy extraordinaire, Beth.

Yea. Just got back from clinic.

Can you believe today?

Not really.

Me neither. I'm not going to school tomorrow.

Seriously? You never miss school.

There's a first for everything. What's detective daddy say about all this?

Don't know. I think he just got home. I'll go eavesdrop.

I like the way you think.

I tiptoe over to the banister and lean against it. Little drips of water roll down my back from my still-wet hair.

My parents' voices are low, rumbling, like they don't want anyone to hear. Of course this makes me even more curious. "…clear message," Dad is saying, his voice tired and soft. "…professional job." Dad must be facing away from the stairs, because it's hard to make out his words. Or maybe he just doesn't want me or my sister to hear. "Took our best guys over an hour to ensure the bomb we found was disarmed."

"Do they think it was a staff member?" Mom's voice, somehow much clearer, and with a sharp edge. I can just imagine Mom facing him, arms crossed, demanding information.

"…not ruling it out…"

"Who else could it be? Who would want to do such a thing?"

"…looking into it…full investigation…possibly ex-employees or ex-students…could even be a current student, but the sophistication of the layout makes that unlikely…You never know though. Some of these kids are really bright."

I creep down the top two stairs to hear better. I can see the light reflecting off Dad's bald head. He's still wearing his work clothes, which look a lot more like business clothes since he got promoted to lead detective.

Mom sighs and suddenly she sounds tired too. "Between this situation today, that note you found, and that poor girl who hanged herself after all that teasing, I'm beginning to think private school is a better option."

Note? What note?

Wait—private school? No way! My ankle cracks as I shift my position.

Dad pauses for a moment but doesn't turn. He's no longer whispering. "Listen, Susan, these things happen at many large high schools. Westmont High had a suicide last year and

9

a big drunk-driving accident with all those cheerleaders. And Blackbury had that six-hour lockdown last semester when there was a domestic shooting in the neighborhood. When you've got two thousand people on the same campus, you get exposed to all walks of life. It happens everywhere."

"You're not comparing apples to apples, Al, and you know it." Mom's voice sharpens. "What happened today is of a whole different caliber. This wasn't just a bomb threat. There was an actual bomb on campus. We could've lost both our girls in one afternoon!"

I rest my head on the banister. My temples are starting to throb.

"Let's not overreact. I don't think this guy actually wanted to harm anyone."

"How the hell do you know?"

I need to take some aspirin. I rub my fingers against the sides of my head.

"This is what I do for a living, Suze. If this guy wanted to blow the place to smithereens, he would've. He *chose* not to. He carefully orchestrated the whole setup so that the bomb *wouldn't* go off. He wanted to send a message."

"Why do you keep saying 'he'?"

"Because nearly every perpetrator of school violence has been male. I study this crap, hon. I know what I'm doing."

"It's just…"

Suddenly his voice softens. "I know you were scared today." I peek down and see him wrapping his arm around her shoulders. He's facing me now, and I shrink back against the banister. "I was too. But early tomorrow morning I'm going to meet with the assistant principals, and we've got some plans about how to proceed."

"What do you mean?"

"That part is highly confidential. But the school realizes they need to do some preventive outreach. The bomb threat and the note were warnings. We've got to catch this guy, and until we do, we have to hold him off by showing him his message was heard."

"How exactly do you plan to do that?"

"Confidential."

"Since when has that stopped you?"

"There are ears everywhere." He dips his head to the right, toward where I am crouched, my hair dripping down and soaking into the carpet.

Damn. Sometimes I hate having a detective for a father.

Stranger's Manifesto
Entry 2

Every year it takes the teachers until winter break
To learn my name.
That's why I call myself *Stranger.*
I am a stranger. To everyone.
Because *no one* knows me.
Or notices me.
Because I don't act like the whiz or the dunce or the shit-talker or
the bully.
Because I listen.
Because I turn in homework.
Because I don't draw demented pictures with guns and blood.
Or carve up my arms.
Or smell like weed or cloves or spice.
Or tweak around and pick at my skin.
Or tag or bang.
So they don't see me either.
No one sees me.
The invisible dust parachute.
Just wait.
They will notice me soon.

3

First thing in the morning, the school sends an administrator to each homeroom. Mine is calculus. Goal—to calm everyone down. It does the opposite. Administrators don't come to hang out in math class unless the world is ending.

Dr. Paisley stands in front of my class and clears her throat. She wears a long braid down her back, with a loose, flowy top and peace-sign earrings. She looks like a hippie love child stuck in the wrong decade. Paisley smiles. "Okay, folks, why do you think I'm here to talk to you all?"

We all know why she's here. But there isn't anything she can say to make us forget about what happened. At least half the seats are empty today. I look around and wait for someone to answer. I feel a little nauseous.

Garth Johnson shifts his massive upper torso in his seat. He looks like the dad in *The Incredibles*—not when he's retired, but when he's in good shape. "You're here to get us to talk about what happened yesterday. Obviously."

"You got it." Paisley points her finger at him. She reminds me of that old-fashioned "I Want YOU for the U.S. Army" poster. "But I'm also here to talk about how to improve our school.

Generally when something like this happens on a school campus, some students knew about it beforehand."

I need water. I am definitely on my way to being sick.

This little pipsqueak kid, Simon or Steven or something, raises his hand. "You're saying there are kids on campus who knew someone was going to try to blow up the school?" He sets his pencil on his desk and it rolls toward him. The sound of the pencil against the desk is louder than I would've thought. He stops it with his hand.

"I'm saying that when experts have studied incidents of school violence across the nation, they've tried to identify patterns. Often the aggressor has told his close friends or made threats." She lets that thought hang over us for a moment. "Unfortunately, sometimes there's a school climate that interferes with those friends coming forward and telling an administrator. We aim to fix that."

"So you want us to rat on each other?" Garth calls out.

A bunch of kids laugh and someone mutters "Petey" in a low voice. Pete Plumber is this brilliant, socially inept kid who thinks he has to tattle about everything to make the world go round. "So-and-so's chewing gum in class," "So-and-so's copying homework," and yada, yada, yada. The other kids have a field day, just messing around with him. I think it's mean, but honestly, it's none of my beeswax.

"Not rat." Paisley smooths back the loose wisps of hair around her face. "Let's use another word."

"Snitch?"

When Paisley smiles, she pulls her lips back too far, making it seem forced. I'm close enough to see one of those clear teeth straighteners over her pearly whites. There's something creepy about adults with braces. Plus it makes her slur. "How about something with a more positive connotation? How about 'share'?"

Exactly how long has it been since she was a teenager? Maybe she's older than she looks. That hippie thing is working for her.

"Here's the thing. If there really had been a live bomb, and if we hadn't been able to defuse it, we would've been looking at massive casualties." Pause.

I look around for a trash can just in case breakfast decides to resurface.

"And let's say hypothetically some of you knew about this plan before it went down...Think of how you'd feel. Think of how it would be to go to one of your friends' funerals."

We all stare. *Well, duh.* We *have* been to other students' funerals. Paisley has only been an administrator at our school for six months, so maybe she doesn't know. But freshman year Alicia Benton died of bone cancer. Sophomore year Jo Moon hanged herself on a tree. Junior year a group of kids got their hands on some bad ecstasy. One died and another fried his brain.

This year, senior year, we've been tragedy free. So far.

Paisley moves around the side of the room and we all shift in our seats. "Here's my point. We need to create a school culture in which people feel comfortable sharing their own observations with the administration. Where students can come to me and tell me their concerns with no fear of retribution from peers."

There is a trash can by Paisley's left knee. I might puke right here in front of everyone.

Paisley fingers her peace-sign earrings. "So we'll be pulling every single student out of class for an individual interview. We'll gather data about how you all feel about this school, what you think we can do to improve the school climate, and so on. If you know anything about yesterday's incident, this will be a time when you can share. We promise to keep your comments confidential."

15

Someone in the back row coughs. Loudly.

"Yeah, good luck with that," someone else calls out.

Paisley ignores this. "I also want to commend you all for coming to school today. With all the support we have from the police at this time, school is the safest place on earth for you. Tell your friends. We'd like everyone back in their seats tomorrow."

"Yeah, good luck with that," I whisper under my breath.

* * *

I text Beth that evening. **FYI, Paisley says "school is the safest place on earth."**

She must have her phone in her hand, because she's quick.
No...that'd be Disneyland.

Disneyland is the happiest place.

Not for me. My happiest place is my bed.

If you'd ever had a boyfriend in your entire life, that'd sound dirty.

LOL! Your mind's in the gutter!

Proudly. Hey, you coming back tomorrow?

Dad's making me. Gotta keep my "eye on the prize."

I'm impressed you stayed home today.

Yeah. Faked a fever.

Clever.

It's okay. School's my happy place too.

I know, you rocking genius.

Look who's talking, Miss Straight A.

That'd be sweat and tears and zero social life.

Study groups are social. There's conversation. And snacks.

Yes—but no kissable boys!

Boys are drama. No time for that. You've got too much to do.

Thanks for reminding me.

The story of my life.

Stranger's Manifesto
Entry 3

Look at me
Writing in a journal
Like I'm Anne freaking Frank.
Like what I have to say matters. Like anyone will care.
But the only reason the world
Gave a shit about Anne Frank's diary
Was because her words documented history.
Pain. Suffering. Strength.

Well, so the hell will mine.
The world just don't know it yet.
But when they do—*and they will*—
I want them to understand. Because if they don't
Then all this—that I've done
And all this—that I'm planning to do next
Will be for nothing.
This journal is my record.
When they find it—*and they will*—
They'll care what *I* have to say too.

What a crying shame
That they don't have the goddamn common sense
To care *now*. When it *could* make a difference.
Before the world goes to shit…
And it's too late.

I get my blue slip in fifth period the next day. AP government. Since blue slips have been floating around like snowflakes, no one bats an eye when I pack up my backpack and walk out of class, waving my pass in the air.

I push open the door to the front office, but it bangs against something. "Ouch!" I hear. I poke my head around and realize why I couldn't open the door. It's because the school is breaking safety code by cramming the room way over capacity. Some guy in a black cotton hoodie and purple Vans scoots over. They haven't timed these blue slips right.

I wedge my way into the waiting area. When the boy in the black hoodie tries to make more room for me, I can smell his gum. Cinnamon.

I swear it's ninety degrees in here. The air's heavy and stale.

"I think I'll just wait outside," I say out loud, but to no one.

I back through the door. The air in the hallway feels cool in comparison. I slide down the wall to the floor. It's gonna take them hours to interview all the people they have in there. If they get to me before the end of the school day, I'll be surprised. I pull my knees to my chest and rest my head.

The door opens. Someone steps out and sits down next to me.

"You've got the right idea," he says with a light accent. His voice is husky.

I lift my head. Black hoodie boy leans back against the stucco. "Might as well take a little siesta." He makes a pillow out of his backpack and arranges himself against it. I can still smell the cinnamon, but now I also get a whiff of fabric softener. He crosses his arms and closes his eyes.

I've never seen him before in my life.

* * *

"Miguel? Miguel Gomez?"

My black hoodie friend lifts his head, looking like he doesn't know where he is. He really did knock out there on the hard hallway floor. His breathing went all heavy and I heard a couple snores.

"*Qué?*"

"Your turn, buddy." It's a cop, but not one I know.

Miguel hoists himself up with sudden energy. He slings the backpack over his shoulder and salutes me. "Later. Nice sleeping with you."

I almost choke on my air. Did he really just say that? My cheeks get sunburned hot and I want to crawl into my own backpack, but instead I check him out. Maybe he doesn't get the double meaning of those words. He's pretty obviously an ESL student, which explains why I've never had a class with him.

He glances back as he heads through the door, and I catch a sparkle in his eye. *No way.* He totally knows what he just said.

Ten minutes later, the cop's back for me. "All right, Gabriella, follow me." He leads me into the administration wing, past the row of offices for our assistant principals and school counselors. Most of the doors are closed for other interviews.

The cop steps into Principal Bowen's office. I've never been inside before. The walls are covered with certificates and awards, evenly spaced. Principal Bowen and his big, bulbous nose are nowhere to be seen. At his desk sits Officer Williams, who looks like she's outgrown her uniform. She's been working with my dad for as long as I can remember.

"Take a seat, Gabi." She smiles at me, but her eyes look tired.

I sit down slowly. It's so quiet that I can hear the ticking of Officer Williams's watch.

"I am going to ask you a series of questions. Please tell us everything, however irrelevant it may seem. We will use our discretion and protect your privacy as much as possible." She takes a sip of her soda. "First, please tell me your experience from Tuesday. What you saw and heard before, during, and after the incident."

I tell her everything. Except for the peeing-in-my-pants part. I keep that to myself.

Then she jumps into a rolling list of questions, scribbling notes with her free hand. The questions blend into each other—"Have you ever heard anyone make a threat against another person? Have you ever made a threat against another person? Have you ever seen a gun or knife on campus…" *Have you, have you, have you.* "If you ever needed to talk, do you know who your assigned school counselor is?" *Well, duh. Of course.* But the question is does *he* know who *I* am? There are three counselors total, and we get like five and a half minutes with them in the spring to plan next year's classes. I've never sat down with a counselor just to chat.

"We'll have extra counselors here at school for the next two days, so please utilize them. Situations like this can be very traumatic, and trauma can interfere with your ability to function— you know, sleeping, eating, concentrating, that kind of thing."

I nod. By the time she reaches her final question, I feel like she's taken a big spoon and stirred my brains around.

"Is there anyone you know personally—or have heard of—that might have orchestrated this threat?"

I hadn't really allowed myself to consider that thought. Faces flash before me. The grungy custodial assistant who talks to himself while he mops the floors and who looks like he stepped off an America's Most Wanted poster. The dropouts who set up shop selling drugs from a rundown rental across from the school. The loner kids who sulk by the band room and get shoved into trash cans. Anyone who's ever been expelled from the school. They should put Petey Plumber on reporting duty. Like a neighborhood watch, only in the school halls. He'd love it.

"No." I can hardly hear my own voice, and when I glance up, I can see Officer Williams looking at me expectantly. "No," I repeat, this time louder.

"If you think of someone, we'll have an anonymous-tip call line. Is there anything else you'd like to add?"

Something to add? Besides the fact that my brain is spinning in dizzy circles like that teacup ride that makes me barf? *Uh…that'd be a big, fat no.*

5
LATE OCTOBER

Funny how quickly things slide back to normal. Except for the three officers milling around campus at all times, and the hand-held metal detector as we walk through the front gates, school is school. Teachers teach, students sleep, I take compulsive color-coded notes.

At lunch Beth waves at me from our table outside the cafeteria. She saves me and Bruce a space every day. Bruce is our "special friend," and I mean that in the kindest way possible. Beth and I volunteered in one of the special ed rooms at summer school after freshman year. Maybe we were overly friendly or something, because after that he wanted to sit with us at lunch. What were we going to say…"No"? We thought it'd be a phase.

Bruce has a crush on Beth, but he's so innocent that it's cute. He sits with us. Or rather, he sits with Beth. Sometimes on her shiny, black hair because, yes, it's *that* long. She shares her Oreos with him and he listens to her nonstop brain-numbing gab. True love.

"You know, Bruce"—she hands him his first Oreo of the day— "this relationship totally works for me."

He crunches in response.

"There's no drama. No interruption of study time. No late-night texts. Plus you're adorable."

He nods politely. And crunches.

"Beth," I say, sighing. "I don't do drama either. But don't you think you're taking advantage of him? Maybe he'd crush on a girl from his class if he wasn't crushing on you. It's not fair."

"What? This is a mutually beneficial relationship. Plus it's the topic of my college admissions essay. And my first novel. Possibly a dissertation."

"You're too much."

"Seriously, Gabi. Neither you nor I have time for a *real* boyfriend. This is as close as I'm gonna get until I finish my double doctorate. Plus I know all my secrets are safe with you two." She offers me an Oreo. I turn it down.

I pretend to be insulted. But she's right. I don't have time to hang out with anyone but Beth, so who would I tell? So I crunch my organic kale salad and listen to her social commentary. As soon as she starts whispering, I know I'm gonna hear something juicy.

"Did you see the way Kikki Todd was all over that guy by the lockers? No shame, I tell you, no shame! That's why nice girls like us get zero male attention. No offense, Bruce." She doesn't expect any response, so I can just zone out.

"Are you even listening?" Beth's voice breaks in. Not sure how long I've been zoning, but the kale salad is nearly gone.

"No." I'm honest. "I'm conserving my brain cells for study group."

"Looks like your sister and her fellow cult followers are trying to get your attention."

I check out Chloe's spot on the grass. Right smack in the center, totally exposed. Her group wasn't lucky enough to nab a nook by the portables or a locker cranny. Most of the fringe groups position themselves in the crevices of campus, so they can people watch while securing their own perimeter.

"No offense, Gabi, but why does your sister hang with the rejects? It's weird."

I never know how to respond to Beth. It seems mean to talk this way, but I kind of agree. Chloe's cronies include this funky mismatch of kids that don't fit anywhere else. Two of them are meditating. Pretty soon they're gonna be weaving anklets out of straw or making their own clothes out of hemp or something equally strange. I usually just say nothing.

"Is she even taking any honors classes?" Beth whispers, then flashes a huge smile at Chloe and wiggles her fingers in a "hi."

"Thanks a lot, Beth. Now I can't even pretend I don't see her," I say. Chloe waves wildly, gesturing me over.

"Bruce and I always got your back, sis."

"Gee, thanks."

I groan and head over to Chloe's "alternative" faction. Because I'm an AP kid and a cross-country kid and a leadership kid, I have special powers to circumvent Central's social clique boundaries. It's like being Superwoman, only I don't let it go to my head. I glance over at the football meatheads. I get distracted by looking though, and my shoulder bumps into someone.

"Oh, sorry," I apologize.

It's that kid Miguel. I see him everywhere now. He's like a leprechaun or something, popping up at random times. Miguel gives me a curt little wave and moves on, running to catch up to someone.

Chloe spots me and pops up from her cross-legged spot. "Gabi!" She's usually not that excited to see me. "Did you hear that they arrested the shop teacher?"

"Mr. Marks? Seriously?" I look around. Besides the random pieces of fruit that are being tossed, I can practically see rumors flying from table to table like sparks, catching on everything and igniting. *He was the mastermind behind the bomb threat.*

"Yep! The reporters are saying that the cops analyzed all the computer records after the bomb threat, and it turns out Mr. Marks has been giving 'extra credit' to certain unnamed female students for 'extracurricular activities.'" Being able to give me the scoop is making her unusually gleeful.

"Gross!" I try to imagine someone making out with Mr. Marks. He's so hairy that it'd be like kissing Cousin It.

"I know!" Chloe bounces a little.

"You are cheerful. I haven't seen you this happy since you got your last T-shirt off Woot," I point out. "Mel"—I nudge Chloe's friend Mel with my foot—"can you believe her?"

Mel nods, pinched and irritable looking. "Chloe's whacked. We both know this," she says. Mel is whacked too, probably more than Chloe, but I don't think it's polite to point this out.

"Come on!" Chloe bounces. "This is drama at its finest. Someone should stage a reality TV show from Central High. I *live* for this shit."

"How are we even related? I have no time for drama. Drama is draining." I look over to Mel to help me make my point. "Right, Mel? You're exhausted just thinking about it, aren't you?" Mel sits like a lump, apparently not impressed. Just getting out of bed in the morning must be exhausting for her, so maybe she's not the best example.

Am I the only one with a more sinister thought wedged in my mind? If the cops arrested Mr. Marks for being a pervert, *not* for making a bomb threat, it means the bomber is still out there. Waiting to strike again.

* * *

I get a blue slip halfway through English and I wonder if I'm in trouble. I stand in Dr. Paisley's doorway, watching as she types rapidly on her computer, her fingernails clickety-clacking against the keys like music. She must be going too fast, because every ten seconds or so she pauses and sighs before she hits the backspace key a bunch of times in a row and retypes something. I stand there for a full minute before she notices me.

"Oh Gabi! Come on in. Shut the door behind you, will you?"

I move over to a chair and sit on my hands.

"So I brought you in today because your name has come up for our new school-climate improvement program." Paisley takes a deep breath like she's about to say something important. "Central High is starting its own crisis hotline. We're handpicking fourteen members. You're one of them, if you choose to accept the invitation."

I nod.

"But in order for the program to work, you won't be able to tell other people of your involvement."

Okay, so I'm honored to be hand-picked, but it sounds fishy. "Why?"

"If callers know who's picking up the phone, they'll be less likely to reach out in this way. It has to feel safe. Private. Anonymous." Paisley shakes her heavy earrings and they bounce against the side of her face. "For that reason, we'll ask you to keep it private even from your family. Your parents will sign a generic consent that allows you to volunteer for a confidential program, but even they will not be privy to the details."

I think about this for a second. It's all very cloak and dagger.

"Time commitment is six hours a week. One shift a week, from four to nine. Staff meeting every Sunday morning from 8:00 a.m. to 9:00 a.m." She must know I want to groan, because she adds, "I know it's early. We had to do it that way to accommodate churchgoers."

I hesitate. My schedule is jam-packed. But saying no is not easy for me.

"You can count it as volunteer experience," Paisley throws out, like she's dangling a carrot under my nose. "Looks good on résumés and applications."

I hate that this entices me. "Doesn't Central already have a peer counseling program?" I ask, taking my hands out from under my butt because they're nearly asleep.

"Yes. We've had a peer counseling program for a few years, but it's sadly underutilized. We think students are afraid of being exposed in some way. That's why we need something anonymous. We've got to make the students feel as if there is someplace confidential they can go when something's bothering them."

I nod. I agree. I'm just not sure I'm the one to do it. I stick my hands back under my butt.

"It'll be fun, Gabi. It's like a secret society."

A secret society? "Okay," I say slowly, half regretting it. "Let me check with my parents."

* * *

Mom says yes the moment she hears the magic words "volunteer opportunity." It's too bad I'm such a good kid. I could get away with anything if I told them it was a study group or a volunteer opportunity. I could probably run a successful Ritalin redistribution business without them having a clue.

Sigh. And once again I'm stuck doing something I'd rather not. I need to practice saying "no" in the bathroom mirror. It shouldn't be that hard. It's only one syllable, for Pete's sake.

Stranger's Manifesto
Entry 4

In a sick way the worst week of my life
Was the best week of my life.
At the funeral, people actually saw me.
Looked me in the eye as if I existed.
Asked me if I was okay. Told me to hang in there.
Hang. Bad choice of words.
They even hugged me—as if I was real.

But it was all a trick. A magic card trick.
A slip of the hand, a freaking illusion with light.
Because they forgot I don't exist
And when they remembered,
I wanted to crawl into the deepest, darkest hole I could find.
Because I knew—for a moment—
What it felt like to be *someone*.
And I liked it.

Everyone's whispering about Mr. Marks,
Wondering about his arrest.
I wonder too. Does he feel famous? Mysterious? Important?
Or does he just feel
Like a toxic piece of shit?

I can't help but wonder how I'll feel when my time comes.
I've pretty much got
The piece-of-shit thing down.

6

The drama room is so cold that every hair on my body prickles upright. Paisley stands at the front of the room, wearing a loose dress that falls all the way to her feet. I hope she doesn't trip.

"If you're sitting in this room, you've made a commitment to better your school," she says to all fourteen of us who got suckered into this Sunday orientation-training. "You've agreed to keep this experience and our purpose entirely confidential."

Why do I feel like I just joined the Secret Service? Is it too late to back out now? Probably. There's a sort of discomfort in the air, no doubt because none of us fully understand what we've gotten ourselves into.

"What if we pick up the phone and it's one of our friends?" someone asks.

Dr. Paisley smiles. "This may happen. In fact, expect it to happen. That's why we've been so careful in selecting you all. We picked students we felt had high moral standards and who came from a diverse number of social groups. We expect that if you recognize a caller, you'll be able to keep it to yourself. And, of course, if a caller recognizes your voice, he or she has the discretion to decide whether to continue the call or not."

I'm not sure I like this.

"We'll give you some basic skills and protocols to follow. You'll work in pairs, so you'll never be alone on a shift."

I don't know about anyone else, but I feel like I've swallowed a golf ball. And there it sits, wedged in the top of my throat, making it difficult for me to breathe.

"All right, let's pull our chairs into one big circle," Paisley says.

I wonder if anyone else is thinking about bolting for the door. There's the obligatory scraping of chairs against the floor as we pull ourselves in to face each other. It's a sorry circle though, looks like we all failed kindergarten. When Dr. Paisley said they'd pulled from all the social circles, she wasn't kidding.

I scan the room. Yep, we've got our football player, our band member, our genius, our emo, our druggie, our student government representative, our loner, our social partyer, our cheerleader, our resource kid, our—wait. My eyes stop on Miguel. He is staring back at me, looking less surprised to see me than I am to see him. His full lips seem to smirk, and I wish I was close enough to flick him with my finger.

I'd figured the kids recruited for this program would be all the regulars. The AP students. The valedictorians. The main players in student government. *Kids like me.*

Dr. Paisley claps her hands together twice to get our attention. "We'll start with a get-to-know-you activity. Everyone will share two random facts about themselves."

Silent groan. Agonizing ice breaker. Luckily she starts on the other side of the room.

Garth Johnson goes first. The boy barely fits in the chair. When he shares that he's a quarterback (sure looks like one) and a vegetarian (definitely does not look like one), I hear whispered gasps of "No way!"

I *hate* things like this. Sure, I'm sort of curious about what everyone else will share, but I'd rather pull out my eyelashes than share myself. Because I'm *boring*. I have no secret interesting facts to share. If I tell people I've never missed a day of school since freshman year, I'll sound like a freak.

"Hi, I'm Eric." I know him. He's the kind of guy who takes every AP class offered, aces all the tests, and plays French tapes to learn a new language while he's sleeping. He doesn't act cocky about his IQ though. "I'm an only child. When I was a kid, I built a five-story apartment building out of toothpicks."

Next is Janae, with funky hair—cut in a way that sounds awful, but she somehow pulls it off. One side hangs low over her left eye, and she flips it out of her face as she talks. The back is buzzed close to her neck. There's a red streak on one side. I wish I could try a haircut like that, but I'd be way too scared it wouldn't look good.

Right away I like Janae, even though I've seen her hanging out by the druggie tree, kicking the druggie ground and joking with her druggie friends. "I'm Janae. I've changed schools eight times since kindergarten and my favorite snack is uncooked noodles." Someone asks if her dad's in the military. "Nope." She shakes her head, her longish bangs flopping over her eye again. "Just couldn't find the right school."

Miguel is next. I've been trying not to look at him, but it's harder than it sounds. When I peek, I see that he's staring straight at me. He is *so* not my type. I wish he'd get a grip. "Hi, I'm Miguel." His accent sounds even stronger than it did the other day. "I love tamales, and I have a pit bull."

When it's Cruz's turn, I can tell right away that he's one of those guys who thinks he's cool. Or he wants *us* to think he's cool. He leans back, crossing one leg over his other. "I like to have a *real* good time." People chuckle. I've heard Cruz throws raging keggers. He's short but buff, and his big teeth give him a squirrel-like look. "And…I'm captain of the wrestling team."

I'm up before I'm ready. I stumble a bit. "Uh, hi. I'm Gabi. I'm on the cross-country team. My sister and I are eleven months apart in age, but two years apart in school." Everyone looks at me politely enough, but I'm groaning inside. I'm *so* boring. I feel my cheeks redden, and I want to cover them with both hands. *How old am I? Five?*

The rest of the members blend together. There's Nate, a wannabe gangster type; Tihn, our student government president and a competitive piano player; Stacey, a squeaky string bean who looks and sounds like a wisp of air; Clarke, an emo type with so much hair I can't see his face; Amar, who was born in India and plays in the high school band; Bryan, who I'm pretty sure was in the resource class that I TA'd for sophomore year; Christina, who's active in her youth group and spends forty dollars a week on smoothies; and Carla, who could double as a multicolored bouncy ball and wears her cheerleader uniform at least once a week.

"Okay, folks. Take five." Paisley calls out. "Then we'll come back together."

I stand up to stretch my legs. That weirdo Miguel is edging closer to me, so I avoid him by going to the bathroom. Janae is in there, leaning in close, redoing her eye makeup. I don't know how she gets it so thick without smearing it. It's a talent. I smile at her in the mirror, feeling strangely shy.

When I step out, Miguel is standing there waiting. "*Hola*," he says.

"How is it that I've never seen you before in my life, and then all of a sudden you're everywhere I go?" I touch my earrings,

32

trying to remember which ones I wore today. Small gold hoops. "You stalking me?" I joke.

He looks confused for a moment. "Stalking?"

Okay, so now I'm way embarrassed. He's totally an ESL kid. And I'm stuck having to find a way to define the word "stalking." "Uh, that means like watching. Watching me."

He smiles, and recognition brightens his face in layers. "Yes!" He nods. "I'm stalking you." There's a certain peacefulness about it—like he's happy or light or something. "It's hard not to stalk someone so beautiful."

Is he for real? If he wasn't so obviously clueless, I'd think he was messing with me. Paisley saves me though. She claps her hands again. "People, gather up! I'm glad you're all getting to know each other, but we've got some more work to get done today."

I give Miguel a mini wave and head back to my seat. He follows me, though, and sits his butt right down next to me. This causes everyone else to shift their seats accordingly.

Dr. Paisley brings out a large dry-erase board. "Here, Cruz. Hold this for me." She grabs the empty chair next to him. "I'll divide you into teams of two."

We all look at each other. The lights suddenly feel way too bright.

"Your shifts will be from four to nine p.m., and we'll be open seven days a week. We'll need to log every call—the time it comes in, how long it lasts, the main topics discussed, and whether you give a referral."

My brain starts to spin.

"There are two ways calls will come in. Via live phone call and via text."

"Do we get loaner cell phones so we can text back?" Christina asks. "Because my parents will flip if I'm texting strangers with my own cell."

"No. The texts will come in through one of the two computers we have set up in the office. They have a secure and encrypted web-based SMS-texting platform. A text will pop up on the computer, and you answer it by typing on the keyboard. You won't be able to see the actual phone number you're texting to for confidentiality purposes."

Yikes. Too much to keep track of.

Paisley goes on. "I suspect you'll find the texting simpler, because that's how you all communicate these days anyway. Plus, you can easily collaborate on how best to help the texter. Live phone calls are harder, because although your shift partner can write notes and suggestions for you on a notepad, ultimately it comes down to you."

Gulp. I raise my hand. "Are both partners taking calls at the same time?"

Paisley beams. "Great question! No. We'll have only one incoming phone line for callers. The computer can accommodate multiple texters at the same time, but we've only got two computers, which will affect the rate at which we can respond."

"What if we need help?"

"Great question. I was just going to get to that. We will have a separate phone line that won't be made public. This line can be used in case you need to consult during a call. Your partner can simply call me on this back line while you're still on the phone with the caller. Then your partner can convey my thoughts by writing them down on your notepad." Paisley pauses as we all sit and digest. "All of you will have access to the back-line number, so that you can reach your fellow listeners during their shift, but I ask that no one give that out."

I wonder if everyone else feels as freaked out as I do.

"Don't look so panicked, folks. You're never truly alone. While one listener is actually talking to or texting with the caller, the other one will be writing ideas for their partner."

We must look confused, because Paisley points to the dry-erase board and whips out a marker. "I'll show you what I mean. Janae, come on up here. You'll be the listener and I'll be your partner. I'll help you. Nate, you can be the caller. You start by saying 'ring, ring.'"

Nate grins. "Yo. A Ring-a-ding-ding!" He says it like he's rapping.

"Uh, hello?" Janae puts a pretend phone to her ear.

"Hold up." Paisley interrupts them with her hand. "Say, 'Helpline, this is Rachel.'"

"Rachel?"

"I recommend that you pick a pseudonym. You don't have to pick Rachel, but pick something other than Janae."

"Okay. Helpline, this is Gertrude."

We all laugh.

Nate laughs too, but looks like he's trying to swallow it down and get into character. He bunches up his shoulders, "I can't take it no more." He sniffles all loud. "Too much drama all over the place."

Janae looks to Paisley. Paisley writes on the dry-erase board. *Validate that. Say, "It sounds like you're having a hard time."*

"It sounds like you're having a hard time."

"I am. Life sucks. My girlfriend's giving me stress, my dog died, my math teacher gives too much homework, and my favorite band is breaking up."

Paisley writes on the board, *You've got a lot on your plate.*

Janae rolls her eyes, "I can't say that. I wouldn't say that."

Paisley sets down the marker. "These are just suggestions in case you get stuck. You can say whatever you want to say."

"Really?" Janae's eyes light up. "Okay. Get a new girlfriend and a new dog. Go to the library after school. And just deal—that's the music business."

A few people start clapping. Paisley holds up her hand for attention. "Which brings me to rule number one. No advice giving—you're not qualified."

"*What?* I thought this was a helpline!"

"We just listen, support, and link the caller to resources."

I hear rumblings of "This is stupid." I have to agree.

"I bet you'll be surprised by how effective listening can be. Okay. Turn to the person next to you. Let's practice reflective and supportive listening." Miguel sits on my right. Christina sits on my left. I start to turn toward her, but she's already started talking to Bryan. "The person on the right will share about a problem they are having. It doesn't have to be something personal, but make it something real."

Miguel looks at me. He starts to say something and then he stops. "I don't know what to say."

I sigh. "What problems do you have?"

He sort of laughs, but with his head bent forward and his chin tucked in, he's laughing into his chest. When he looks up, his eyes are dangerously close to my face. "No problems. My life is perfecto."

"Make one up."

He tries flattery. "How am I supposed to concentrate when I'm sitting next to a beautiful girl?"

"No chance, asshole." I surprise myself. And judging from the look on his face, I surprise him as well. "Give me a problem."

"Yeah? Okay. The love of my life is ignoring me."

I make a face and stretch my brain to find a validation. "That sounds...hard."

"It is. In a lot of different ways." He winks and suddenly I realize the double meaning in my words. "And that validation sucked."

Who is this guy? I can't figure him out, and he's irritating. Like an itch you can't scratch because it would be impolite and people would stare. So I take a risk and ask, "Did you really not know what the word 'stalking' meant?"

He grins, and his smile tells me all I need to know. "You asshole," I say again.

"Hey. You're cute when you're feisty, you know that?"

I turn away. "I'm going to ask for another partner."

We haven't even gotten to the texting practice yet. It's going to be a long day.

7

It looks like someone puked fliers all over the school. Every blank space on every wall has some variation of the *Central's Peer Helpline—We're Here to Listen* advertisement. We all worked together to make the fliers, but Paisley posted them after hours so we wouldn't blow our secret cover.

She ran an ad in the local paper too.

So officially, we're now in business.

Too bad we don't have a clue what we're doing.

My locker is across from a particularly colorful slathering of fliers. There's a playing card precariously wedged in one of my locker slats. I pull it out and look at it. A joker. There's tiny, black writing, block letters that look so neat and square I wonder if they have been printed around the edges of the card. I turn the card counterclockwise to read all the words. It says, *Remember stranger danger from elementary school? I am Stranger.*

I have this sudden urge to get the card as far away from me as possible. I drop it in the nearest trash can and back away. People these days have a twisted sense of humor. *Sick.*

* * *

I feel like I'm sitting in a closet. Probably because I *am* sitting in a closet. A converted storage closet with a futon, a desk, two computers, two chairs, and two phones. The whole room is smaller than my parents' master bathroom.

I'm highlighting my AP government textbook, using my three-colored approach. Pink for possible vocab words, yellow for dates, and orange for facts. Janae is sprawled across the futon, paging through a magazine. Luckily I avoided being paired with Miguel.

"*Why* did we sign up for this again?" She rolls over onto her back.

I laugh. "I was wondering the same thing myself." The phone hasn't rung once. We've been parked in this tiny room for over an hour. About as much fun as getting orthodontic braces tightened. At least I'm getting some good studying done.

"Nice ankle bracelet," I tell her. It's pretty, made of baby-blue seashells and tied together with some kind of twine that resembles hay.

"You like?" Janae grins and holds up her leg for me to examine more closely. "I made it."

"Seriously?" I look closer. She doesn't seem like the jewelry-making type. She seems more the weed-smoking, rave-going, bleach-your-hair-in-the-sink type.

Janae unhooks the bracelet and turns it over in her hands. "Yeah. This is a good one. I made a bunch a while back when I was living away from home." Her eyes lose focus for a moment, like she's remembering something. "I can show you how, maybe next shift?"

"That'd be fun," I agree. "It might help to pass the time." I wish I could offer some cool art project of my own, but my artistic skills are limited to creative highlighting techniques. I should show her my color-coded textbooks. They're pretty.

"I'm starving." Janae sits up and unzips her backpack. "But it looks like I am *way* unprepared." She pulls out a granola bar. "I don't suppose we can order a pizza?"

"Yeah, having a delivery boy show up kind of blows the whole secrecy thing." I spin around on my swivel chair like a little kid, considering our top-secret helpline office space. Our converted supply closet is hidden way back in C wing, a section of the school that's been empty ever since those massive budget cuts two years ago when they increased class sizes. At five minutes to four, each shift team has been instructed to enter the C building casually and make sure no one is in sight before going down the back corridor to the janitor's closet.

Today Janae and I both lingered at the school library after school. We didn't study together because we have no classes in common, and we'd probably draw unnecessary attention to ourselves. At our school, friends sort of match together like puzzle pieces. Not Janae and me.

The door to the closet-office sports a combination lock. Not the twisty kind they put on school lockers, but one that's actually inserted into the door, with numbered push buttons that have to be pressed in a certain order to release the lock. At first glance our code (4–3–5–7–5–4–6–3) just looks like a random grouping of numbers. But the numbers correspond to cell phone letters, spelling out "H-e-l-p-l-i-n-e."

Janae's face brightens. "You know what we need in here? A mini fridge. We could stock it with sodas."

I nod. "We need to decorate. It'd be like decorating a backyard fort."

"Right?" Janae laughs and plays with one of the little studs in her left ear, twisting it in a circle. "The neighbor kids and I made these massive forts in the laundry room at our apartment complex.

Until some cranky old lady called the landlord. She said it was a fire code violation."

"Bummer."

"It's okay. We egged her car," Janae says, practically beaming.

"No way. Really?"

"Yep. If there's a prank that needs pulling, you just come to me. I'm the prank queen. Speaking of eggs, I'm so hungry. And snacks just aren't gonna cut it." Janae rolls onto her side. "I'll just go pick us up some Mickey D's."

"You can't leave a shift." This comes out kind of whiny and of course it's true, but what I really mean is that she can't leave me alone on a shift. "What if someone calls or texts while you're gone?"

"Doesn't look likely at this point."

"They might."

Janae's already standing up, and I have the urge to lunge for her ankle to hold her there.

"Let's text Eric or Garth. I've got their numbers." I grab my phone. I've had classes with Eric since freshman year. And Garth Johnson was on my team for our euthanasia debate in government. "They both drive."

"Good thinking. Here, hand me your phone. I'll text them." She holds out her palm expectantly. "There," she announces.

"Did you text both of them?"

"Why not?"

A half hour later, we smell onions and pickles, then hear the metallic clicks of the door code being entered. Garth plops down next to Janae on the futon. The futon tilts with his weight. He pulls out a few sub sandwiches and spreads them out on the sandwich paper.

"Dig in!"

41

Within a few minutes, Eric's there too, unpacking a Taco Bell bag.

Looks like Garth and Eric think they've been invited to stay, and the room feels suddenly crowded. It's quiet for a while, with just the sounds of us chewing. So we all jump when the phone rings. *Riiiiing. Riiiiing.* I scramble for the seat by the desk. *Riiiiing.*

I grab the phone, standing up and trying to catch my breath. "Helpline, this is…Vanessa." I hadn't picked my pseudonym before this moment.

"Hi." Soft voice. Female. Hesitant. I sit down. Eric shoves a stack of loose paper in front of me, and Janae hands me a pen. I try to remember protocol. It's too hard to listen and think of what I have to say next and write notes for the others all at the same time. This is mental juggling, and I just might have too many balls in the air. I draw a circle with a plus sign attached to it, so the others will know it is a girl.

"Hi," I say back.

Quiet on the other end. I can hear breathing. Janae slides a chair over next to me. She picks up another pen, a different color from the one I'm using, and starts to write, *How old?* I answer with a question mark. I can't tell yet.

"You can talk about anything you'd like. I'm here to listen." This I try to say calmly. Slowly. Like we practiced in our role-plays. Garth leans over my shoulder and draws a big happy face. *Good job.*

"Are you a student?" The voice surprises me with this question.

"What?" We hadn't practiced answering personal questions. But I know we're supposed to be anonymous, so I better figure out a way to tap-dance around anything that might identify me personally.

"Here. At Central. Are you a student?"

42

"This is a peer helpline. We're all students." I try to keep my voice even. Steady. Janae writes, *Tell us what's happening. We'll help you.*

The caller makes this strange noise, this *mmhmm* from deep in her throat. And then she goes on. "So basically, you don't know shit." I hear an edge now to her voice.

I take a breath in, like she's socked me. I write what she said in quotes. *You don't know shit.*

"Maybe not. But if there is something you want to talk about, I'm happy to listen."

We can't all fit around the desk, so Eric sets a paper down next to me. *None of us know shit. Ha! You're doing great by the way. Ask her what's going on? What made her call tonight?* I tilt my head up to Eric and try to smile my thanks.

"What I want to know is, does anyone remember her?"

"Who?" I am confused. This is harder than it sounds.

But the girl goes on as though she doesn't hear me. "She was famous for a week or so. But now that it's all over, does anyone remember her?"

Say what? I repeat, "So you're thinking about someone who was well-known for a while, and now you're wondering if anyone remembers her." I sound like a complete idiot.

The girl's words are tight now. Like she's keeping her mouth closed while she talks. "She didn't matter to anyone. That's why she offed herself. She didn't matter then, and she doesn't matter now."

She must be talking about that girl, Jo, the one who hanged herself sophomore year. But the question is *why* is she talking about Jo? I get a strange feeling in my stomach. "She must have been very unhappy."

"No shit. Everyone saw those pictures." Her voice wavers. "I

43

mean, her life sucked, just like everyone else's, but the pictures put her over the edge."

I didn't really know Jo except from having P.E. with her one year, but I definitely knew *of* her, even before she hanged herself. Everyone knew her as "that beanpole dyke." She was seriously awkward, with stringy, greasy-looking hair, but nice enough. Until that group of cheerleaders made her the punch line of their practical joke. One of them pretended to be into her, tried to seduce her, and then took pictures. And posted them all over the Internet.

She lasted three days after that.

Everyone at school saw the pictures within twenty-four hours. It took two days for her parents to find out. Word was that they were ashamed. Ashamed that she'd been so stupid. Ashamed that she was a lesbian. They kicked her out of the house, but she had nowhere to go. So she left a note basically telling everyone off. Then fastened a noose around her neck and checked out.

I am not sure what to say to the caller. I write on my paper, *Help!* Janae leans over and writes, *You sound really upset.* Eric adds, *Tell me more.* I shake my head. Neither of these are right.

Luckily, the girl saves me by going on. "The question is, would anyone remember me if I checked out?"

I gasp. Out loud. Then cover my mouth. I hope she didn't hear. There isn't anything I can do but ask. "Are you thinking of hurting yourself?"

She laughs. In a sarcastic, "life sucks" kind of way. "Every freaking day." I can feel my heart pounding in my eardrums. "Don't worry. *Thinking* is one thing. *Doing* is another. I'm scared shitless. With my luck, I'd mess it up. I'd wind up in a coma or be a human vegetable forever. Worse than death. Worse than life. So no, I won't do it. But that doesn't stop me from wishing I could."

And suddenly I get this funny feeling in my gut. I know that voice from somewhere. But I can't put my finger on who it could be.

Help!?! I write. I'm not sure I'm cut out for this.

Referrals for counseling? Janae scribbles.

I ruffle through a pile of papers on the desk, thinking we probably should've organized this office *before* we got our first call. "Would you like a referral to a low-fee counseling center?" I ask before I've even gotten my hands on the referral list.

She laughs again and says, "I don't need a shrink. I need a new life."

And what exactly am I supposed to do with that?

Thank goodness she clicks off, because I do *not* have a good comeback for that one.

I sit with the dead phone to my ear for a full minute, just thinking. Until Eric nudges me with his shoulder and writes, *Are you okay? What's she saying now?* Then I take the phone from my ear. "She hung up."

No matter how much the others tell me I did a good job, and what a challenging caller that was, and all that encouragement crap, I can't shake the feeling that I know her voice from somewhere.

And the phone doesn't ring again all night.

We get a text though, five minutes to closing. **Are you still there?**

Janae scrambles to sit down at the desk. **I'm here.**

The texter doesn't respond, so after four minutes, Janae texts again. **I'm here if you want to connect.**

Nothing.

Strange.

* * *

"Look." Chloe corners me in my room, reaching her hand into her back pocket and struggling for a moment, probably because

45

her jeans are so ridiculously tight. Finally she gets a small piece of paper out.

It's a playing card, similar to the one I'd found in my locker earlier. It's a queen, only someone drew on the card with Sharpie. The queen's mouth is re-drawn like a dark, open hole, and her eyes are enlarged into blackened circles, making her look demon-like. There is a crude bomb by her feet, and the words *Tick-tock, tick-tock* in neat block letters.

"Did you draw that?" I ask her sharply. "God, Chloe, after what we've all been through, that's kind of sick."

"No," she retorts, and I can tell from the way her eyes narrow that she's pissed. "I found this. I'm showing it to you because I *found* it."

"Where? Where did you find it?" I'm suddenly worried about her. Maybe this whole bombing thing affected her more than I thought it did.

She hesitates a moment, picking at her black fingernails. She opens her mouth and then closes it, like she isn't sure she wants to tell me.

"Spit it out."

"Dad's wallet. It was in Dad's wallet."

I start to ask her what she was doing sneaking through Dad's wallet, but I can read it in her face not to go there.

So I don't ask.

I examine the card carefully, turn it over a few times, and then hand it back to Chloe.

"I guess you'd better put it back then."

Stranger's Manifesto
Entry 5

Last year
I gave the lunchtime "Games" Club a try,
Dorky as that sounds.
At least it was an air-conditioned place to park my butt
During the *agonizing* forty minutes of lunch.
But get this—while there were at least six simultaneous card games,
No one seemed to have space at their table
For *me*.
I'm not sure they even noticed me standing there.
Waiting. And waiting.

Until I was tired of waiting.
Until I whipped out my solitaire cards as a last resort
And dealt my own hand.
So it wouldn't look like I was sitting all alone.
So I wouldn't have to remember
What it was like when I *used* to have
Someone to sit with at lunch.
So I wouldn't have to remember that feeling of hope
That I might not be on the bottom rung
Of the popularity ladder forever,
Because I know all too well
That feeling can burst.
All it takes is someone with a sharp pin.

8

The next morning, Chloe is texting and eating breakfast cereal at the same time. "You're making a mess," I inform her and swipe a rag across the milk-splattered tabletop. Maybe it's our near-death experience, or maybe it's because going through Dad's wallet makes her a budding delinquent, but I feel this sudden need to get to know my sister. Like, who is she texting so desperately at seven o'clock in the morning?

I grab a banana and sit close enough to see the screen. I must've gotten too close, because she snaps up the phone and presses the off button on top. Rats. She's got the phone password protected, so there's no reading her texts on the sly.

"When did you get so paranoid?" I throw out, more irritated than I should be. I am trying to *connect* with her after all, not piss her off.

We hear Mom vacuuming upstairs. Every morning she uses a little handheld DustBuster to snatch up any loose hairs after she's done washing, drying, and styling.

"Oh, around when Mom got so neurotic." Which has been, like, forever. Chloe grins, and now she doesn't look pissed at all. She's hard to read, my sister. I'll have to keep trying. We connect best when we're making fun of our parents. It's a pastime.

In that spirit, I hold up the sticky note that Mom has left on the counter. *Wipe down fridge. Unload dishwasher. Water plants.* Chloe rolls her eyes. "That's what I'm saying."

The note is not for us. It's for Lucia, who comes once a week to clean. Her note sits on the kitchen counter, where Mom always leaves extra instructions and the check. Mom feels weird about having a cleaning lady, I guess, so she basically pretends Lucia doesn't exist. She manages this by avoiding all interaction with Lucia, except by sticky notes.

"Ya gotta love her, right?" I wink, re-sticking the note onto the counter.

"That," Chloe says, sighing, "is debatable."

* * *

Heat seeps through the bottom of the cardboard pizza "to go" box, warming my fingers. I just finished a mega cram session with Beth. It's seven thirty, and I'm bringing Garth "payback pizza," sustenance for his shift tonight. There are four cars along the darkened street, probably belonging either to neighbors or to my fellow helpline members. We've agreed not to park in the lot so that we don't attract unnecessary attention to ourselves.

As I approach the building, I wish I'd parked closer. The overhead lights seem few and far between, and the darkness envelops everything. I can hear my own footsteps against the concrete. Suddenly I think about how stupid this is, coming here so late and by myself. Maybe my mind is playing tricks on me, but I think I hear someone behind me. I'm tempted to stop and whirl around. Instead I move faster. I clutch my car keys in my right hand, thinking I can use them to gouge someone's eyes out.

I push through the outside door of the C building and slip inside. If someone tries to follow me in here, I'll definitely hear him.

There is no way to open that heavy outside door without being heard. I think I'll feel safer once I'm indoors, but it's dark inside too. Only the emergency lights dimly mark my path.

I grip my car keys so hard that my fingers hurt, and I barrel toward the storage closet-helpline office. I type in our secret code and then slip inside as quickly as possible. The bright lights nearly blind me.

"Welcome!" Garth opens his arms wide and accepts the pizza box from me. He tips up the lid, and the smell of spicy sauce and melted cheese wafts out. Janae was apparently invited too, because she's sprawled across the futon, shuffling a hand of playing cards. The sight of a queen, face up, startles me. *God, I'm jumpy.* I can't even lay eyes on a deck of cards without thinking of those creepy notes. Once Garth catches sight of me, his smile fades. "What's wrong with you?"

I'm embarrassed, but I can't hide my shaking hands. "Oh, I just got creeped out walking in."

Janae nods. "It is pretty dark out there. Coming in alone mid-shift is probably not smart."

Garth sets down the box. "My bad," he apologizes. "I didn't even think of that when I texted you guys."

"No worries," I assure him. "I mean, you brought us food the other night and it was no big deal."

"Yeah, but it was about an hour earlier, and it's a little different for me to be walking around late at night than it is for you… no offense."

"There'd have to be at least four guys to take you down, huh?" Miguel swivels around at the desk. I hadn't noticed him when I walked in. How funny that I'd just assumed Garth and Eric were partners. Miguel's wearing those purple Vans again, and for the first time I notice that he's doodled all over them. Neat block letters in Sharpie, so small that I can't make out what they say.

"It's okay." I stumble over my words. "I'm okay. Just being paranoid."

Garth shakes his head. "Someone threatened to blow up our school two weeks ago. There's no such a thing as being too paranoid. If you both can stay until our shift ends, I'll walk you to your cars."

I really shouldn't stay, but I don't want to walk out alone either. I look to Janae. "I can stay," she offers.

I have a ton of reading for English, but maybe I can fake it in class even if I don't finish. "I can stay too." I text Mom that I'm volunteering tonight, and then I settle back on the futon. Janae plays with my hair, and I listen to them talk about random things. I haven't just hung out in forever. I forgot how nice it feels.

Riiiiing. We all freeze. *Riiiiing.* Garth and Miguel scramble to get themselves set up. *Riiiiing.* "You can take it," Miguel offers.

"Nah, you go first," Garth volleys back.

I'm just about to pick it up myself when Miguel grabs the phone. He takes a breath and then speaks in that calm, slow voice that we've practiced. "Helpline, this is John." The quality of his voice surprises me. It's deeper, thicker, and more fluid. I don't hear any trace of an accent. Miguel spreads the note-taking pages out so that we can all reach them.

"What a joke." I hear the voice on the other end of the phone, far away but still clear enough to identify. Miguel holds the phone slightly away from his ear.

Miguel pauses for a moment, looks up to us, then goes on, "I'm here to listen."

"Listen, my ass. You're here to spy."

"Excuse me?" Miguel lets his accent slip a little.

"This is all a sorry-ass attempt to investigate people. I know you've got wiretaps." Miguel looks up again at us. *Wiretaps?* he writes.

I lean over to scribble on the notepaper. *To record phone calls.*

"I'd—uh—I'd like to hear more about that." Miguel stumbles. Garth draws a happy face on the paper.

"I bet you would." The voice laughs. "You think I'm an imbecile? I know you're just a setup to try to catch the bomber."

My heart catches. I look at Janae, and her eyes are wide. Miguel writes a big question mark on the paper. *Talking about bomber. Don't know what to say.* I lean over again to write. I can smell Miguel's cinnamon gum and something else, maybe aftershave. Miguel's got a little stubble going on. I write, *What did you call to talk about?*

"So, uh, what would you like to talk about tonight?"

Again the caller laughs in a hardened way. His laugh sounds old, but his voice sounds like a high school kid. A bitter, angry high school kid. "I'd like to talk about what a shithole mess Central High is."

Pause. "I'm here to listen."

"What are you, a goddamn robot? Can't you think for yourself? You just gonna parrot back all the crap they taught you at whatever ridiculous little training class they made you go to."

I see a fine line of sweat build along Miguel's upper lip. "You sound angry."

"You'd be too if you had to deal with the crap I have to deal with."

Miguel's voice is smooth as pudding. "What kind of crap?"

The caller cackles again. "Wouldn't you like to know?"

Miguel swallows hard, and I feel sorry for him for a moment. He takes a breath and says, "I'd like to help you talk about it."

"I bet you would." Another cackle. "All I'm gonna say is that things had better change around here."

"What do you mean by that?"

"Nice try." The caller slams the phone down and Miguel jumps. We all sit in silence for a moment, digesting.

"Gabi, your dad's a cop," Janae says slowly. I see Miguel's eyes flick toward me and back to Janae, surprised almost. "Do you think they're using us to gather information? Are they tapping these calls?"

Everyone looks at me expectantly. "Would that even be legal? To advertise this as a confidential helpline, and then tap and trace the calls? I don't think they can do that."

"Not even to investigate someone who made a terrorist threat? Not even to save lives?" Janae presses. Miguel's rich, brown skin looks pale in the fluorescent light.

"I don't think so," I repeat, but even as I say it, I'm not sure. Suddenly their eyes feel mistrustful, and I shift in my seat. "Would it make that much of a difference if they were? I mean, people can still call to talk about their problems. We can still support them. If the bomber calls, and the police figure out who he is, then isn't that kind of a good thing?"

Janae unclasps her ankle bracelet and examines it. "Do you think that guy who just called…Do you think *he* is the bomber?"

We all look at each other for a long time.

I think we're all grateful that the phone doesn't ring again. But just before we head out the door, we get a text, same as last night.

Are you still there?

Garth types back, **I'm here.**

And then…nothing.

9

"Why do people run to watch a fight?" I nudge Beth. We watch excitement catch like fire, and kids racing toward the B wing, as if someone's tossing free money in the air. "We all know it's gonna get broken up. Yeah, someone might be bloody, but who cares?"

"It's our voyeuristic culture." Beth takes a tiny bite of her sandwich. "That's the whole basis of reality TV. Everyone likes a good train wreck."

"Not me." I set down my Greek yogurt.

"Train wrecks are bad," Bruce chimes in mid-crunch.

"Well, you're smarter than the rest of these idiots," Beth tells him, and he smiles. There's a tiny bit of Oreo in his teeth, but he's still cute.

Some kid's barreling toward the fight so fast that he nearly collides with our half-clad Native American statue. "You ever wonder why our mascot is a 'warrior'?" I ask.

"Duh. Because this was all Chumash land, way back when."

Beth looks like she's about to launch into a history lesson, so I stop her. "Yeah, but don't you think they should've picked something more PC? Less violent?"

"Hah! Good point." Beth tucks her hair behind her ears. "How do they expect us all to get along when they've got this image of war greeting us every day?"

"Someone should suggest we change our mascot to Buddha." I imagine this. "Wouldn't that be cute, to see him sitting there, happy in a diaper with cute, little fat rolls and a big smiling face?"

"Maybe we'd all get along then. You could suggest it." Beth gives me a big, fat wink. "You know you're the kinda gal who can make things happen."

"Somehow I doubt the football team would go for a fat-man-in-diaper image."

"Forgot about that." We chew quietly for a while.

* * *

Our Sunday morning helpline meetings break four rules. We (1) enter the public library before it's open (2) through the "staff-only" door, (3) talk above a whisper, and (4) eat and drink break-fast foods. Apparently Paisley is dating one of the head librarians. Pretty soon she'll (gasp) tell us we can check out more than ten books at a time. We're living it up. *Yeehaw!*

We're parked in the children's section, which is built to look like a pirate ship. The ceiling is high and sloped, and there are wooden benches along the sides. A mast rises through the center of the floor, and large murals of ocean scenes line the walls. Janae has settled herself on my left, with a twisted glazed doughnut and a cup of orange juice. She leans into me and rests her head on my shoulder.

Paisley sits on one of the benches, facing us. She holds a large jelly doughnut over a paper plate. As she takes a careful bite, jelly squirts out the other side. She doesn't notice.

"Okay, guys!" She steps in front of a dry-erase board. On one side she's written *What's working* and on the other side *What's not working.*

"Everyone has had a chance to manage a shift in their pairs by now, so you've gotten a taste of the program. This is a work in progress, so I anticipate we'll have our fair share of glitches." Paisley takes another bite of her jelly doughnut, and more of the red, gooey middle leaks out the back. I watch it roll down her plate. No one says anything.

We establish pretty fast that we need food (mini fridge) and entertainment. I feel like a wimp, but I raise my hand. "Safety issues." I say. "It's dark outside when we're walking out, and we had a creepy caller."

Cruz calls out, "We had a creepy caller too."

Nate and Eric say, "So did we."

"Really?" Paisley asks, her jelly doughnut poised midair, forgotten.

I add, "We got a caller that accused us of gathering information for the cops. Like we're trying to catch that bomber guy or something."

Paisley sets down her doughnut. "This is a campus improvement project. We have nothing to do with police officers. If someone calls up and confesses, you should try to get them to turn themselves in." She scans the room as if looking for comprehension. "But please know that the purpose of this line is to support people. Sure, it's a response to what happened on this campus, but it is run by *us*, not the police."

I want to believe her. I really do.

"What should we do when we respond to a text, and then the texter leaves us hanging?" Cruz asks.

"Nothing," Paisley says slowly, like she's surprised by the

question and has to think it through. "The texter knows you're there and will text back when he or she is ready."

"So what happens if that person texts back after we're closed?" Garth calls out.

"Great question." Paisley wipes her hands on a napkin. "They get an automated text back, just like the callers get an automated answering machine saying we're closed for the evening and here are our hours."

"That's good," Cruz jumps in. "We had a last-minute texter who just said, 'Are you still there?' and then after I texted back there was nothing."

"That happened to us too," a few people call out.

"Huh." Paisley scans the room. "By a show of hands, how many people got a text like this right before closing?"

Every hand in the room goes up.

Stranger's Manifesto

Entry 6

What's this?
A helpline?
Come on. *Really*?
I'm insulted.
Call me cynical, but I say,
"Too goddamn little…too goddamn late."
Just who the hell is it supposed to support?
A sicko like me?
Might be fun
To watch them try.

10

Dad sits cross-legged on his bed, playing solitaire. I stand in the doorway, digging my toes into the carpet. He looks up from his game. "Oh hey, baby. You all set for bed?"

"Almost." I sink down next to him, and my weight makes the cards shift position. Dad has played solitaire since I was a little kid, but I wonder if the cards have new meaning to him now. Does he see the blacked-out mouth of that queen? The ticking bomb by her feet? I consider asking him about it, but I don't want to get Chloe in trouble. She'd probably been digging through his wallet to scavenge for a loose ten or twenty, hoping he wouldn't miss it.

"Dad, did you hear about that helpline the school set up?" My throat closes up a little.

He deals the cards out again. They look so white against the dark navy comforter. "Yeah. I think it's up and running." He says it as casually as if he's talking about pulling a bunch of guys together for a game of two-hand touch football.

"Could the police department place a wiretap on something like that?" I touch the bedspread.

"Why would they want to?" he asks, studying the cards

before placing a few down. "Aren't those crisis lines supposed to be confidential?"

I am purposely vague. "Uh, maybe if there are risk issues or something like that."

"Oh, you mean if someone's suicidal and says they just slit their wrists or something?"

Not really, but okay. I just wait for him to go on.

"I think in an emergency like that, and with the person still on the line, the police could trace the call to save the person's life. That would be considered a kosher reason to invade someone's privacy."

"Oh."

"Why do you ask?" He looks up from his cards.

"No reason." I kiss him good night on the forehead, and he returns to his game. But I peek back at him as I leave the room. His hands are holding cards, but his eyes are watching me. When he sees me looking back, he quickly looks down.

* * *

We have a safe under the desk in Mom's office. My parents keep private stuff in there. Documents, passwords, projects from work, and Dad's gun. Dad always says when you're a cop in a small community, you never know when you're gonna need your weapon. So he keeps one locked away.

I know the code to the safe. I'm not supposed to know it, of course, but I do. I'm responsible about it though. It's not like I'm gonna tell anyone. But I do sometimes take a peek. I know my parents each have wills. And that they have a document that separates their finances. And that Dad sometimes brings home photocopies of evidence so that he can study them after hours.

I don't touch the gun. I never do. Dad did a good enough job of scaring me away from guns when I was little. Guns and motor-cycles. I won't touch either.

But tonight, after everyone's asleep, I creep down and look at Dad's work file. I find a photocopy of another playing card. A joker. It looks just like the one I'd found in my locker, with neat block letters in Sharpie edging around the perimeter. *I still hold a thousand lives in my hands. But you will never find me. I am invisible. I could be right under your nose, and you know it.*

After I read it, I wish that I hadn't.

I put everything back carefully, then scramble upstairs. I'm so spooked that it feels like the shadows have eyes and the corners of the banister are pulling at me with bony arms. *Yikes.* I try to laugh at myself, but fail. It feels a little too convenient that one of those same playing cards just *happened* to be in the slats of my locker. The bomber's got to be planting them. For me. For Dad. And maybe for other people too.

So even though I have no clue who *he* is, he knows who *I* am.

He's playing a game.

A game that I don't want to play.

And now I'm totally losing my mind, because I hear this clickety-clicking sound coming from the hall, like mice are tap-dancing on Chloe's dresser. I move forward and peek through the crack in the door to her room.

Chloe's up. She's typing on her computer, and since all the lights are out, there's a bluish glow emanating from the screen. The screen lights up her face with an otherworldly tint. I get the profile view, because from my position at the door, I just see the side of her face. I can't tell what she's typing, or even what site she's on.

I inch the door open, craning for a better look.

The door creaks. Her head snaps toward me. "Hey." She seems surprised and quickly moves the mouse to close out of whatever she was doing. Her hair is sticking up in all directions, and she's wearing the nighttime retainer that makes her slur. "You can't sleep either?"

"Nah," I lie.

"Wanna have a party?" When we were little and got scared at night, we'd sleep over in each other's rooms and call it a "party."

"Sure," I say slowly, thinking that it's been at least four years since we've done this. "My place or yours?"

"Yours." She's moving the mouse around again, shutting the computer down completely. "I don't want you sleeping on the floor in your old age."

"Very funny."

Five minutes later, I'm in bed with the covers pulled up to my chin. I can hear Chloe shifting around on the carpet beside me. We've laid out comforters and pillows, and basically done everything but move her mattress over here. Chloe's breathing evens quickly. I try to match mine to hers. Try to take myself back to a time when nighttime sleepovers were the norm and my sister and I shared all our secrets.

When life was simple.

It feels so long ago.

Stranger's Manifesto
Entry 7

I found her, you know.
Jo.
Hanging like a puppet from the tree.
Swinging in the wind.
Eyes bulging and pointed right at me.
Accusing me.
Like somehow I could have stopped her.
Like somehow I *should* have stopped her.

I hate that
Shoulda-woulda-coulda feeling.
It weighs down my chest
Like an avalanche of dictionaries.
But now, *I'm* in charge
And things will be different.
This time I'll deal the cards
In *my* favor.

11

EARLY NOVEMBER

"This is harder than it looks," I complain. I'm sitting cross-legged on the futon, holding a tiny purple bead between two fingers and trying to thread wire through the microscopic hole. Janae searches through the pile of beads in the center of the futon.

"You want some help?" Miguel asks from my left.

Miguel and I were somehow paired together when Paisley made the executive decision that all helpline shifts would be run in coed teams. To "remedy safety concerns."

Janae raised her hand in the meeting to say that bombs and bullets were equal opportunity killers. Walking out with a guy didn't necessarily increase her safety. But Janae's not complaining because she got paired with Garth. I made Janae promise to come with me for my shifts so I wouldn't have to be alone with Miguel. I told her I'd pay her back and come to her shifts too.

"Go for it." I say, holding out the jewelry. Miguel takes it from me, his fingers brushing against mine. His skin feels hot, and the tips of his fingers are rough to the touch, but not in a bad way.

Miguel grins, his teeth flashing white against his dark skin. "I've rethreaded my mother's sewing needles a hundred times." I watch as he licks his finger and then slips the wire through the small hole.

Riiiiing. We all jump. We've got to stop being so jumpy about getting phone calls. That is, after all, the whole reason we are here. *Riiiiing.*

"I'll take it," I say.

I sit in the chair, take a deep breath, and pick up the phone. "Helpline, this is Vanessa."

"Oh, hi." The voice sounds surprised, like maybe she didn't expect anyone would answer.

"Hi," I tell her. "What's going on tonight?"

"Uh…" Her voice is shaky. "It's nothing really."

"I'm here to listen," I remind her.

"Okay, it's just that I moved here midyear, and no one at this school has ever heard of being friendly!"

I am momentarily offended. Of course we're friendly. I write on my paper: *Lonely. New to school. People unfriendly.*

Janae scribbles, *How does that make you feel?*

I hate these pat answers and questions. They feel so forced. But I can't think of anything else to say. "So you're new to school." This sounds even more ridiculous, but luckily the girl doesn't seem to mind.

"Yeah. I hate it here. I've been eating my lunch in a bathroom stall, because there's no place to sit. No one seems to want to get to know someone new."

Miguel writes on the paper, *Get involved in a club? Or a sport?*

I'll have to remind him later that we're not supposed to give advice. "Are there any groups you'd really like to hang out with?"

"At my old school I hung with the theater kids."

"We have a drama program here too," I point out. "The drama teacher lets people eat their lunches in her room if she's in there."

"Really?" I hear the slight lift in her voice. "But I'm not in drama. And I haven't auditioned for any plays."

"As far as I know, there's no rule that says you have to. As long as you clean up your own trash, it shouldn't be an issue."

I'm not sure if I just gave advice, but whatever I did, it worked. The girl chatters for a few more minutes, saying she has nothing to lose so she might as well give it a shot. Anything beats eating lunch in the bathroom. And my friends each give me a pat on the back. Mission complete.

At five minutes to closing, *Ping!* A text comes in. The words glow on the computer screen. **Are you still there?**

Miguel types, **I'm here.**

"Anyone in a hurry tonight?" I ask. "Let's just stay here another twenty minutes and see if this person texts back."

Everybody's game, so we kick back and wait. It takes ten minutes. Then *Ping!*

I can't fall asleep. I can never fall asleep.

That must be really frustrating.

You're still there? I thought you guys got off at nine.

We do. But if you know that, why do you text after we're closed?

I don't know. Then a few seconds later. **Because I can't fall asleep. I just keep thinking and thinking, and it makes me feel like I'm going crazy.**

Are you stuck on a thought tonight?

It's embarrassing.

No worries. This is anonymous.

I keep having nightmares about that lockdown. I wake up all sweaty and panicky. Thinking about it makes it hard to fall asleep.

That sounds awful.

Seems ridiculous that it's still bothering me.

I bet you'd find other people are still reacting from the lockdown too. Have you talked to any of your friends?

Well, that's the other thing. I'm losing my best friend.

Tell me more.

She's just moving on. That happens, I know. But it sucks.

Agreed. Have you talked to her about it?

No. But what's she gonna say? She's too nice to hurt my feelings. I can just tell she's moving on. Too bad this thing is anonymous. I'd like to link bathroom-lunch-eating girl with losing-my-best-friend girl.

That must make you sad.

Yeah. Then a few seconds later, I'll let you go. Thanks for staying late for me.

Sure.

12

The next morning in homeroom, Garth stops at my desk before the bell rings. I stare at his Nikes for ten seconds before I register that he's there to talk to me. His feet are the size of tennis rackets. "Got a question for you."

"It better not be about the physics exam, because I know *nothing!*" I feel like crap—I'm wearing sweats and a baseball cap to hide my unwashed hair. "I tried to cram last night when I got home, but it was too late and I couldn't concentrate for anything."

"Physics is a nightmare," Garth agrees. "But that's not—"

"I'm gonna fail." I cut him off. "My parents are gonna kill me!" My voice is shrill. I've never been this unprepared for a test.

I must sound panicked, because some scrawny kid I don't even know says, "I got a cram sheet if you want to see it." He's wearing a heavy jacket, so big that it could practically swallow him up.

"For physics," he asserts again, shifting his camera strap. Those yearbook kids wear cameras like accessories. "You can use my cram sheet." He pulls some crumpled papers out of his backpack.

"Thank you," and then I pause. I can't remember if his name is Simon or Samuel, which is embarrassing because I've had science classes with him since sophomore year. I take the papers from him. Looks like a worksheet of some kind.

"No prob." He smiles and moves on.

"And who says people aren't nice these days?" I scan the page, realizing how little I know about today's test and how royally screwed I am.

"Gabi—" Garth pauses like he's uncomfortable. "You think Janae has a boyfriend?"

"Where did *that* come from?" I look up from the cram sheet, surprised. "And why do you care?"

"Will you ask her?" Garth's cheeks turn pink.

"Depends. What do I get in return?" I just might have fun with this.

* * *

"How middle school!" Janae complains, trying to hide a smile with her hand. "He can't ask me himself?"

I turn to my locker and twist the knob. "Maybe he's just shy."

"Shy, my ass. How 'bout coward-ish?"

"That's not even a word," I tell her.

"So? You know what I mean, so it works." Janae readjusts her Dickies skinny pants. I can see her belly button ring. "You know we're gonna have to pay him back for being such a loser."

"No. No. No! I don't know that." I shake my head to make my point. "I'm not getting anyone back. I've already committed one crime for the day, and that's enough for me."

"Wait. Crime? You committed a crime?" The corners of Janae's mouth twitch, like she's thinking something funny. "You mean something other than having the world's messiest locker?"

I make a face. My locker is messy, sure, but there's no need to be mean about it. I sigh. "I cheated on a physics test."

"So?"

"So I've never cheated on a test in my life."

"Oh, boohoo." Janae wipes fake tears from her eyes and gets all dramatic now, holding her hand to her face. "So now your moral code has gone to shit like the rest of us."

I ignore this. "It's so weird. This kid I hardly know gives me a study sheet. But that sheet *was* the test. Same formatting and everything. How he got a copy of the test I don't know, and I don't really want to know."

"You're a trip." Janae slings her arm around my shoulder. "Where have you been? Everyone knows Cooper reuses tests. Probably half the kids in your class crammed with the same info you did. Anyone who has an older brother or sister who's taken the class, or a neighbor or a friend...There are probably thirty copies of that test floating around campus. So give yourself a break, why don't you, before you have an aneurysm."

"Is that supposed to be comforting?" I ask, but honestly, I'm relieved. If I go down for cheating, so will half the senior class.

"This is good for you, Gabs. You got to loosen up." And then she gets this gleam in her eye. "Get comfortable with being less than perfect, Gabi, because you are about to be a part of something totally sneaky and fantastic. A prank war."

* * *

Janae works fast. By the following day at lunchtime, we're cramming ninety-seven dollar-menu hamburgers into Garth's locker. We could have fit at least twenty more if we'd smushed them together and hadn't run out of money. Janae texted as many people as she could, asking them if they'd pitch in a buck for a dollar-menu cafeteria burger and a good laugh.

Janae and I lean against the lockers across the hall from Garth's, just waiting and watching for him to come along. I'd begged Garth's best friend to tell us his locker combo. It took him about ten seconds to give up the combination once I explained the prank war.

Word has spread and now this hallway is way crowded. I see Garth ambling down the hallway, all big and bulky with hands like bear paws. Janae hugs me. "Are you ready?"

I am. I've already got my phone out. My job is to capture the moment with video so that we can post it online.

If Garth notices anything strange, he doesn't show it. He walks with his whole body, like he can't just move his feet, and it takes his shoulders to move him down the hall.

When Garth twists the knob on his locker, I've got the phone out and pointed at him. It all happens in slow motion. The burgers are so crammed in there that as the door pulls back and away, they tumble forward and out. He steps back instinctively, and I move at an angle so I can catch his expression. Kind of a what-in-the-hell, do-I-have-the-wrong-locker look.

I'm standing in his line of vision though, and I can see him taking in the cell phone camera. He scans the room in slow motion. People start to clap slowly, but it builds up. Garth calls out, "I hope these are veggie burgers!"

Stranger's Manifesto
Entry 8

You think best friends know everything about each other.
You think I should have known what she was going to do.
You think she would've told me.

She did.
She did tell me.
But she'd been saying shit like that for years.
Years.
Talking death. Emo crap. Black eyeliner.
The whole bit.
Playing her game.
What's the best way to die?
Being slammed on the train tracks?
    Instantaneous.
    But they'd find pieces of you for miles.
    And what would your parents bury?
Slitting an artery?
    Slower.
    Pain not so bad.
    But messy as hell.
    And who cleans that up?
Gun in the mouth.
    Quick.
    Effective.
    Also messy.
    And where does a tenth grader get a gun?

Pills.

Easy to get. Easy to take.
But if nobody finds you, you choke on your own vomit.
Kind of repulsive.

She never mentioned hanging.
Never.
And she never said this was more than a game.
Never.
But I should have known.
A better friend would have known.

That's my daily ride on the guilt train.
My mind circles the track
Over and over
The *chugga-chugging*
Sounding a whole helluva lot like
Shoulda-woulda, shoulda-woulda.
I can never get off that train.
It's the worst when I'm in bed
And the silence of the house is suffocating.
The only way I can distract my brain
Is to plan
My next move.
There's one thing I've learned from Jo—
That sometimes someone has to die
To make a point.

13

Our library is always freezing. I don't complain though. It keeps me awake.

"You ready for the test in government?" Eric stacks his notes neatly on the library table.

I look up. "No. That'd be why I'm cramming during lunch." I'm trying to refocus on my schoolwork. Kick senioritis to the curb. Beth's sampling a new lunchtime club.

"Want help?"

"Unless you can magically beam the answers into my brain, I doubt any kind of help can rescue me now. I'm just bracing myself for the parental lecture I'm gonna get when I bring home a B. All about getting my priorities straight and yada, yada." I rub my arms because the goose bumps are having a field day.

"The problem is that you've spoiled them by bringing home all A's. Now they expect it."

I grin. "Maybe."

"If you started out with C's, they'd be thrilled with B's."

"Good point. Maybe I've been going about this all wrong." I look back at my book. I have so much left to read. I don't want to be rude, but I want him to leave. I really do need to cram. "I don't think you're a good example though. You're in the running for valedictorian, aren't you?"

Eric shrugs like it's no big deal. He drags back a chair, scraping it on the ground, and sits himself down. He pulls my textbook away from me and I'm about to protest, but I see the librarian shooting us the evil eye from across the room. We are too loud.

"Here," he says, turning the pages. "Focus on this section. If you have this part down, you'll do fine."

"Okay. I guess I can't get through it all anyway." I move the book back in front of me. He stays in his seat, watching me. "Not to be rude, but I can't concentrate with you sitting there."

"Okay, okay, I get the hint." He stands up. "You'll do fine."

I read the section twice, and skim the headings and bolded words in the rest of the chapter. I hope Eric is right. The warning bell rings and I suddenly feel the warmth of a body next to mine. I almost laugh out loud. Has Eric been waiting for me all lunch?

But when I look up, I don't see Eric. I see Miguel. He's holding a single rose.

My skin prickles in an oh-my-god-is-this-really-happening kind of way. I have never been given a rose by a boy in my life.

It feels so completely cheesy that I can hardly take it from him.

But I don't want to hurt his feelings, and he looks so vulnerable standing there holding it. So I reach my hand out and take it. I murmur something that vaguely resembles a "thank you." It's so awkward I can hardly meet his eyes, so I scramble to pack up my books and jam out of there. Halfway to my locker, I prick my finger on a thorn. I spend half the government test sucking on the finger so it won't bleed all over my paper.

* * *

Chloe has perfected the art of parental manipulation. The girl should win an award. She has a whole strategy.

Step One—Secure parental sympathy (slink around in room groaning about PMS, I'm so depressed, and no one understands me).

Step Two—Spring the big question (which may vary based on situation).

One time her strategy backfired and they made her see a shrink. Today, however, she's having a sleepover. The living room has been taken hostage by sophomores, with their pillows and blankets, nail polish, cell phones, and magazines strewn all over. I smell burnt popcorn kernels and nail-polish remover. Ice-cold sodas decorate the coffee table, and I have this irresistible urge to slide coasters underneath them so that they don't leave rings.

Beth and I are standing in the doorway with our mouths open. We've got three tests next week, so we thought we'd get a head start on prepping.

Chloe waves me in, all enthusiastic. "Hey Gabi! Come kick it with us."

I try not to groan. "Uh, no thanks. We've got to study."

"It's Friday night—live a little. We'll give you a makeover!" She says this like it's a good thing, then rips off a piece of red licorice with her teeth.

"You're not touching my hair." I tell her, sinking down onto a mound of blankets and sleeping bags. "My toes maybe, but not my hair." Beth sits stiffly on the very edge of the couch.

"Deal," Chloe agrees. "Does Beth know everybody?"

I look around. "I think so," I tell her, but I introduce Beth anyway. They're all girls Chloe has been friends with since middle school. They're like a funky mismatch of lost socks, each without a mate, but hanging out together makes them one of a group. That

76

girl Mel sits with a sour face in the corner, painting her toenails black. She seems like even more of an outcast than the others.

Beth watches half of *Scream 4* and then takes off, mumbling about due dates for essays and upcoming quizzes. I hate to see her go, but I'm not in the mental space for studying anyway. I allow my toenails to be painted silver by a girl who is bouncing off the walls.

"God, you're such an idiot, Chloe. When Mom sees this room, she's gonna be hella pissed."

"Yep." Chloe grins. "That's pretty much the point."

Mel surprises me by joining our conversation. She drops down onto the couch. "Why do you want to piss her off?"

"Have you seen her get worked up? It's hilarious. True entertainment."

"You're lucky she gets worked up," Mel says. "One time I went on a silent shower strike. I didn't shower or talk for a week, but no one noticed. I'd planned to wait until someone said something, but no one ever did."

"What finally happened?" Chloe asks.

Mel shrugs. "I got so tired of my own stink that I gave up and showered."

Chloe and I laugh at this, but not for long because Mel isn't laughing. Dad walks in just then. I can tell by the way his gait falters and then speeds up that he is as surprised as I was to have our living room taken hostage. He covers it up, though, with a curt, "Hi there, girls," followed by a brisk walk to the stairs.

"He even walks like a cop," Chloe says.

"How exactly does a cop walk?" I ask.

"The way he does. Like with his whole body."

"Does your dad have a gun?" Mel asks, all curious. Her fingernails

77

are nonexistent. Either she bites them or she files them down really low. It looks ridiculous, because she's painted them black, and all you can see are these tiny blobs of black on each finger.

Chloe answers like it's the most obvious thing in the world. "All cops have guns."

"No—I mean one that he keeps at home?"

"Yeah." I kind of thought all cops had guns they kept at home.

"Trippy." Mel chews on her lip, and then she whispers, "Have you ever touched it?"

"No," I answer fast, and then wish I hadn't. I wonder how Chloe would answer that one. "He keeps it locked up." I don't mention that I know the combo. And then because I can't help it, I ask Chloe, "Have *you* ever touched it?"

She doesn't make eye contact right away, and that tells me all I need to know. She slides her eyes up toward mine, and then she says, "Nope. Never touched it." If she hadn't looked away, I'd have believed her. But she did look away. And now I know she's a liar.

I can tell Mel knows too. She makes this strange *mmhmm* noise and gets this glimmer of a smile, so slight that after a minute I'm not sure if it was really a smile at all. First time I've seen her smile today.

It creeps me out.

* * *

"Want to grab a pizza after our shift?"

Miguel has asked me out ten times in the last week. In ten different ways. To ten different places. I've made up ten different excuses.

I sigh. I've been considering asking Paisley to swap partners, but maybe I should just be a grown-up and talk to him.

I face him. "Miguel, this may sound strange to you, but I've never really dated anyone."

78

I can tell by his expression that he thinks this is just excuse number eleven. It's not. "Look, my dad's a cop, and he sees all kinds of crazy things out there, so he's super strict." Plus Mom has always wanted me to stay focused and avoid drama. Keep my "eye on the prize."

So I don't date.

Not that I've had a lot of opportunities anyway, but I don't tell Miguel that. He's nodding again, and I can tell he's not going to give up on this one. What, is he waiting for his quota of rejections?

"How many times do I have to tell you I'm not interested?" I ask Miguel. I feel brave because Janae's in the office with us. She's beading and she has her earphones in, but I can tell she's really listening to our conversation anyway.

"Only once." He sits down close to me.

"I've already told you a million times!" I almost scoot away. But his bare arm is touching my bare arm, and it makes me tingle. I'm not sure if it feels nice or uncomfortable, but I stay anyway.

"You've lied to me a million times. I *know* you're interested."

"You're full of yourself."

Miguel stops, and I think maybe I've offended him. He repeats what I said. "Full of myself? I am not familiar with that expression."

Janae snorts. She unplugs her ears. "You're a riot," she tells Miguel. He winks at her. "A riot? What does that mean?"

Janae throws a bead at him. "In case you didn't know it, Gabi, Miguel likes to play the new immigrant thing. It's his dating act."

"What you mean by 'new immigrant thing'?" Miguel holds his hands up flat, all innocent. Then he reaches over and grabs Janae's foot.

79

"He thinks it makes him cuter." She kicks her leg to try to get him off. "Has he tried the rose shtick yet?"

I look back and forth between Janae and Miguel. Miguel's face has turned a dark shade of purple, which is hard to do since his skin is so dark in the first place. But he's not pissed. His eyes are practically twinkling. He turns to me. "Anyway, I *know* you're into me. *You* just don't know it yet."

"Screw you," I tell him as firmly as I can. I try to ignore the tingling on my arm from where our skin connected.

"Okay." He grins, palms flat up in the air again. "That sounds fun."

Stranger's Manifesto
Entry 9

I knew.
I freaking knew.
Not in my brain.
But somewhere deep in my bones.
I *knew.*
And I did nothing to stop it.
The *shoulda-woulda* of the guilt train
Reminds me
Every time I close my eyes.
That's why I have to do something now.
Even if people hate me for it.

Implementing my plan is painfully easy,
Because there are perks
To being invisible.
No one feels the heat of my eyes watching
Or wonders what I'm doing out of class.
No one sees me lurking by lockers.

So planting playing cards is a freaking piece of cake.
I've got to practically wave the clues under their noses.
That's how stupid they are.
Or maybe just how
Inconsequential
I am.

14

MID-NOVEMBER

A-minus on the government test, 89.99 percent.

Eric moves past my desk after Mr. Thurber hands out the graded exams.

"See?" he whispers. "I told you not to worry."

"How'd you do that?"

"Magic." He winks. "I have my ways." He slides into his own seat.

I shake my head and smile.

Eric follows me at passing period and corners me at my locker. "If we're study partners, I guarantee you'll ace all your government tests."

"Yeah?" I say, trying to pull the trash out of my locker. I've got to keep my grades up, at least until I get my acceptance letters. Then maybe I can let things slide. "Want to form a study group? If we invite Beth she'll bring Oreos. Her mom buys them in bulk."

"How about just you and me?"

I look up, and Eric's all shifty, like he just asked me out on a date or something.

Life is crazy. For seventeen years no guy has ever noticed me, and now all of a sudden I've got two who want to hang out? Mom might be a little more approving of a study-date kind of thing, and who could be more brilliant than Eric?

"I don't have much time," I tell him.

"Well, you have to study, right?"

"Good point. I get home from clinic at seven thirty on Thursday. Want to come over then?" Mom won't mind, I don't think. She'll be happy I'm studying, and we'll sit at the kitchen table so there isn't any stress about bringing a boy into my room.

"Sure," he says, like this is what he's been waiting for.

"My mom's a health-food nut, so don't expect chips or candy. You like carrot sticks?"

He looks at me like I'm kidding.

* * *

Mom is buzzing. Zipping around in the kitchen, hovering by the fridge, then organizing our junk drawer and fixing some snacks of veggies, hummus, and sliced triangles of whole-grain pita bread. "Eric is such a focused young man." The study date meets her standards, apparently. Mom has known Eric since junior year's academic decathlon, when he blew everyone away with his brilliance.

"You're not going to hang around here while we study, are you?" I ask her.

Mom says "no" so trigger-fast that I know she's lying.

"I am." Chloe smirks. "Should be fun."

"You can't interrupt them, Chloe," Mom warns, pretending like she wasn't planning to do exactly the same thing.

"I won't interrupt them. I'll study. You want me to study too, don't you, Mom?"

Mom is stuck. I can see her thinking through her answers, wondering how she can tell Chloe to stay away from us without insulting Chloe's academic potential, and without implicitly con-doning Eric and me spending time *alone*. So she just shrugs and says, "As long as everyone's staying productive," and continues buzzing around the room.

An hour later, Eric and I sit at the kitchen table, nearly elbow to elbow. "I thought you were kidding about the carrot sticks." He grins.

"Nope," I say cheerfully, crunching one loudly.

Mom has disappeared from view, mostly. She buzzes in and out periodically to make it clear that she is *supervising*. I'm embar-rassed, because I'm seventeen after all. *Please*. Chloe sat with us for the first twenty minutes, her math book open and her pencil poised, clearly prepared to watch the show. But then when we really did talk government, I could see her excitement melt away. Eventually she slunk into the other room to watch TV.

I look at Eric. He's sort of cute, I guess. At least he might be in a few years if he fills out and figures out a way to do his hair that doesn't make him look like a little boy. Why is it that brilliant guys are so clueless about how to use hair gel? Maybe academic brilliance is inversely related to fashion sense.

Eric reaches for a carrot stick and chomps down. When he sets his elbow back on the antique table, he puts it directly against mine. It feels cold and smooth.

I look up and he is staring at me. *Way to make me uncomfort-able.*

But I'm struck by something.

I have no tingles. Touching his arm doesn't gross me out or anything, but I feel nothing.

I might as well have my arm against a telephone pole.

* * *

"Eric would have some cute potential, like, in a nerdy way, if he'd just wear something other than Star Wars T-shirts," Janae says, all encouraging as we walk between classes. Some people do double takes as we stroll past. I guess we're an unlikely pairing.

I can't help but smile.

"He's only got like seven different ones, and he recycles through them every week. Dude, at least alternate the day! Don't wear them in the same order every single week." She turns around and walks backward, facing me.

"I'm just not feeling it," I tell her. "Sure, I'm happy for the help studying, but I'm not into him, you know?"

"I know who you *are* into." She stops me, putting both hands on my shoulders.

"Shut up."

"And so does everyone else. It's obvious. Give poor Miguel a break. How hard are you gonna make him work before you break down and kiss him?"

"Shut up," I tell her more firmly now. "Focus on your own love life, why don't you?"

"That," she says, eyeing Garth from across the quad, "is an excellent idea."

* * *

Chloe has way more experience with dating, kissing, you-name-it than I do. By far. So although it seems strange to go to my little sister for advice, I find myself lingering near her bedroom door. I knock softly a couple times, but she must have her earbuds in because she doesn't answer. Unsure if I'm going to walk in on her half naked or picking her nose or something, I place my hand on the doorknob and open the door slowly.

She's sitting cross-legged on her bed. Her back is turned away from me, and she does have her earbuds in. The bass is so loud that I can hear it from the doorway.

But something stops me short. She's holding a playing card in her hand. It's a queen, with black Sharpie drawn on it like the others. She lifts the card up toward the light. The queen's eyes are crossed out with *x*'s, her tongue is hanging, and there is a noose drawn around her neck.

What the hell? Did Chloe draw that?

Just as I step in closer, she throws the card across the room, or tries to. The card is too light, so the throw looks pitiful, and the card sort of floats to the floor. She draws her legs up to her chest and pushes her head down into them.

A lump crawls into my throat, and I feel suddenly sad. I step back and slowly close the door.

Stranger's Manifesto
Entry 10

I know what you're thinking.
You're wondering what's so wrong with me that I only have one
friend.
Had.
Had one friend.
You're wondering, do you smell?
Do you have some major case of B.O.?
Do you pick your nose? And eat it?
You're wondering what's wrong with me, what makes me such a
loser?
Man, if I had the answer to that question,
I'd sure as hell do something about it.

Let's just say it took me until the third grade to figure out
That talking out loud to myself was strange.
And when my mom left in the sixth grade,
There was no one to make me take a bath all regular,
So I went weeks in between contact with soap and water.

But now I know better.
I shower, I brush my teeth, I don't walk around talking to myself.
And still…I have no one. No one real, anyway.
The only one who ever really talked to me like an actual person
Is dead.

15

I corner Chloe in the morning before school. We're crowded in the bathroom, both trying to blow-dry our hair and apply makeup. We're plugged in on opposite sides of the bathroom, each of us in front of our own sink, our blow-dryers loud.

My eyes are red rimmed, and they feel raw every time I blink. I hardly slept, and when I did, I dreamed of Chloe, playing cards, nooses, and bombs. Had Chloe taken another card out of Dad's wallet? I'd been snooping through his safe, so I couldn't really judge her if she'd been doing the same thing. But seeing her with that horrible card in her hand? It made me worry.

Members of my family have come into contact with at least four creepy cards in the last couple weeks since the bombing attempt. The one in my locker, the one Chloe found in Dad's wallet, the one I found in the safe, and the one I'd seen in Chloe's hand yesterday. *What in the world is going on? And why is my family such a part of it?*

I watch us both in the mirror, look at our faces, and marvel at how different we are. But are we different because we have truly opposite personalities, or are we different because Chloe has purposely made herself as opposite from me as possible? If I liked red, did she decide to like blue? Since I got A's, did she decide C's were her goal?

Chloe must see me staring at her. She sets down her hair dryer, still running full blast. "What?" She asks me.

I turn mine off and set it down.

She keeps staring.

"Can you turn off your drier?" I shout, because that's the only way she'll hear me.

She does. "What?" she asks again. "You have the strangest look on your face."

And now that I have her attention, I have no idea how to start.

"Are you okay?" I ask her.

"Yes. Why? Do I look sick?" She leans forward to the mirror to examine her face. She pokes at imaginary circles under her eyes.

"No—I guess you've just seemed a little down lately and I wanted to check in."

And then I wonder if she's heard me right. Because she starts to laugh. Hysterically. Like I'm the funniest person in the world.

I'm offended (a little) and alarmed (more than a little). "Why are you laughing?" I snap.

"Oh—sorry." She dabs at her eyes with a tissue, and now she really does have circles underneath them because she's managed to smear her eyeliner. "I'm fine, Gabi."

"Why are you laughing?" I ask again.

"Because you sounded like a shrink." She giggles. "But no worries. Right now I'm fine." She tosses the wet tissue, now a dark gray, into the trash. "Things are good."

"I'm glad." And then I get curious. "Why are you fine right now?"

I can tell by the way her lips purse that she's going to joke around. "Because God made me fine." She tosses her hair dramatically. "Fine ass, fine face, fine, fine, fine."

I catch myself rolling my eyes in the mirror. "At least you've got good self-esteem."

"No—I'm fine because I have a new boyfriend." She winks at my reflection.

"Really? Who?" Super curious. I didn't know she'd dumped that freshman.

"Not telling yet. I've got to get to know him better first."

"Oh, okay." And I smile. Because I'm thinking of Eric. And Miguel. And wondering if I might have a boyfriend of my own pretty soon. I'm warming up to the idea.

"Why are you smiling?"

"No reason." I try to even out my lips, and I can't. "I guess I'm just thinking I better ask how you're doing more often."

We're both still facing the mirror, but she scoots over and slaps my butt. Hard.

"Ouch!" I complain.

"You'd have a fine ass too, if you gained five pounds."

Now it's my turn to laugh.

Chloe's fine, I reassure myself. She's not depressed. She's not the kind of person to draw a noose around the neck of a queen of hearts. She probably just dug through Dad's stuff, and I did the exact same thing, so who am I to judge? And as to why she looked so upset yesterday? Seeing a creepy card like that would be upsetting for anyone. It's normal.

Chloe's fine.

Honestly, she's probably better adjusted than I am. She's funny, laughing, dating new boyfriends. At least she knows what kind of guys she's into. I'm clueless. Maybe I just need some experience to know what I'm looking for. I used to swear up and down that mint chip was the best ice cream in the world. Until I tasted double java chip, which is, hands down, a million times better. Maybe I won't really know what kind of guy is my type until I take a risk and start to date.

16

My "risk" comes sooner than I thought.

I'm not prepared.

Eric and I sit at the kitchen table talking government and working through some calculus problems. My sister lies sprawled across the couch in the next room. We had a half day today, so he came over right after school.

Mom keeps buzzing in and out of the room for random things she "forgot," and after she buzzes out for the zillionth time, Eric leans over and catches my mouth with his. Quick, determined, and mostly close-mouthed—although at the end he pushes his tongue in and it surprises me. I'm stunned, and all I can think is, *Did he really kiss me?*

He pulls back, almost embarrassed-like, and looks at me. "You are *so* pretty," he whispers, looking at me like I'm not real and he wants to touch me to make sure.

Okay, so this is awkward. Because what am I supposed to say back? Am I supposed to try to repay the compliment and say something nice to him? *And you're brilliant!* Or, *You might be cute in a few years.* Or, *Gee, thanks.* None of those sound right. So I say nothing. Instead I just lean back in and give him a peck on the cheek. His skin feels sandpaper rough to my lips, like maybe he had some stubble there that he'd shaved off.

Eric sits the rest of our study date with this goofy half-smile, and I swear the kiss has vacuumed his brain cells away, because he doesn't know his government from his English lit. And I'm sitting there thinking, *That was all right. Not great, not horrible, but all right.* And I'm hoping he can hold on to some of those brain cells and still help me keep an A in government.

Eric takes off an hour before my helpline shift. He squeezes my hand before he goes and looks like he wants to kiss me again. But Mom is still buzzing around, and there's just no time for that, so I stand there wondering whether I even *want* him to kiss me again. *Maybe. As long as he doesn't drool on me.*

But the moment passes, and he wraps his arms around me for an awkward hug, even though my mom's standing right there. She doesn't say a word. Maybe if I only date guys with IQs higher than mine, she'll be cool with it. He heads off, his backpack strapped to his shoulders and looking like it's carrying a library full of books. For some reason, this is a bit of a turn-off.

My phone buzzes on the table. Text from Janae. **Can't make it to the shift tonight. Got the flu. Hope I didn't already give it to you.** That means Miguel and I will be on our own.

Thank goodness the shift starts with a bunch of easy calls. "My best friend's using drugs, what should I do?" Since we can't give advice, we just read down a list of referral numbers for counseling and for drug treatment. "My boyfriend broke up with me and boohoo." Piece of cake. Just listen and validate feelings.

When Miguel answers the phone, I scoot my chair in so I can reach his notepaper. When he speaks, there is something soft in his voice that lulls me. Maybe it's just his attempt at being supportive. He speaks in low tones, and I quickly stop paying attention to what he's saying, so his words run together, but they almost sound musical.

Ping! **Man problems. Need advice.**

"I'll take this one." I elbow Miguel.

"Not sure you're qualified." He elbows me back. "You don't date, remember?"

Good point. "Well, I'm more qualified than you!"

Men! What's up? I type.

Why do they always seem so nice at first?

I look pointedly at Miguel. "Okay, maybe you *are* more qualified. Answer this question: What's up with this nice-guy act?"

"Ahem. I can only speak for myself. I am truly nice. Can't help it."

We must have taken too long to respond, because she (I'm assuming it's a she) texts again. **But when they get what they want, they morph into assholes! Explain this to me.**

I look at Miguel. He holds up his hands. "Those guys give men a bad rap. That's not me."

Again, I'm not going fast enough for her. **Advice?**

So I'm not actually allowed to give advice. But I can give you a referral for counseling.

Seriously? I don't need a shrink. I just need someone to talk to.

Is there anyone at home you can talk to?

Uh, no. That'd be why I'm texting you. No one at home would understand. They're all perfect, and they already think I'm screwing up my life.

What's more important is what YOU think. That must've caught her attention, because she doesn't text back right away. **What do you think?**

I think I deserve to be treated better than this.

You go, girl! After I press Send, I gasp. "What if that wasn't a girl? It could've been a guy."

Miguel smiles. "True. Good point."

Hopefully I didn't offend him-her, because he-she texted back. **Thanks.**

In between calls we decorate the office, joke around, and tack our homemade bracelets to the office walls in a great, big peace-sign shape. Miguel's arm keeps bumping into mine. I pull away. I feel like he's got some kind of electric current running through him, and every time he touches me I get shocked. It's not a bad feeling exactly, but it surprises me, and I'm not sure what to make of it.

Miguel stands back from our peace sign and studies it. Then he turns and studies me. "So you survived almost a whole shift without your bodyguard," he jokes.

"Who, Janae?" Now that's funny, because Janae's about my size. "If I wanted a bodyguard, I'd have picked Garth. Besides, I can protect myself." I go to sock his arm, but he grabs my hand and pulls me toward him. He smells so clean, like always, like he just stepped out of the shower and his clothes are fresh from the dryer.

"*¿Puedo besarte?*" he says, reverting back to his new-immigrant persona.

"What?" I'm stalling. I've had four years of Spanish. I know what that means. I step away. He's not my type. But what's my type? And wasn't I just telling myself to take a risk? To experiment a little to see what I like?

Miguel's grinning. Like he already knows I want him to. "Look, I'm not like one of those guys our texter was talking about. I'm a nice guy. I promise." I see a tiny dimple in his upper right cheek that I never noticed before. "And you are *muy bonita*. Can I kiss you?"

His shirt is pretty tight. I try not to notice how his chest presses against it. He looks like he's fit underneath it—not like he lifts weights, but more just naturally fit. He waits expectantly. *Crap.* I answer in Spanish, as corny as that sounds. "*Está bien.*"

He pulls me in again, and he doesn't hesitate. I hold back at first, tense. *Take a risk, take a risk,* I tell myself. I close my eyes and allow myself to relax. Then I'm melting into his arms, my mouth melting into his mouth, and every single hair on my body is standing on end. So electric. The rest of the world blurs and there is only him. His hands cupping my face, moving to my shoulders, and settling around my waist. Our hips touch and my body is on fire. So *this* is a kiss. I want more. I am hungry for more.

When we pull away I have no idea how much time has passed. Was that one kiss? Or a marathon of kisses?

"Wow," he whispers in my ear. His breath sends tingles down my arms. "We got to do that more often."

I don't say anything at first, just stand there, catching my breath and drinking him in with my eyes. "I think you have a point."

That seems to be all the invitation he needs, because suddenly I'm melting into him again, feeling warm and cold and tingly and like I'm floating. Everything I see bleeds into something else, all my senses are on overload, and my thoughts are ricocheting around in my brain. Like I might lose my footing at any moment.

Even after we stop kissing, the goose bumps last twenty minutes. And the tingles last an hour.

* * *

When I get home, I realize something terrible. I'm a player. I can't believe I just kissed *two* different guys in *one* day. Or, more accurately, two guys kissed me. I'm the kind of girl Beth and I normally hate.

Both the kisses were nice. But Eric's kiss was all about the physiology of it—lips meeting lips, tongue meeting tongue. Miguel's kiss involved all the same body parts, but the end result was tingling electricity. No comparison. Just the thought of Miguel's minty taste makes my body light up again.

And suddenly it feels *wrong*. I feel wrong.

I can't be kissing two guys in the same day. Especially not two guys who know each other. That's a recipe for disaster! It's the kind of reality-show drama Chloe would love. And the kind I avoid like the plague.

I'm not sure if I'm feeling panic, or my heart is just racing because I'm thinking about Miguel's kiss. But I know I have to do something right away. *Take a risk*, I prompt myself. If I want to try dating someone (and I most definitely do), then I need to decide which one.

But it's not a decision. My mind was made up from the moment our lips connected. I want to be with Miguel.

So I corner Eric at school the next day. And I lie. A great, big, fat lie about why I don't want to study together anymore.

I don't mean to lie. I mean to give him a mostly true explanation about valuing his friendship and not wanting to mess that up. I think through at least five different ways to say it, but none of them sound right.

And then because I start to tell him without thinking it all the way through, I lie. I say, "I'm just not into guys right now."

I see him digest this meaning, and I know within seconds that he thinks I just told him I'm gay. I'm not, of course.

But I don't correct it. Letting him believe this about me seems like an easy way to let him down.

As long as he doesn't find out otherwise.

Stranger's Manifesto
Entry 11

I stand corrected.
I have a friend.
A *new* friend.
Guess it depends on how you define "friend."
I send her messages.
I give her presents, if you can call them that.
I talk to her on the phone.
Granted, it's a tad contrived.
Oh well.
Got to take what you can get.
Besides, she's a part of my plan.
She just doesn't know it yet.
Because my bomb threat
Was like a tidal wave,
Surging, rising, powerful, strong
But it fell flat. Forgotten already.
Perhaps the school
Needs a little reminder.

17

EARLY DECEMBER

Beth takes tiny bites of her turkey sandwich, edging around the crust. "Gabi, as your best friend in the universe, I'm compelled to share my concern."

I'm scanning the campus for Miguel. We're officially "together" but we haven't transitioned to eating lunch together at school. Mostly because when I picture Beth's reaction to Miguel, my stomach sinks to my toes. I won't be able to keep our lives separate for too much longer, because this weekend I'm supposed to go to a family party with him.

"Seriously," Beth goes on. "I'm no doctor of course, but I'm diagnosing you with a raging case of senioritis."

"This is possible." And perhaps a complete personality change, because even though I've considered Beth a "best friend" all through high school, we suddenly don't feel that close.

"You've lost your focus. Forgotten your mantra. Remember 'keep your eye on the prize'?" She pauses appropriately, but I'm still looking for Miguel. "Bruce and I are worried about you. We're considering an intervention. Right, Bruce?"

He nods.

I interrupt. "Bruce, speaking of which, what's the name of that cute girl by the snack bar? The one who keeps looking at you?"

Bruce glances up from his lunch. "Katie Smith."

"Let's invite her to sit with us, Bruce. I think we need to expand our horizons. Stop being so separatist," I say. "Whaddaya think?"

"O-kay." He's easy to please.

Beth sets down her sandwich. The crusts have been nibbled away. "Gabi, I've been wanting to talk to you about this for weeks, and you're not even taking me seriously."

"As your best friend in the universe, I have the right to ignore your advice."

"Maybe. But what if you get a B? You'll never forgive yourself."

"Beth, what if we go through our entire high school existence and we never feel like we *lived*? Think of the opportunities lost. What if we graduate this year and Bruce never gets to know Katie? They could be soul mates."

Beth crosses her arms. "They say people change, but I never thought *you* would. It's your senior year, Gabi. I just don't want you to have any regrets."

"My point exactly," I tell her, and then dump my quinoa salad in the trash on the way to introduce myself to Katie Smith.

* * *

I stand in line at the taco cart, the beat of salsa music thumping in my ears. I'm wearing my white strappy sandals, because thanks to Southern California weather, it's in the high seventies—and I move my toes in time with the beat. I've somehow lost Miguel in the crowd, but it doesn't matter. I'm happy not to know anyone, because it means I don't have to fake any kind of small talk. I just get to listen to the sizzle of the tortillas on the outdoor stove, to the lyrical words in a language I don't understand, and to the music I can almost see when I close my eyes.

Arms slip around my waist, and I feel Miguel's mouth near my ear. "I bet this is the best *quinceañera* you've ever been to."

I get the tingles again, but we're in public and I don't want him to think he can get too comfortable too fast, so I turn far enough to sock him in the arm. "You know this is the only quinceañera I've ever been to."

"Then it's automatically the best."

I breathe in the onions, the spicy *pico de gallo*, the fresh corn tortillas, the melting cheese, and the fresh ground beef. "It definitely smells the best."

"I'll help you make a plate."

"I *have* eaten Mexican food before. I'm not a complete idiot."

"Going to Baja Fresh doesn't count." Miguel grabs a white paper plate, the thick kind that can handle heavy food without disintegrating. He shovels on rice, beans, guacamole, and a funky fruit salad with cucumber, orange, and jicama. "You've got to try this salad. It's got a little kick because it's made with pico de gallo salt, but it's the bomb."

We sit under a large tree with sloping branches. Dried pinecones have fallen all around, and as we talk, I pick them up and break them into small pieces. Miguel chews slowly. "I hope we see my mom soon so I can introduce you. You nervous?"

"A little." Meeting his mom seems like a big step. There's no way I'm ready to introduce him to my parents. I'm pretty sure they'll flip. I think I'll wait as long as possible.

"She'll love you."

I try a tiny bite of the fruit salad. I cough. "You weren't kidding. This really does have a kick." I've never had fruit salad that didn't taste pure sweet. But somehow this wakes up all my taste buds and sends them spinning. "So what's your mom like?"

Miguel just looks at me for a moment, a long moment, and his face is as proud as if he'd made the salad himself. "*Mi madre.* She's awesome. She's my idol."

"Really?" I've never heard anyone say that about a parent. Mostly we all complain. Too strict. Too mean. Works too much. Drinks too much. Irritating.

"Check this out. She came to this country with twenty dollars in her pocket, and eight months pregnant with me." Miguel takes a sip of his drink. "She came over twice actually. She got deported when I was in middle school. Took her a couple years to get back over here." His voice catches. "We've been through so much shit together, so I try to do right by her."

"That's sweet."

"It's not sweet. It's just right. I can't disrespect her no more." Miguel moves his fork around his plate, mixing the foods together.

"What do you mean?" I set down my fork.

"You ever wonder why you didn't know me before this year?"

"Actually, yeah." I'd wondered that a hundred times at least.

"It's because I was sent to a county school for sophomore and junior year. I was here at Central freshman year, but I got kicked out the first semester of sophomore year."

"No way." County school? That's where they send kids who've been expelled. I've never kissed anyone who's gone to County. Of course that's not saying much. If you count Eric, the total number of people I've kissed is a whopping two. "For what?"

"I got caught with a knife in my backpack."

"What?"

"Just a pocketknife, nothing serious. I carried it for protection. We live in a tough neighborhood. My mom cleans houses; she doesn't make much money, and half of what she does make she

102

sends home to her parents in Mexico." Miguel looks up at me through his thick, guy eyelashes. "That's all in the past. All that matters is that I do right by my mom from now on. She's been working her ass off for seventeen years to give me *opportunity*. I can't waste that by getting shot or stabbed or locked up."

"Shot or stabbed or locked up?" Miguel is sounding more and more complicated. Don't ask me why, but something about it is sexy.

"All in the past, Gabi. All in the past." He looks like he's trying to change the topic. "So did you like the food?"

"*Delicioso*," I say, touching his hand. Someone must have cranked the music up, because I can almost feel it vibrating through the ground. I tap his hand in time to the beat.

"You wanna dance?"

"Only if you ask me in Spanish. It sounds way cooler."

Miguel grins, and this time his smile reaches up into his eyes, giving them a copper-penny shine and making the corners crinkle up. "*Quieres bailar?*"

"*Sí.*"

I feel the music pumping through my veins. This kind of dancing is so different from the ballet I took as a kid. My body parts move in opposition instead of in unison. My hips pulse back and forth, my head tilts, my hands and arms move, but in the opposite direction from my feet.

Miguel holds my hand, and I notice right away that even though he's moving fast and breathing hard, his hands are not sweaty. His movements look easy, natural, as though they're an extension of his body. He spins me around, in and out, and around again.

Before long I find I'm only looking at his eyes. My body moves without my awareness. Even the nuances of the music blend.

Except for the beat and except for his eyes, there is nothing.

* * *

I come home from the quinceañera high as a kite. I know that sounds like I smoked weed or something, but I didn't. I'm high off some combination of salsa music, spicy fruit salad, and being spun in circles by a hot boy who thinks I'm beautiful. There was such a flurry of people that I never got to meet his mom. That's okay. The lightness in my heart and brain is infectious, and I practically float up the stairs. I'm thankful that the house seems empty, because I don't want anyone or anything to bring me down.

I'm brushing my hair when Chloe's voice breaks in through my thoughts. "*I hate you!*" she screams. She's so loud that at first I think she's in my room, yelling at me to stop being so self-obsessed. I whirl around, and it takes me a moment to get my bearings. She's yelling from next door; it's just that the bedroom walls are thin. Is she talking on the phone? Or to herself? Is someone over?

I stand, frozen for a moment, my brush caught halfway through a chunk of my hair. I feel like I'm eavesdropping, and maybe I am. I should've been louder coming up the stairs so she'd know I was home.

I wait to hear more words, but all I get is muffled sobbing, like she's crying into a pillow. And then the bang of something being thrown across the room. And more sobbing.

My quinceañera high is sinking. It feels like someone tied a brick to the tail of my kite, and I'm no longer flying high. No longer flying at all.

I step carefully toward her bedroom, my feet silent on the thick carpet. She's left the door to her room wide open, so she must have thought she was alone in the house.

I peek in, and sure enough, she's flung herself onto her bed, her face pushed deep into her down pillow. I stand there for a minute, debating about whether to go in or not. I want to.

But Chloe's crying like this because she thinks she's alone.

So I carefully pad back down the stairs. I open the front door softly, wait a beat, and then slam it closed.

I pick up and drop a pair of shoes by the door, so she thinks I'm just getting back. And then I purposely pound my way up the stairs. When I get to the top, I step into my room and turn on the music.

And I listen.

Chloe is totally quiet. I wait five minutes and then poke my head into her room.

"Hey, Chloe. I didn't know you were home. What's up?"

She looks like she's napping. Long, deep breaths, her arm flung over her face.

She's faking.

I sit on the edge of the bed and put my hand on her leg. "Hey, Chloe." I shake her, pretending I really think she's asleep. "I'm gonna make popcorn. You want some?"

She fake-stirs. "What?" She acts sleepy.

We should be actresses. We are both so good at this. "Oh, sorry to wake you. I'm gonna make popcorn. You want some?"

"Nah." She shakes her head and turns away from me.

"Hey, Chloe, are you crying?" Her face is red and puffed up like a freaking balloon, so it's a perfect opportunity. Her fair skin has always betrayed her that way.

She opens her eyes then. Even her eyelids are puffy. I can see her weighing her options, but she can't very well lie. It's obvious she's been crying. "Yeah. Just some stupid boy drama. I'll get over it."

I pet her hair like she's a puppy or something. I know it's corny, but I can't think of anything else. "You wanna talk?"

"Nah." She shakes her head. "Thanks for asking though."

And because I don't know what else to say, I add, "Drama sucks."

I stay in her room for at least an hour, stroking her hair. I turn on some music. I can't stop wishing she'd tell me what's really going on. And I can't stop wondering how well I really know my own sister.

* * *

I know it's sneaky but I don't care.

I'm going to snoop.

I wait until the following night when Chloe's out with friends and my parents are on a date. I search Chloe's room first. I yank open her closet doors and examine the row of holey jeans and ridiculous T-shirts. I pore through her desk drawers, realizing what a total slob she is. I sift through her panties and bras in her dresser drawer. I don't know what I'm looking for exactly. Weed? Razor blades? Cigarettes? Cloves? Those morbid Sharpie-filled playing cards? I don't find any of those things.

I scan the walls. There's not an inch of uncovered space. Chloe uses pushpins to tack up everything and anything she thinks is cool. Whenever she's got something new to add, she has to take something else down. There are posters from different bands, movie tickets, Pooh Bear and retro early childhood stuff, menus from her favorite restaurants, and random pages from magazines.

As a last-ditch effort, I lift up the side of her mattress. There, wedged underneath, is a diary. A locked diary. I never would have pegged Chloe as a diary kind of girl. As much as I would love to read whatever she's writing, I know I can't open the book without

106

breaking the lock. So I wedge it right back under the mattress and creep out of the room.

On to the next snooping area.

I crouch by my dad's safe and twist the combination. On the top shelf there are two photocopies of cards clipped together. The original plus an additional one. Even on my best, most-perfect-daughter day, there's no way I could have not looked. I don't even feel bad about it.

It's a joker again. This time the Sharpie has been used to draw him an extra arm, holding a lit bomb. The block letter words edged around the outside say, *I can obliterate the entire school with the push of one button. Oblit-er-ate. ¿Comprende, amigo?*

I feel a rush of panic shoot through every vein in my body. The Spanish scares me. Like, why did he write in Spanish at the end? Miguel's sweet face pops into my head. But every college-bound kid at Central takes Spanish or French for at least two years. Not to mention about a fifth of the students live in bilingual homes. So it can't mean anything. But still, this note is pretty scary. What if my dad is wrong? To me, it sounds like this guy will try again no matter what. And Chloe and I and all our friends will be sitting like ducks on a shooting range, waiting to be pegged.

Stranger's Manifesto
Entry 12

If my teachers could see
The meticulous notes I'm keeping,
They'd moan and cry about
My wasted potential
And how far I could "go" if I really applied myself
Toward something that "really matters," like school.
They'd kick themselves for
Overlooking me all these years.

I'm taking notes on people,
Studying them.
Talking to them and dissecting their reactions.
Figuring out what makes them tick.
Figuring out how to draw them into my plan.
I will coax them in
Until their feet are glued and they are stuck.
They are way too stupid to think of taking off their shoes.

18
MID-DECEMBER

"Maybe I can fix you up," I offer to Beth at lunch. "Apparently I'm quite the matchmaker." I point to Bruce and Katie, sharing their lunches.

"No time, Gabi. No time." She's eating her own Oreos today. "Must stay focused. Life is a race. Don't want to fall behind." Apparently this includes talking in truncated sentences.

"I'm dating someone," I blurt out.

"What?" She sits, frozen. "Who?"

"You don't know him. He's not in any of our classes, but I wanted to introduce you. Maybe we can all eat lunch together."

"Well, that'd be awkward." She shifts to face me.

"Not if we add to our group. I can bring a few friends to join us. It'll be fun." Although as I'm saying it out loud, I realize that merging my two factions of friends may be mission impossible.

I catch a glimpse of Miguel by the far tree, laughing it up with some buddies. "Here. Do you see the tall guy over there, wearing the white tee?"

"Yeah," Beth says slowly, like I'm explaining a complicated calculus equation and she doesn't quite get it.

"That's him!"

"That's who?"

"The guy I'm dating!"

Beth turns to me with worry etched across her forehead. "Oh Gabi." Her eyes soften. "You don't have to get all desperate on me. Lots of girls don't have their first real boyfriend until college. You're not behind schedule."

I swallow hard, feeling suddenly scolded. "I'm not worried about being *behind* schedule. I wasn't looking for a *boyfriend*. I just like him."

Beth makes a disapproving sound. "You don't need that kind of drama. No wonder you're losing focus on your classes. Besides, he looks like a player."

"He's chill," I insist. "I'll get him to bring one of his buddies. Haven't you ever wanted a Latin lover?"

"Only if he'd teach me Latin. I could bump up my SATs." Beth busies herself packing up. "Gabi, I'm busy. I'm not trying to be rude or anything, but I don't have time to make new friends. Plus, why bother when I'll be away at college in a year? Besides, they asked me to chair the lunchtime Green Team meetings. So I won't be around at lunch anyway."

"That'll look good on your college apps," I say, knowing her early action applications were sent in long ago.

"Exactly my thinking." She pats my shoulder, looking sad.

As she walks off, my throat tightens up and I want to cry. I feel like I'm losing my best friend. Maybe I am.

* * *

When the phone buzzes, we all jump. The shift has been busier than usual, probably because people are beginning to realize the helpline is really a resource. *Like, hello? We actually exist.*

It takes me a minute to realize that it's not the helpline number, but the back line, RAPP, that's ringing. No one knows RAPP exists except for us, the people on the line. The first three numbers are the same as the line's number, which are 555, and the last four numbers are 7277, which spell out RAPP. Miguel pointed out to me that it also could spell PASS or SAPP or PARS or SARP, but RAPP sounds the coolest. The RAPP line buzzes instead of rings, just in case we're on a call. It buzzes again.

Garth picks it up. "What's up?" he asks into the phone. "Oh, hey, Cruz." He listens, then turns to us, his eyes all lit up like we just offered him a tofu steak or something. He tucks the receiver under his chin and says to us, "Raging party tonight. BYOB. Cruz's house. Wanna go after our shift? It should be really kicking by then."

I lean into Miguel on the futon. It's the four of us. Miguel and me because it's our shift, and Janae and Garth because it's more fun that way. Janae has her head in my lap, and I'm braiding a small section of her hair.

"I'm up for it. Let's go!" Miguel wraps his arms around me. I breathe him in. Fabric softener plus spearmint gum.

Garth grins and tells the receiver, "We'll be there, bro."

Janae sits up, rigid. "Sounds like kid stuff, if you ask me. Why would we want to sit around watching everyone get plastered off their asses?"

Her cheeks are pink, and she almost looks like she's about to cry. Of the four of us, I'd assumed Janae was the only real partyer. I've never been to a hard-core party like this in my life—the kind you see in made-for-TV movies, with everyone loud and drunk, and people chugging beer through beer bongs and girls dancing to music so loud it rocks the floor. This is not the kind of party a good girl (like me) attends. I can't *wait* to go!

111

"I've got to pee," I announce, standing up. "Buddy system."

"What's up, Janae?" I ask after we slip out of the office. The halls are darkened, except for the emergency overhead lights.

"Nothing." She walks next to me, scuffing her feet against the floor.

"Come on, Janae. I think I know you pretty well by now. Something's up."

She pauses for a moment, and all I hear is the squeaking of our feet. Then she says, "I can't party anymore. My dad sent me away to rehab ten months ago."

"Oh." This I didn't expect. *Rehab?*

"That's where I learned to bead jewelry," Janae drags her fingers against the wall.

"Wow." I see Mom's face in my head all of a sudden, tsk-tsking because here I am surrounding myself with friends who've been to county school and rehab. "Congratulations?"

"Yeah. Well, when I first got out, I didn't know who to hang with. Most of my old friends still party. They say they understand, but they don't. I thought that by hanging with you guys, I wouldn't have to deal with the whole party scene. I know I can't slip up, because my dad will send me away again."

"Oh." We push into the girls' bathroom. "Why don't you just tell Garth that? He'll totally understand."

Janae stands in front of the mirror, messing with her hair. She flips her hair one way. Then the other. "I'll scare him off."

"What?"

"He's like a...a quality guy. I don't want to scare him off. If he knows how screwed up I am, he'll jam."

I stare at her reflection. "Okay, first of all, no. He won't *jam*. And second of all, we're all screwed up, so welcome to the family, and third of all, who cares?"

Janae whips eyeliner out of her back pocket and relines her eyes. It doesn't look much different than it did when she started, but I don't say anything. Instead I put my hand on her shoulder. "Me thinks you need a prank to lighten the mood."

"What?"

"You and Garth have this prank war going on, right?" I pause long enough to let her nod, and she does, with a confused look on her face. "So come up with some crazy prank—you know you love that kind of thing."

"Yeah, but what? Hot sauce in his beer?"

"Won't that turn it red?"

"Maybe."

"You could plant your bra in his jacket pocket when he's all buzzed and then accuse him of cheating on you."

"Ooh." Her grin spreads all wide, and I can tell she's imagining it. "You're sneaky for such a goody two-shoes."

"What's that supposed to mean?" I try to fake being pissed, but I can't help smiling and I know she's right. "Let's go together then, and I won't drink either. Beer makes me gag anyway. We'll stick together and hang out with the guys. Then we'll show off our master prankster skills. You think you can pull this off?"

"I'll be so good I'll even have you convinced." She winks.

Our **Are you still there?** text comes in at 8:55, right on schedule.
I'm here
Nothing.
I text again. **I have to leave at nine tonight.**
Nothing.

19

The "rager" party is just a dark house on the beach, with people crammed in so tight that there's scarcely room to breathe. Cruz's parents are out of town. There are cars lined up and down the street, double and triple parked. We pull into a spot about a block away. I can hear the bass of the music from there. Janae has thickened her makeup, and her face is plaster-stiff, almost like she's wearing an invisible mask of powder and mascara. If she moves her face, it might crack.

Garth and Miguel keep poking each other, like they're kindergartners again and just can't keep themselves still. I slip my arm through Janae's as we walk. She squeezes it. I squeeze back.

The house smells. Mostly like B.O. A little like spilled beer. And a faint odor of puke. *Lovely. This is what I've been missing?* Cruz is shoving someone out the porch door. "No smoking zone, buddy. You can only smoke outside." The guy is stumbling and nodding.

Cruz sees us and frog-jumps onto Garth's back. "*Mi familia!*" He shouts to Miguel over the eardrum-shattering music. "Help yourself to the keg in the back. Free beer for family only. You guys count."

I am flattered for a moment in a strange kind of way. That he considers us family. Strangely enough, I feel the same way. Something about it—the secrecy, the excitement, having a common goal, I don't know. But I feel like Cruz is family too, and I've only said maybe twenty words to him in my whole life.

We all follow Cruz through a dark hallway and into the kitchen. It takes about five minutes to figure out that there is only one refreshment at this party. Beer. There are no pretzels or chips or bottles of water. Just beer. The kitchen looks like it used to be decorated all fancy, with old-fashioned pictures of roosters and matching hand towels and baskets of fruit. But today it's dirty. Wet and muddy footprints tracked all over the tile floor in twisted patterns. Beer spilled across the counter, making it shiny and wet. Plastic cups everywhere, some half full, some empty.

Cruz pours large plastic cups for Miguel and Garth, who politely pass them to us. I shake my head slightly and say, "We're sticking with water tonight."

"Seriously?" Miguel looks guilty. Like somehow us not drinking means he can't drink.

"Go ahead," I tell him. "Have fun. We don't mind. We'll be your chaperones tonight."

Garth is already chugging. He nods and offers us a thumbs-up. "Good thinking. You'll be our designated drivers tonight, and we'll swap next time around."

I act like I'm agreeing. I take a peek at Janae. Her face is relaxing, her plaster mask melting.

"You got some soda?" she asks Cruz.

"Check the fridge," he tells her. She rummages around in this funky, fancy fridge where the freezer is on the bottom and the fridge is on the top. She grabs two root beers and tosses one to me.

"Janae!" I scold her, totally teasing. "This is going to spray all over the place when I open it."

She puts her hand to her face, fake shocked. "Oh no!" she gasps. "We don't want to make a mess. This place is goddamn immaculate."

"Right," I agree.

Miguel sets down his plastic cup, the beer frothing over the sides. He wraps his arm around my shoulders. "Are you okay here? Because we can leave."

"I know we can, but I don't want to." I pop the top on the root beer, and it does fizz out. I jump back and hold it away from me.

"Is it good?" Miguel asks after my first sip.

"Delicious."

"Will you share?"

I offer him the soda, but he shakes his head. "Not like that." He turns his body toward mine, and I see his face coming closer, his eyes open and soft. He stops about an inch away from my face. I've never kissed anyone in public before. "Is this okay?"

It's more than okay. It's fabulous. I don't answer, just press my lips into his, turning my head to allow his sweet tongue into my mouth. The rest of the world disintegrates into nothingness. All my senses are connected to his tongue and the way he tastes all pure and fresh and root-beery. I'm so grateful he hasn't sipped his beer yet. I close my eyes, and the buzz of the party disappears. I feel his hands rest on my hips, securing me there. This is our most amazing kiss so far, and we've been getting lots of practice.

I only stop because of the cheering. Janae and Garth and Cruz and a whole mess of other people are standing around us, clapping. Hooting. I pull away from Miguel and wipe my mouth. When exactly did this kitchen get so crowded?

116

I'm just about to ask Janae this question, when my eyes stop on a familiar face. Eric. I swear his features have turned to stone. His nose. His cheekbones. His eyes. They are hard as rocks. He is staring at me, though, looking as if I'm the one who has turned to stone in front of his eyes. And maybe I have, because I have no idea what to say. Or what to do. I stand there, frozen by indecision, hearing my own words echoing in my head, "I'm just not into guys right now."

Eric reaches for a plastic cup, his eyes still on me. "So where's that free beer?"

* * *

I'm not in the mood to watch Janae's prank unfold. She whispers in my ear. "Now? You think he's drunk enough?"

I shrug. Janae has lent me her plaster face mask. Because the more comfortable she seems to get, the more I feel my own body tighten up.

"I'll go take it off," she whispers. "Then I'll try to find the right moment to stuff it in his pocket." Garth is wearing a hoodie sweatshirt with one of those big front pockets. Perfect for hiding a bra.

I nod, wishing I could have more fun with this. I'm too busy worrying about Eric, who has apparently decided to drink his body weight in beer. His eyes have totally lost focus, he can hardly walk, and I feel totally responsible. I follow him around like a lost puppy dog.

Garth, Miguel, and Janae head over to play pool in the other room. Janae winks at me as she goes, and I know she's going to plant the bra. I am sitting in the kitchen on a stool, suffocating from the fumes. Beer breath, spilled beer, and puked-up beer—it's all around me.

117

If I thought the house was crowded when we first arrived, I didn't understand the true meaning of the word. I think half of Central High is in this house. And most of the county school too. People are parking their trucks and vans all over the front lawn. Cruz is too hammered to understand the full ramifications of this mess, and it's probably good he's enjoying himself, because I'm guessing he'll be grounded for the rest of his high school career when his parents figure this all out.

Eric won't talk to me. Or look at me, no matter how many times I try to explain.

My root beer has long since lost its fizz. The syrupy sweet taste clings sluggishly to my tongue. A heavy arm drapes over my shoulder, and I turn to look.

Eric. He bends his head toward me, and the smell of beer slams me in the face. Maybe he's now intoxicated enough to face me. "You don't like guys, huh?" He leans into me, all unsteady. "Maybe you just don't like *me*."

"No, it's not like that," I protest. Because it's not that I don't *like* him, it's just that I'm not into him. There's a difference.

Eric grabs my shoulders then and the drunkenness makes him rough. I fall backward against the kitchen counter, feeling the sting below my shoulder blades. Eric's a small guy, his body all long and wiry, so skinny that his muscles pop through his skin, even across his face. But as his hands squeeze my wrists, it's like he's suddenly made of steel.

His jaw is tight, his eyes intense, and there is sound coming from his mouth, but I can't identify what he is saying. His hair is plastered across his face, wet with beer or sweat. I don't know which. But as he comes toward me, the smell of it makes me gag. I turn my face away.

I scan the room, looking for Miguel or Janae or Garth, anyone who can pull Eric away from me. I know Eric's not a bad guy. He's just drunk. And hurt. And the two aren't a good combination. I tell myself I'm not scared of him, that it's just Eric, the guy who ate carrot sticks at my house. And we're in a room full of people, so it's not like he's going to hurt me or anything. But still, my wrists burn. And I can't get away.

Somebody yanks Eric off, hard. He slams against the opposite wall and shatters a vase that should've been moved hours ago. Some guy cuts the music and hits the lights. I've never heard the sound of knuckles against muscle and bone before. It's a thick, hard sound, a sound that makes the center of my stomach sick, and I hear it over and over again. Each hit a slightly different tonality, as the fist connects with bone, then flesh, then gut.

My eyes focus. It's Miguel. He's punching Eric. Over and over again. *Stop!* I think. *You're hurting him.* Eric's not the kind of kid who's been in many fights. He's the kind of kid who wins the spelling bee and hacks into school computer systems for fun. Miguel pulls Eric up to standing and cocks his arm back again.

"*Stop it!*" I scream, because no one else is helping. Even Garth, with all his bulk, who could pull Miguel back with one pinky, is watching. My words must have been louder than I thought, because everyone's eyes flick toward me for a moment, almost in unison, and then they slide back to Eric. Miguel looks at me too. Then he turns back toward Eric and slams his fist into his cheek. He must have also hit Eric's nose, because all of a sudden, blood spurts out all over the place. Eric covers his nose with his hand, as if he can stop it. The blood drips down his Star Wars shirt like someone's twisted idea of coloring in the lines.

At first I think the blow shocks Eric out of his drunkenness.

And maybe shocks Miguel too. He looks back at me with something like remorse. Miguel shakes his hand out and then grabs
a wet rag from the counter. The rag is damp from mopping up
spilled beer. Miguel holds the rag up to Eric's nose.

Eric pushes his hand away.

"Back off, asshole." He starts for the sliding screen door. And then
he turns back to the room. "Screw you all." But his eyes are pointed
at me. And they are madder than any eyes I've ever seen before.

* * *

Miguel looks old, somehow, as he walks back toward me. His face
is nearly gray. He has pulled the hood up over his head, and he
walks like his legs are filled with cement. "I'm sorry. I lost it." He
reaches out his hand toward me.

I step back. "You scared me."

"I know. I'm sorry." He pulls my arm and tugs me away from
the crowd. "He was getting rough with you. I couldn't watch him
do that to the girl I love."

This catches me completely off guard.

Miguel goes on as though he didn't just drop the *L*-bomb. "I
had to defend you."

"What about just pulling him off me?" I ask, still thinking
about the fact that he said he loved me. "What about just cussing
him out? You didn't have to break his nose!"

"I couldn't let him punk me."

"You?" What is he talking about? I see Janae and Garth watching from the corner, Janae's face all bunched up and worried,
Garth with a lacey white strap hanging out of his pocket.

"You're my girl."

"I don't belong to you." I wiggle out of his grip, which is tighter
than I want it to be.

"Don't be like that." He tilts his head to the side and steps toward me.

I step away. His breath smells like beer now and it makes me feel ill. "You're drunk. You just beat up some dorky whiz kid, a kid we have to work with on the Line for the rest of the year. What the hell were you doing?"

"You're overreacting. I had to put him in his place." He's too close to me. I wish he would chew a piece of gum or something. I can hardly breathe.

"It's a big deal to me. That's not how people solve problems in my world."

"Well, it is in mine."

"Maybe we're just too different." I say this all fast, and it makes me sad when I hear it out loud.

"Don't say that." He shakes his head, and I might be imagining it, but I think I see tears in the corners of his eyes.

"I need some space," I tell him. "I need to think."

* * *

The cops come within the next ten minutes. Four of them. Brusque and bothered, acting as though their whole evening is ruined by having to come out here to break up a party. I can't say I'm too disappointed, until I realize they're writing down everyone's names.

When the young cop with the badge reading C. Murphy gets to me, I mumble my name with my eyes pointed at his shoes. The pen scratches against his tablet but stops mid-word. *Crap.* "Al's daughter?"

I nod, my heart sinking to my knees like quicksand.

"He know you're here?"

I shake my head, daring to meet his eyes. *Crap.*

"I think I'll give you a ride home, young lady. Make sure you get there safely." Murphy looks about nineteen. Super young. And sort of familiar, like maybe he even went to Central High before the police academy.

Janae entwines her fingers in mine. She's been standing with me ever since Miguel took off. "My friend is coming with me. Buddy system. I promised not to leave her alone at a party with all these drunk guys."

Murphy considers me, his mouth all smirky. "All right then. I'll escort the two of you home when I'm done here. You take a seat on that couch while I finish up."

It's my turn to be frozen, but Janae leads me over to the couch. "My life is over," I whisper.

Janae pats my hand like she knows I'm right but doesn't want to say it.

20

"Trust is one thing we've never had to worry about with you, Gabriella." Mom's face has been swallowed up by wrinkles. She wears these smoothing patches on her face when she sleeps most of the time, and they make her look like a zombie, her face all taped up. Forced relaxation. Apparently she can't relax it on her own.

They called Janae's dad to pick her up. Her father came, looking grungy like a truck driver and not seeming at all surprised to find his daughter in a strange friend's home in the middle of the night. He reeked of cigarettes. This did not impress my parents. Neither did Janae's short-short skirt, piercings, or ankle tattoo.

And now I'm alone with them, watching them plan to torture me. I say the same thing I have already said four times now. "I was at a party but I didn't drink. My friend Janae doesn't drink." Of course I don't mention her trip to rehab. Methinks that might not get her on their good side.

Mom drums her fingers on the table. It sounds like a firing squad.

I decide to get a head start. "I'm sorry." I'm so glad I never introduced them to Miguel. Now I won't ever have to deal with that issue. It's over.

Dad pinches the bridge of his nose between two fingers. "I'm glad to hear you say that. Because you have to remember who I am."

I never forget who my dad is.

His eyes are intense. Not mad exactly, but intense. It makes me want to look away, but I don't. "It's embarrassing to have you brought home by one of my officers. And particularly Officer Murphy. He's fresh out of the academy. Smart as a whip, but he's got a chip on his shoulder, and he's been out for me ever since I wrote him up a few months ago. He won't hesitate to use this against me. This will be all over the squad by tomorrow."

"I'm sorry," I say again, and this time I really am. "I wouldn't have gone to that party if I'd known it would end this way. I was just excited to have some new friends."

Mom looks at Dad. I see her eyes harden and the lines in her face firm. "Well, you won't have them for much longer. I'm pulling you out of that school."

My heart misses at least three beats and I forget to breathe.

Dad puts his hand on Mom's. "That's something we should discuss first."

I swear Mom's eyes flash. Won't be long before she's breathing fire. Mom and Dad step out of the room to "get on the same page." I sweat and plan my counter-argument, all the reasons why I should stay at Central. Before, I'd have counted Miguel as a reason to stay. Not anymore.

I've seen them do this before. It's funny because Dad is this tough-guy cop, but as a parent he's much more of a softie than Mom. I scrape my fingernails against the lines in the table. It's supposed to be an antique. My parents spent three months visiting antique stores, looking for the perfect kitchen table with distressed wood. I don't know why Mom is so big on distressed wood. Maybe it makes her forget how distressed her face is.

They're gone for less than ten minutes. When they sit back down, I dare to look up. Mom's lips have disappeared. I think she's swallowed them. Apparently she will not be the one talking. I shift my focus to Dad.

"Gabi," he starts out, stern but quiet. "Your mother and I agree that you're a good kid. All honors and AP classes, all A's, volunteer obligations several days a week. We understand that you will make mistakes from time to time. And that you *will* learn from them." Big emphasis on "will." "You *have* learned from this mistake, haven't you?"

I nod rapidly, trying not to look as eager as I feel.

"And you won't be making the same mistake again, will you?"

Quick shift to head shaking.

"Okay, then. Grounded for two weeks, except for your volunteer obligations."

Mom looks like she's trying to hold in a flood of words. I hightail it up to my room before the flood has a chance to break loose.

Chloe is waiting on my bed, wide spanking awake. Wired, in fact. Grinning from ear to ear like a freaking Cheshire cat.

"Welcome," she greets me, spreading her arms wide.

"God, Chloe, I'm not in the mood. I almost just got both our butts shipped off to private school."

"Welcome," she says again, smirking, like she's been planning her comeback for hours, "to the club."

"What club?"

"Teenagehood. You are now officially a real teenager. You had your first 'We are disappointed in you' lecture."

"It sucked." I sink down on the bed next to her.

"They generally do," she agrees. "Still, *I'm* proud of you."

"Well, that makes one of us." I slip off my shoes.

"Oh, come on. You can't tell me you aren't just a tiny bit proud. Did you get drunk?"

"No." I rub my feet.

"Smoke weed?"

"God, Chloe. No."

"Stick your tongue down some guy's throat?"

"No." Well, yes, but I'm not ready to tell her about Miguel. And I may never have a chance to stick my tongue down his throat again.

"Down some girl's throat?"

"*No!*" Now I am getting irritated. It's late. I'm tired. "You're having way too much fun with this. But I'm exhausted. I'm not used to being a delinquent. I'm going to bed."

"Okay, fine. But first tell me what you did."

"Just went to a party."

"That's it?" She sounds disappointed.

"A party that got broken up by the cops."

"Oh." She still sounds disappointed.

"Come on, Chloe. You haven't done much worse yourself." I almost smile. Wouldn't Mom be proud? Here we are competing against each other. I think she'd always hoped we'd compete over grades or looks or anything really. Instead, Chloe opted out of the competition. Forged her own mold. Now we're competing over who's more of a rebel.

"I haven't been *caught* doing much worse. That doesn't mean I haven't *done* worse."

I consider her. This is the sister-to-sister connection we need. Finally I can talk to her about how she's really doing, only I'm not sure where to start. I pull my legs in toward myself and shift to face her. "Don't tell me you're smoking weed."

"I tried it."

"Chloe…" I sigh. She's so sassy that it's hard to read her true feelings. "You're too much. You're not on the brink of some kind of hormonal teenage breakdown, are you?" I pause. "Are you okay?"

She smirks. "We covered this already. I'm not just okay, I'm *fine*. Fine boobs, fine ass, fine—"

And then I feel the need to shut her up. So I tell her, "Well, I got escorted home in a cop car."

"Really?" Her face lights up like I just bought her a bag of clothes from Hot Topic.

"Really. And I did kiss a hot guy. In front of about thirty people."

"No *way*! Maybe we have more in common than I thought!"

And then I decide I am just a teeny, tiny bit proud. And a whole hell-of-a-lot confused.

* * *

I am dead asleep when my cell phone vibrates on the nightstand. At first I'm not sure whether it's real or a part of my dream. I try to wake up, and it feels like I'm pulling myself through water.

My eyes are bleary but I recognize the number right away. Janae. I pick up the phone to read her text. **Wonder when Garth will check pockets and find bra?**

I don't have the energy to think about this, even though I know she's trying to cheer me up. **What if his mom finds it? In hamper?**

She texts back right away. **LOL.** Then a few minutes later she texts again. **You okay?**

I respond. **Been better.**

The phone buzzes again, and I expect to see Janae's number. But it's Miguel. **I'm sorry.** The text reads. **Lo siento.**

I don't text back, even though my fingers are itching to reach for the keys. Instead I lie there in the dark with my comforter wrapped around me like a cocoon, feeling the tightness in my throat that means I want to cry, but somehow I can't.

And then I get pissed. Royally pissed. Who the hell does he think he is? He probably broke Eric's nose. I don't even really know him. Who knows what else he's done. What else he *could* do.

I'm an idiot. Blinded by him because he's a good kisser? I mean, come *on.* Am I really that stupid? It's over. I should've known this wouldn't last. I should've known better than to let myself get sucked into high school drama. *Sheesh.* I pull the comforter over my head and hate my life.

Stranger's Manifesto
Entry 13

Ever been to a party?
A high school rager? A kegger?
It shouldn't surprise you that
I don't get invited formally.
My only invitation is
The pounding of the bass from down the street,
The smell of beer and puke in the air.
Sometimes I go anyway
To try to pretend I fit in.
I time my arrival for after
People are sufficiently drunk,
Plastered enough to think I belong.
And before the
Wailing of police sirens
Breaks the whole thing up.
Crazy things happen at parties.
The regular rules of the world
Don't apply.

21

When I get home from clinic the next night, Mom is grating squash for some kind of casserole. I can tell she's pissed by the rate of her grating. I know this because I stood outside the kitchen for a few minutes, trying to get the guts to walk in. The grating was slow, tired. *Grate...grate...grate.* Like that. But now I'm in the kitchen, avoiding eye contact, opening the fridge to study its contents. And she's grating faster, probably because she knows I'm there and she has a zillion things she'd like to say, but she won't break down and say them. *Grate-grate-grate-grate-grate.*

I grab something so she doesn't bark at me for standing there with the fridge door open, wasting energy. *We all have to do our part to be green, don't we, Gabi?* she'll say. I shut the door and sit at our distressed kitchen table, feeling more than a little distressed myself. I open the blueberry container and eat one at a time, wishing I'd picked something else. They've been in the fridge for a few days and the skin is soft, so when they burst in my mouth it's a slow, leaky kind of thing instead of a strong, big burst like it's supposed to be. I chew slowly. I think antioxidants.

Mom's back is turned, hunched a little, although she's always after us to stand up straight.

"I really am sorry about last night, Mom," I say. "I messed up."

Now the grating is supercharged. *GrateGrateGrateGrateGrate.*

"People are allowed to make mistakes, Mom. That's part of growing up, isn't it?"

When she spins toward me, I automatically shrink back, like she's gonna throw the grater at me or something, although she's never done such a thing and I doubt she ever would. What I see etched in her face surprises me. It is not anger and disappointment, like I'd thought it would be. It's something else. Sadness maybe. Regret?

"Someday, when you're a parent, you'll understand," she says. She sets the grater on the kitchen table too hard, and little flakes of grated squash rain down. Her tone hardens. "You're just like any other teenager, Gabi. You'll think you're invincible until you find out you're not."

"God, Mom. You act like I'm going to run out and do something irreversible or something. I'm a pretty good kid. Nothing I do is going to be irreversible."

"Nobody ever thinks it will be. That's the whole untouchable fallacy of youth."

Whatever. "Look. I'm sorry, Mom. I'll be more careful, okay?"

Suddenly her hand is gripping my wrist. Hard. "You are the only Gabi I have. I've centered my whole life around you two. Given up the things I wanted for me."

No one asked you to, I want to whisper. *We're big now—you can go back to school. Or back to work.* But I don't say a word.

"You better be careful. The world is full of invisible booby traps."

I want to laugh at the word "booby." It sounds so foreign coming from her mouth. I don't though. Not even a giggle.

* * *

131

I get seventy-three texts today. All with the words, I'm sorry. I don't answer a single one.

* * *

"He hasn't said anything about the bra." Janae whispers to me the next day at lunch. "Not a word. Maybe they just found it in the wash and thought it was his sister's."

"Possibly," I tell her, focusing on peeling my orange and specifically trying not to look toward where I know Miguel is sitting. The lunchroom feels like a battlefield with land mines everywhere. I don't want to accidentally make eye contact with bruised-up Eric either. Although I rarely see him in the cafeteria. He's probably one of those guys who eats lunch in the debate room. Maybe Beth's eating there too. She's clearly avoiding me. Except for in class, when she keeps her nose in a book, I haven't seen her at all. Life is getting complicated.

"But what a waste!" Janae complains. "That had the potential to be one of the best pranks I've ever pulled." She grabs my hands, orange and all, and turns me toward her. "Plus that was an expensive bra!"

I nod blankly.

"Oh, come on, Gabi! Snap out of it." She waves her hand in front of my eyes. "Just go talk to Miguel."

I shake my head.

"You're being a total bitch. No offense." She takes the orange out of my hands and sets it on the table. "So he screwed up. Aren't you the one who told me that we're *all* screwed up?"

I nod again, but she's not convincing me.

"So Miguel's got a temper. So he's a fighter. You got to be if you grow up in the barrio. But he was defending you, right? What did you want him to do, let some guy attack you and just stand there like a lump? I'm telling you this as a friend, so hear it. Get over yourself, or you're gonna miss out."

"I think we might be too different," I tell Janae. "We come from totally different worlds."

"Opposites attract." Janae picks the orange back up and breaks it into pieces for me. "Besides, look at him. He's pining over you." I glance up and see him, all puppy-doggish, and then I look back down. "You've got to share a shift with him anyway. Have you thought of that?"

"You'll come with me, won't you?" I ask.

"I'm probably enabling, but what the hell. Yes, I'll go with you." She sighs, like I'm impossible. "Here, eat this orange. You've got to keep up your strength."

We dump our stuff in the trash and head out of the cafeteria, only to come face-to-face with our school mascot, the statue of a bare-chested warrior, wearing a lacy white bra. Janae's bra.

Janae squeals and hugs me. Despite my mood, I can't help but laugh.

22

Every time I see Eric, he pretends the night at the party never happened.

At first I think he doesn't remember. That the whole thing was one big, drunken blur.

That he doesn't know how his nose got bloodied and his face bruised.

But he doesn't ask me to study anymore.

He doesn't stand next to my desk and offer me tips.

And he doesn't look me in the eye.

Ever.

* * *

"Helpline, this is Torrie." I'm experimenting with new aliases. I glance at Miguel to see what he thinks, but he keeps reading his magazine. After a total of 233 *I'm sorry* texts, he stopped trying. Suddenly there's this coolness about him, like there's some kind of on-off button to his heart, and all he had to do was flip the switch to disengage from me forever. Now I am rethinking my decision not to respond to any of his texts.

My thoughts are flying so it takes me a while to realize no one is talking. I say again, "Helpline, this is..." I forget my pseudonym.

Janae leaps over to the pad of paper and writes *Torrie* with an exclamation point. I've got to start writing my name down when I say it. "This is Torrie."

Silence on the other end.

I have less patience than I used to. In my six weeks on the Line, I've had my share of crank callers. "Hello? Anyone there?" I am just about to hang up, when I hear something that stops me. Sounds like sniffling.

"Sorry. I'm here." The voice is soft.

"What's your name?" I ask.

"What does it matter?" I recognize her voice. I probably have a class with her. I hope she doesn't recognize mine.

"It matters," I insist, even though I know how hokey that sounds.

"That's a load of crap. Nothing matters, but some people matter even less than others. I am one of those special someones who doesn't matter to anyone." There's sarcasm there in an ugly kind of way.

"I bet there's a friend out there who really cares about you."

Janae waves her hands in front of my face, almost panic-like. She draws a big stop sign on my paper. *You are not a shrink. Stick with what we practiced.* I stick out my tongue at her. She returns the favor.

The voice laughs, all brittle and angry. "There are no such things as friends. There are people who pretend to be your friend so that they don't have to sit alone at lunch. But no one really cares. If you think they do, then you're as suckered as the rest of them."

"It sounds like you're feeling really discouraged," I say, following Janae's advice.

"No shit."

And then I feel mad. Because here I am, talking to this girl on the phone, trying to be supportive, and she gets sarcastic with me?

"What are you hoping to get from calling tonight?"

"What?"

I reword and try not to sound as irritated as I feel. "How can I help you?"

"You can't help me. No one can help me."

"How can you help yourself?"

"If I knew that, I wouldn't be calling you. Don't they train you guys?"

I grit my teeth. *Help!* I write on my paper. Then Janae writes the smartest thing. So smart, I promise myself I'll remember it for another time. I read it to myself once, and then I read it out loud. "You took the time to call tonight, which shows me that a part of you wants to help yourself."

She makes this strange noise, this *mmhmm* that brings to my mind an instantaneous mental image. Of a girl. A girl that I know.

I am talking to Chloe's friend. To Mel. The one who reminds me of Eeyore. The one who smiled when she asked if we'd ever touched our dad's gun.

I soften my tone. I'm not trained for this. Paisley told us if we recognize a caller, we should pretend we don't. Proceed like normal. But now that it's happening, I feel panicked. "What were you hoping would come from your call tonight?"

"Honestly? Nothing. I have no hope that you can talk me out of anything. I just want to share the misery."

I have to reach deep into the recesses of my mind to come up with a response. "It sounds like you're looking for some kind of connection."

"I guess. I wonder if that's what she was looking for too."

"She?"

And then I get another flash. This is the same voice I spoke to during my first call. Mel was the caller talking about Jo Moon,

136

the girl who hanged herself. Mel, who thinks friends are not really there for her. Mel who smiles when she thinks about guns.

I take a risk. "Would you be interested in a referral to a community counseling center?" Because this girl needs a shrink.

"Why? You tired of talking to me? You trying to shove me off on someone else?"

This takes me totally off guard.

"Well, guess what? I'm tired of you too." And with that, she hangs up. How rude!

Moral dilemma. I know the caller. But the Line is confidential—so what am I supposed to do with this information? It's not like I can go to her house and follow up. *Crap.*

"You all right?" Janae's voice is sharp. Worried.

I'm shaking. I try to straighten the desk, but my hands are shaking too bad. Miguel puts his hand on my arm, and I grab on to it with both of my own. I don't know if I've forgiven him, but I do know it feels good to have his touch. His hands are warm and rough.

"Just some girl wanting to vent. I wonder how many times she's called the Line. I know I've spoken to her at least twice myself."

"Do you want to call and consult with Paisley?" Janae asks. "We're supposed to debrief if we're upset."

"I'm okay," I lie. I don't want to tell anyone that I recognized the caller. Not until I figure a few things out for myself. Like who I can truly trust, for one. This will take time. Because I'm suddenly struck with the realization that I have no idea who the hell I can trust in this crazy world. The bomber is out there somewhere. Maybe it's no one I've ever met. But what if it's someone I know? What if it's someone I think is my friend? What if it's one of my sister's friends? What if it's even a grown-up with a revenge agenda?

I'm ninety-nine percent sure I can trust everyone in this room. Even though I'm pissed with Miguel for breaking Eric's nose, that doesn't mean he's not a trustworthy person. And Janae is reaching best-friend status here really quick. But still there's so much I don't know about her. Garth's the one I've known the longest, and that brings with it some kind of automatic trust. But he's also the one I know the least.

Bottom line, the only person I know I can trust a hundred percent is myself. And so I say nothing. Mel has called before. She'll call again. I will pocket this piece of information. And watch. And wait.

Ping! **Are you still there? It's 8:55.**

I'm here.

Nothing.

Miguel types, **We close at nine. Maybe tomorrow you can text earlier?**

Nothing.

* * *

"Can I buy you a piece of pie?" Miguel asks as we walk out at the end of our shift. He shoves his hands in his pockets all deep, and for a second he reminds me of a little boy.

"I don't eat pie," I tell him, partly because it's the truth and partly because I don't want to make this too easy.

"Come on. Pie is supposed to be this American favorite. You know, like apple pie, pumpkin pie, lemon meringue…"

"The boy has a point," Janae interjects. She's a few steps ahead but clearly eavesdropping.

"You should at least *pretend* to mind your own business." If I could see Janae, I'd kick her. But it's so dark I can't even see my fingers when I hold them up.

Garth jingles his car keys. "You call it, Gabi. Because I'll drop Miguel at home if you'd rather skip the pie."

And then of course he's got me. Because I *want* to make up with Miguel. Even if it means sitting at some lame coffee shop with a piece of stale pie.

"Nah. Wouldn't want to force you and Janae to give up your alone time," I tease.

And so twenty minutes later I'm sitting in a dark corner of an all-night coffee shop. Miguel rearranges the packets of sugar and sugar substitute for the third time. He doesn't talk. I'm not going to make it easy for him. The waitress comes and stands towering over us, putting on the pressure for us to order. I scan the menu and pick a scoop of fruit sorbet. Miguel orders chocolate cream pie.

"So you weren't kidding about the pie," he says, smoothing his napkin across his lap. "I have to ask. Why don't you eat it?"

I shrug. "It's like eating a stick of butter."

"I *like* butter."

"Yeah, well, I like being able to see my feet." I pick up my fork and shake it at him. "Do you actually enjoy being this irritating?"

"Kinda." Miguel sighs in a way that makes him seem way older than he is. "Crap. I royally suck at this."

"At what?"

"At apologizing."

"*This* is supposed to be an apology?" My voice rises an octave, and I sound more pissed than I really am.

"Well, this plus my thousands of texts have to count for something."

"They make you seem like a stalker. One or two texts would have been plenty."

"A stalker? I am not familiar with that term." And it's déjà vu, because he's used this line before. I roll my eyes, but he pretends not to see. "I'm buying you dessert, and I'm telling you that I'm sorry I overreacted. I care about you, Gabi. I couldn't stand by and watch someone try to overpower you."

I nod. I trace the napkin holder with my finger.

"So I'm sorry." He lowers his eyes.

"I'm all done being mad," I say softly. "And I never got a chance to say thank you. Not for hitting him, but for getting him off me."

He looks up suddenly, as if he's surprised. But not as surprised as me, because that waitress is back with four of her cronies, belting out "Happy Birthday" at the top of their lungs. It is not my birthday. It is six months from my birthday.

I start to explain that this must be a mistake, that they have the wrong table, to turn away the perfectly good piece of brownie à la mode, and then I catch Miguel's expression. He looks like he's about to burst.

My cheeks are hot as hell, but I manage to smile at the waitresses, accepting their birthday wishes. When they disappear, I point my finger at Miguel. I'm not even sure what to say.

He grins. "There's no good reason Garth and Janae should have this prank thing all to themselves. I can pull a prank as good as anyone."

I shake my head, still searching for the right words.

"Apology accepted?" Miguel asks, curving a fork into the soft brownie. He brings it to my lips. It's still warm. I accept the bite and it just might be the best thing I've ever tasted.

"Oh, what the hell," I tell him, exasperated. "You know it's on though now, don't you? You better watch your back."

"I'm ready," he says, looking happier than he has all night.

23

LATE DECEMBER

My hands are on the steering wheel, and the music's pounding. Chloe's got the flap to the mirror up so she can recheck her eye makeup. Chloe usually gets a ride to school from one of her friends, but they had an argument last week, so she begged a ride from me. I'm glad.

I turn down the volume. "So tell me about your boyfriend," I begin, thinking how strange it is that I don't know how to start a conversation with my own sister.

She turns the music back up.

I turn it back down.

"Come on, Chloe!" I scold, sounding way too parental as she turns it up again. "I want to talk to you."

"Fine." She turns it back down. "I was just messing with you anyway. That's what I do to Mom when she corners me in the car to talk."

"Nice. Well, I didn't corner you, and you were the one who asked me for a ride, remember?" I flip on my signal to pull into the parking lot.

I turn my head to peek at her and she's grinning. Wide.

"So spill," I command.

"Okay. I'm still figuring him out, but he's a hottie."

"Define 'hottie.'" I see a parking spot up ahead, a good one, and I speed up to nab it.

"Yeah, well, your hottie and my hottie are definitely different." She holds on to the door handle as I accelerate.

"Clearly," I agree, thinking of the guys she's dated in the past. "Define your hottie."

"Great eyes. Quirky sense of humor. Older."

My antennae perk up. "Define 'older.'" I ease into the spot. It's tight, but oh well. We'll just have to be careful not to open our doors too wide.

"God, who are you? Mom? He's older. Not like illegal older, just older."

"Got it." We are parked now, car still running, but I don't want to shut off the engine.

"He's got his own style, kind of grunge. Brilliant under-achiever, just like me."

I laugh. Not because she's not smart. She is. But because some-how being a "brilliant underachiever" is a compliment in her mind. "Sounds like a winner." My voice is a teeny-weeny bit sarcastic.

"He is." Apparently she doesn't pick up on my sarcasm.

"How's *your* boyfriend?" she asks.

"Great." And it's true. Ever since my pseudo-birthday à la mode, Miguel and I have been hanging out almost every day. I tell Mom I'm going to study group. She buys it, which makes me feel a little guilty, but whatever.

"Maybe we can double date to prom," Chloe teases. I turn to look, and she socks me in the arm. "Just kidding. You know I hate school events." She flashes me a smile. "Okay, okay. Enough with the bonding, Gabi. You've done your sisterly duty. I feel loved, okay?" Chloe wraps her arm around my shoulder for an awkward hug. "Turn off the car, already. Haven't you ever heard of global warming?"

I take the keys out of the ignition. She's right.

Miguel's waiting for me by the flagpole, so Chloe rushes off ahead, her left eyebrow arched high. She flips around after she passes him and walks backward for a moment, giving me a thumbs-up. So now she knows Miguel is my boyfriend. I need to figure out hers. I wonder why she's being so secretive about it.

"Hola, bonita!" He greets me with a smushy peck on the lips. Why does that always make me tingle? But now whenever he kisses me in public, I think of Eric and wonder if he's nearby. God, I really messed that up.

The warning bell rings, and Miguel gives me a second peck. "Adiós, bonita!" He spins around and walks backward for a moment, nearly crashing into two clueless freshmen, who narrowly escape his path. Then he turns on his heel and books it toward the math wing. I have to laugh.

When I round the corner to my locker, Beth's leaning up against it. "What's up?" I ask her, sort of breathless.

"Oh hey," she says all casual, like she wasn't just standing here waiting for me.

"Hey." I set down my backpack. "Can you scooch over while we talk?" I ask. "I just have to grab a book."

She does.

"So what's up?" I ask again, while I twist the combination lock.

"I know things have been weird between us."

A *little. No—a lot.* I crack the locker door open so that nothing spills out.

She goes on. "But we used to be close, and I just have to tell you that I'm worried about you." She leans in when she says it, and something about her tone is insulting.

"About me?" I close my locker.

"You're acting strange, Gabi. You're changing. Don't let some stupid puppy love make you forget what matters." She fiddles with her backpack strap. "Don't forget who your friends are."

I'm not forgetting. I'm just changing my definition of "friend."
"You're still my friend, Beth. I'm not ditching you. Let's all eat lunch together."

"Gabi, come *on*." She lowers her voice. "You're hanging out with losers."

The *L* word catches me like a fish on a hook. "*What* is your problem?" I snap.

"What?" Beth turns to me, her eyes wide, like she seriously has no clue what just happened.

"God, Beth. What do you think gives you the right to pass judgment on all kinds of random people? Just 'cause they're not like you? That somehow makes them less worthy as human beings? What kind of holier-than-thou shit is that?" My voice is too loud. I try to rein it in, but fail miserably. "You're *mean*. And I'm *mean* for listening to you all these years and not telling you what I really think."

Beth's face turns white, and I worry she might pass out. "Are you serious? Ask anyone on this campus. They'll tell you how nice I am. You know that."

I can't stop myself at this point. All that I've wanted to say is just bubbling out like a science experiment gone wrong. "Yeah, but they don't *know* you. Not like I do. You think that because you took Bruce under your wing, that somehow gives you license to talk shit about everyone else? What a hypocrite!"

144

"Bruce is special. You know that." Beth whispers this all softly, like she doesn't want anyone to hear.

"Sure, Bruce is special. And so am I. And so is my sister. And my boyfriend. And every person on this freaking campus. We're all special." For a brilliant person, she sure is stupid.

"Come on, Gabi. I shouldn't have to censor with my best friend, should I?"

"What makes us best friends, Beth? Because I've sat here and listened to you spout off social commentary for the last four years? Because we cram for tests together? When high school's over, what are we gonna remember? How we aced a physics test? God, I hope there's more to me than that."

Then Beth's eyes completely well up, and she flees to the girls' restroom. My eyes burn with tears. *Shit.*

I jerk my locker open again, this time all the way, and a landslide of loose papers floats down to my feet. I bend to gather them up, and as I stack them, two playing cards slip out of the pile, face down. I turn them over slowly, my heart thumping.

Two queens.

Same as before, black Sharpie scrawled over the images, making the bottom halves of both queens look like ducks. And their hair drawn long and flowy. Just like mine. And Chloe's. And Beth's. And eighty percent of the girls at Central.

Printed in neat capitals around the top edge are the words *pretty sitting ducks.*

I glance around to see if anyone is watching. The halls are empty. Who put these here? Did someone get here before me and slip them in through my locker slats? I try to remember who was near my locker when I walked up. Well, Beth, of course, but was there anyone else I recognized? Miguel and I have this prank war going on, but this isn't prank material. It's heart-attack material. I stand there, leaning against the side of my locker, chewing the heck out of my lip.

The tardy bell rings, scolding me.

I drop the cards in my backpack and stand there with my hand on the door, frozen.

I can't remember which book I need for class.

* * *

The helpline office is looking more like a college dorm room every week. We all keep adding to it—our own decorations, posters, our bracelet peace sign, and so on. Janae's on a call. She's got this reflection thing down and she sounds like a pro. She ends the call by giving some referrals for low-fee counseling centers. The girl is a natural.

Miguel jams out for a bathroom break. Shortly after, the phone rings again. Janae scoots away from it, and I pick up. "Helpline, this is Gina." I write down the name Gina at the top of the page.

"Gina." The voice is fake gruff, like a teenager trying to talk like a man. Or disguise his voice. "Is that your real name?"

This catches me off guard. I fumble around for an answer. "I'm here to listen."

"Gina, were you on campus for the lockdown?"

I don't see any harm in answering this one. "I was."

"Where were you?"

I don't like the way this is going. I try to shift directions. "What exactly did you want to talk about tonight?"

"I want to talk about how scared you were. Were you scared enough to piss your pants?"

Okay, so now this totally freaks me out. Because I did, you

know. Piss my pants. Just a little, but still. "Why do you want to talk about that day?"

"Because I need to know if it worked."

"What?" My voice is shrill.

"Did it have the effect I wanted?"

Omigod. I am talking to the bomber. Or someone pretending to be him. *Help!* I write to Janae. *It's HIM. Use RAPP to call the police. Can we have this call traced?*

Janae writes back with a question mark.

I ask, "What do you mean?" I think immediately of the two playing cards I found this morning, still sitting in my backpack.

"I think you know," the voice speaks quietly. "And I don't think your name is Gina. Although it just might start with a G. Funny thing with aliases. People usually pick a name that has the same first letter as their real name."

My mouth dries. Does he know who I am? "What made you decide to call tonight?" I'm stalling.

"Your voice is familiar," he says.

"I just have one of those voices." If he knows me, do I know him? "Let's get back to talking about what made you decide to call tonight." I point at the sentence I wrote on my paper, and I nudge Janae. I need her to call the police.

"I *told* you. I need to know if it worked." He pauses. "Can I stop now? Or do I need Phase Two?"

"Phase Two?" I ask. Janae leaves my side and I hear her picking up the RAPP line.

"The second act. I have it all planned out. The question is, can you stop me?" Now he laughs, sarcastic. "You are a *helpline,* aren't you? Can't you *help* me?"

"You need to talk to someone about what's going on." Garth is scribbling on my paper, wanting more info. I ignore it.

"I *am* talking to someone. I'm talking to you."

"No, I mean, a professional."

"What I need to do is hang up the phone."

"No, wait." I plead.

"I know your tricks, and I'm smarter than you. I'm smarter than everyone." Then he clicks off. And I am stuck with two thoughts in my mind. The first—*does he really know who I am?* He called my bluff about my name. He recognized my voice. The second—*Phase Two?*

Janae whispers loudly, "Did he hang up? I don't have anyone on the line yet."

"Never mind," I tell her. "He'll call again and we'll be ready."

Stranger's Manifesto
Entry 14

Do you remember
Pressing your nose up
Against the toy-store window?
Wanting something so bad
You'd swear your heart was about to
Shatter into a zillion pieces
Just from the sheer pain of it?
And everywhere you looked,
Other kids had just the thing you wanted.
You watched, you craved, you seethed with the wanting.
You ached with the unfairness of it all.

I see it happening around me still.
People laughing. Kissing. Playing around.
And here I am, wanting that for myself.
Too bad it's no longer simply toys I want.
What I want is a little harder to come by
Than an overpriced toy-store buy.

In my world, I've learned that
No amount of pretty-pleasing
Does a damn thing.
That's why I've taken the situation
Into my own hands.

EARLY JANUARY

I wait until everyone's asleep except for Dad. I pad down the stairs quietly, my pajama bottoms soft against my legs. He's sneaking a massive bowl of ice cream from the carton he hid in the back corner of the freezer behind the frozen chicken that's been sitting in there so long it's crusted with ice.

"A little hungry?" I tease.

He startles, then smiles a guilty smile and holds out the spoon. "Want a bite?"

"Okay." I take it from him, and for a second it feels like we're doing something really taboo, like sneaking a smoke. It makes me want to laugh. I want to ask him how a man who runs an entire police investigation has to sneak a bowl of pistachio ice cream in his own kitchen. But I don't. Instead I hold out the two sitting-duck cards.

His face changes instantaneously. He sets down the spoon. "Where did you get these?"

I lie. I don't know why. Something about the way he asks me makes me wish I hadn't brought them. "In the school parking lot."

"Where in the parking lot?" He's in interrogation mode, and

now I fumble, afraid of getting caught up in my lie and not sure why I'm lying in the first place.

"On the ground. I just picked them up."

He turns them in his hands, holding only the edges, and I notice right away how clean they are. They don't look like they'd been dropping in a parking lot. Does he know I'm lying?

"Did you show them to anyone?"

"No."

"Okay," he says, seeming relieved. "Thank you for bringing them to me. I'll see if there are any fingerprints on them besides yours."

He turns and heads to his office, leaving his bowl of ice cream on the counter to melt.

* * *

Chloe and I veg on the couch. She is painting her nails black. They were purple yesterday. I'm trying to cram for physics, but her T-shirt of the day keeps distracting me. Light yellow with two half-eaten chocolate Easter bunnies facing each other. The bunny with the bite out of his rear says, "My butt hurts." The other bunny has the bite taken out of his ears. He says, "What?" Every time I look at it, I want to laugh.

"Don't you *ever* crack a book?" I grab the polish, wondering if I can pull off black nails.

"Not if I can help it," Chloe says. "How 'bout you just do my homework for me? I'll let you borrow my 'Smile if you're not wearing undies' shirt."

"Tempting." I spread the polish along the toenail, but the black clumps in the corners.

"Here," She takes the nail polish from me. "I'll fix your nails and you do my math."

"Even more tempting. Go find your math book."

An hour later, Chloe holds scissors up to my forehead. "I can't believe you're letting me do this." Painting my nails somehow led to cutting my hair.

"I can't believe I'm letting you do it either. I must have completely lost my mind."

She wets my hair and combs it straight, then pulls it out between two fingers, measuring it against itself. "I won't go that short. That way even if I screw up, there'll be room for a professional to even things out."

"You're really boosting my confidence here." I'm glad I'm not facing the mirror.

Sniiip. Sniip. Sniip.

"You're awfully quiet, Chloe. It's making me nervous."

"Sorry. I'm concentrating."

"How well do you know Mel?" I can't help myself.

Sniip. "What do you mean? She's been hanging with our group since freshman year. You know that."

"I know. I guess I'm wondering if she's, uh, stable."

"Stable?"

"Yeah, like emotionally stable."

Chloe comes around to my front and lifts my chin. "News flash, Gabi, none of us are stable. That's why we hang out together. We're all losers."

"*You* are not a loser," I remind her.

"Says who? Miss perfect AP student and volunteer extraordinaire?"

I start to roll my eyes, but I stop because I don't want to accidentally move my head and wind up with lopsided bangs. "A loser is someone who has no ambition. Or no morals. Nothing that matters to them. That does not describe you." *Or Janae. Or Miguel*, I add to myself.

"Oh, so if I look up the word 'loser' on Wikipedia, that's what it'd say?"

"Come on, Chloe. Please tell me you don't really think you're a loser."

She stops cutting and studies her work. "Mom thinks I am."

"Oh, stop it. She does not. But we're not talking about her. We're talking about you. Do you really honestly think of yourself as a loser?"

"I don't know. I'm certainly no Gabriella." There's a hint of sarcasm there, and it makes me sad.

"Would you want to be me?"

"No, not really. But sometimes I like the things you have."

"Like what?"

"Like the grades. The skills. The body. The sexy Latino boyfriend." Chloe nudges me with the back of the scissors. I introduced Miguel to her last week at lunch.

"Chloe, you can have all of those things. Except for the boyfriend. You can't have mine. Besides, what about the guy you're dating? The older, but-not-illegal-older mystery man?"

"Don't want to talk about him."

"Why?" I press.

"You're irritating me," Chloe warns me. "Don't forget I'm holding scissors to your head. All I need is one little *oops* and half your hair is gone."

"Very funny. I don't mean to come off like I'm lecturing. I'm just saying the only difference between you and me is the choices we've made."

"And, um, like our entire genetic makeup. What about our personalities?"

"But you win on the personality," I tell her. "I'm so boring. I hardly ever have an opinion on anything. You have an opinion on everything."

"True."

"And look at our rooms."

Chloe smiles. "Yeah, I guess my room has a tad more personality." Chloe's room is overloaded with random memorabilia, while my room, on the other hand, is totally devoid of any personal touches. Mom designed it for me. I had no opinion, just agreed with everything she suggested. Tiny green-and-peach flowers on the walls, antique desk with roll-up cover, peach rug, and a wall of collectibles.

"Maybe we can invite Mel over sometime," I suggest. Chloe goes to the back of my hair, apparently satisfied with the bangs.

"You're spending way too much energy worrying about a girl you hardly know. You ought to spend more energy worrying about whether you'll like your hair."

I'd forgotten about my hair. I hold my breath while I use the handheld mirror to check out the back.

It looks pretty good, actually, but I fake-gasp to freak her out.

"What's wrong? You don't like it?"

I stand up, and little bits of my hair flutter to the floor.

"Relax. I like it." I toss it over my shoulder and watch how it falls in the mirror. "If Mom and Dad ever disown you, you can work your way through college by cutting hair."

"I'm not sure whether to say 'thank you' or hack off the rest of your hair out of spite."

* * *

The next day I bring Miguel over for the first time. "Are you sure your parents won't be home?" He hangs back as I step through the front door. "I hear your daddy has a gun."

154

"He's at work," I promise Miguel, grabbing his hand and pulling him forward. "And my mom is hiding from the cleaning lady."

"Okay, explain that one to me."

"I would if I understood it. Just one more example of how my mom is completely nuts."

"Try me." Miguel glances at the row of shoes by the door and slips his own off his feet, carefully rolling up his socks and stuffing them inside.

"Okay. So my mom used to clean herself when I was little, and she'd be a raving neat-freak lunatic for hours after. Finally my dad convinced her to hire someone. But it's like she can't admit she needs help. So she leaves these notes out for the cleaning lady. Notes and a check. And then she hides. Usually in her office or something. But today she's volunteering at the free clinic. So the coast is clear."

I drag him up the stairs. "God, what are you eating these days? Lay off the tamales, okay? I can't believe I'm trying to get you alone in my room, and you're dragging your feet."

"This feels so wrong." He hangs on to the banister. "Especially now with your new haircut. It makes you look even more innocent."

"Just because I've never brought a guy into my room doesn't mean I've never *wanted* to bring a guy into my room."

"You're talking me into it."

Lucia is wiping down the counters in the bathroom between my sister's and my room. I call to her back, "Hola, Lucia." Lucia has been coming to clean our house for the last two years. Before that we had a husband-and-wife team.

She waves the back of her hand toward me, barely looking up from the counter. "Hola, mija."

But Miguel freezes at the top of the stairs. I'm about to question his manhood, because, come on, how hard should it be to get the guy in my room for a little tongue twister?

"Well, *that* just killed my mood," he grumbles under his breath.

Apparently he has issues with hired help too. Lucia looks up this time, really looks up, and her eyes brighten.

"Hola, Mamá." Miguel starts toward the bathroom. "*Te quieres ayuda?*"

We spend the next two hours helping Miguel's mother clean my house. Miguel tells me it's nothing personal. That it's about respect. He can't very well roll around on the bed with me while his mother is slaving away with Lysol and disinfectant. I tell him I understand. I do, but I'm definitely bummed.

And our relationship just got a whole hell of a lot more complicated.

25
MID-JANUARY

Janae and I arrive early to our Sunday morning helpline meeting. We're poking small holes in the bottoms of jelly doughnuts and scooping out as much of the jelly as we can.

"Isn't this overkill?" I half ask, half complain.

"No such thing," Janae assures me.

"How do you know Garth will even eat a doughnut? He's kind of a health nut."

"Good point. I'm ten steps ahead of you though. These are whole-grain doughnuts. And the jelly is organic."

"No kidding?"

"Totally kidding, but that's what I'm gonna tell Garth."

I laugh. "He'll be lucky to make it through a bite." I suck the doughnut crud off my finger.

Janae brought a turkey baster, and we're replacing the jelly with barbecue sauce. Extra spicy. When Garth and Miguel take bites of their "whole-grain, organic jelly" doughnuts, they won't know what hit them.

Twenty minutes later Garth lumbers into the library, looking like he didn't shower or brush either hair or teeth. Janae practically charges the guy, pushing the doughnut box toward him.

"Too early," he groans. "I can't eat anything so processed this early in the morning."

Miguel peers over my shoulder. "Oh come on, bro. Live a little."

Janae wraps her arm around his waist. "I bought them for you, babe. They're organic."

"I need a helpline!" Garth grabs his chest all dramatic. "It's peer pressure. To eat lard and sugar!"

"*Organic* lard and sugar," Janae reminds him.

"Oh fine. Hand it over."

"With pleasure," Janae says.

I lock eyes with Miguel as he bites down, the barbecue sauce dribbling out the back end. I wish I'd thought to video it with my phone. I laugh so hard I can't stand. Our fellow helpliners circle around us, high-fiving and back-slapping.

The guys laugh too. Only later. Much later.

I don't notice until after I get back home that Eric was absent from our meeting today.

* * *

I barely survive the most awkward dinner of my life. It goes like this: Lucia feels compelled to inform my parents that her son and I are "friends." Then Mom feels compelled to break the silence barrier and invite her to dinner. Which means Mom then feels compelled to have a spotless house. And forces me and Chloe to clean the house with her (since we can't very well hire Lucia to clean the house so that *she* can come to dinner). During which Mom's a Nazi-maniac cleaning machine, and I briefly consider leaping out my second-story bedroom window. A broken leg might get me out of this mess.

The dinner conversation alternates between parental interrogation and meaningless small talk. Miguel and I basically keep our mouths full the entire time to avoid having to make conversation. If it hadn't been so uncomfortable, it might have been fun to watch Mom try to connect with the woman she'd been avoiding for the last two years. I almost suggest we bring out note cards so she can get in her comfort zone. They could just write notes back and forth. "So…nice weather, huh?"

I spend most of the dinner chewing and thinking that if this wasn't so epically bizarre, it'd be comical. Chloe certainly seems to find it funny. She keeps kicking my feet under the table, and she nearly chokes on her salad twice.

* * *

Janae and I are carrying our trays through the cafeteria when rough hands cover my eyes. The world goes black. There's this moment of panic, where I think, *Omigod, I'm being kidnapped. How loud can I scream?*

But then I hear Janae giggle and say, "Unhand me, you beast!" and I know immediately what happened. Garth's got Janae. Miguel's got me. I can smell his fabric softener.

Miguel uncovers my eyes and spins me around. He and Garth have wrapped a cafeteria table. Wrapped it. In gift wrap, with crème-colored wedding bells in diagonal lines. I look up at Janae, who also seems dazed but totally amused.

"Am I missing something?" I ask her. I know Janae and Garth are close, but I'm hoping not that close.

"Don't mind the paper," Garth apologizes. "It was all I could find at home."

I tap my fingers on the wedding bells. "So…is this a prank or a date?" I ask.

Miguel and Garth look at each other. "Both," they decide.

"Well, if it's a date, you've got to work on your presentation," I tell them. "And if it's a prank, it's not all that funny."

"You think you can do better?"

"Maybe," I say. I see Beth walking through the cafeteria with a girl from AP English. My wedding-wrapped cafeteria table makes me pretty hard to miss. But Beth pretends she doesn't see me, and that snags me. I make a mental note to text her later.

"Well, I bet you can't. In fact, I'm ready to argue that Miguel and I can outdo you on practically anything." Garth nods at Miguel.

"No way." Janae sways her hips. "Girl power."

"Just watch. But first, I'm buying you each a soda. What do you want?"

Janae picks Orange Fanta. I pick Diet Coke. Garth disappears into the cafeteria line and returns with our drinks in fountain cups. Plus his own iced tea, and strawberry lemonade for Miguel. He forgets the lids and the straws, but I don't complain.

"I bet you two can't do this." Garth places his hands palms down, flat on the table. Miguel sets a full fountain drink on the back of each of Garth's hands. They wobble a bit but don't fall. "Here, Janae. Put the other two on Miguel's hands." She grins and places them on his hands. The cups are sweating condensation and they look slippery. They balance, although I bet Miguel is wishing Garth hadn't filled them quite so high, because they're sloshing around.

"See?" Garth pronounces.

"We can *totally* do that," Janae says. "In fact, I bet we can do it without spilling any."

"Oh yeah? Show us."

"Okay." Janae takes the cups off Miguel's hands and sets them on the table. She does the same for Garth. The bell rings, and there is a flurry of activity around us, people dumping their leftover trash in cans and laughing.

I'm glad. Fewer people to watch my humiliation. I can find the derivative of a differentiable function in five minutes flat, but I am not sure about balancing a full glass of soda without major spillage. Miguel places the lemonade and Diet Coke on the backs of my hands. They're cold. Garth sets the Fanta and iced tea on Janae's.

Except for feeling like my hands will freeze off, it's all good. They balance. No sloshing. I look up to smirk. Only the smirk on Garth's face is at least ten times as big as the one I feel on my own. My smirk melts.

"Have a nice day, ladies." Garth pats Janae on her back. "Too bad you picked white jeans."

And suddenly it hits me. *This* is the prank. We are stuck here with both hands balancing full cups of colored soda. Neither of us can move our hands without spilling all over ourselves. The cafeteria is thinning out. No one I know to come to our rescue. Only bystanders to laugh and point.

"Seriously?" Janae's face is turning red under all that makeup. Then she yells at the guys, "Payback, fellas. Just you wait."

Ten minutes go by before the custodian rescues us. I earn my first tardy in government.

* * *

I flop onto my bed, and take a deep breath. Time to text Beth. **Want to study for physics tonight? I'll bring carrots!**

I know she's got her phone by her side, like always, but she waits a full thirty minutes before texting me back. **You sure you want to?**

She's still pissed. I text again. **I wouldn't ask if I didn't want to.**

She responds, **I might say something mean, you know.**

Hmm. How to handle that one? **That came out wrong. Sorry.**

I wait five minutes, but she doesn't text back, so I add: **We're still friends, you know. I didn't mean to hurt your feelings.**

Nothing back.

You're right. I am changing. I think it's good for me. Like positive growth.

Nothing.

If you hung out with us, maybe you'd like them. You're invited. I'm not trying to ditch you.

Nothing.

If you don't want to, it's okay.

Nothing.

I just want you to know that I still want to be your friend.

Nothing for a long time. I almost fall asleep. Then, Thanks, Gabi. And shortly after, **I'll keep it in mind.**

Stranger's Manifesto
Entry 15

Most people are idiots
They walk around
Locking their car doors
But leaving their keys
Out in the open.
Securing their front and back doors,
But forgetting to latch
The sliding glass door
On the side of the house.
Plugging in combos on their lockers
But leaving the code
In the notes section of their phones.

People pass around their cells in class
All the time
To share pictures
Or funny texts.
If you know where to look
And you're not afraid to try...
You can find out almost anything.
Believe me, I know.

26

EARLY FEBRUARY

I check the mailbox on my way home the next day. Thick manila envelope from Georgetown. I'm in. Early action. Mom will be ecstatic. And I should be bouncing off the walls in elation. So why do I feel like I just ate some bad mayonnaise? Washington, DC, is practically on the other side of the world. I'd have to leave everything I know. I shove the envelope deep in my backpack. I need some time to think.

When I enter the kitchen, Mom's washing vegetables for a salad even though they're prepackaged, prewashed, and organic. Lettuce. Cherry tomatoes. Green onions. Mushrooms. Baby carrots. All "ready to eat," but she's washing them again.

I sit down and open one of Chloe's trashy teen magazines. I despise this kind of gossip, but lately it's been sucking me in. *Chop-chop-chop*. Mom's turning baby carrots into tiny orange pellets.

Chloe slams into the kitchen with one iPod earbud in and the other one dangling down to bounce against her leg. She pops the top on a Sprite, and carbonated soda spews out like a frothy volcano.

"Chloe!" Mom's voice warns. Chloe makes a big show out of slurping the spilled soda directly off the counter. Mom holds up one hand. "I'm not even going to comment on that."

Chloe grins at me. I try not to laugh. I really do. Unfortunately, swallowing that laughter makes it come out my nose, and I sound like I'm blowing my nose into my hand.

Mom just looks at us both for a moment, her lips so tight that I can see little wrinkle indentations around them. That almost makes me want to laugh more, but this time I hold it in. Mom lowers her gaze back to the vegetables and begins to slice the cherry tomatoes in quarters. They spurt juice everywhere.

"Mom," Chloe begins, and I can tell she's about to say something she thinks is funny, because her nose wrinkles up. "I don't think you actually need to slice cherry tomatoes. They're like grapes. No one slices grapes."

And then so suddenly that I don't see it coming, Mom throws the salad bowl across the room. Like a Frisbee almost. Thank god it's Tupperware. It bounces off the wall, and bits of sliced carrots and gooey cherry tomatoes and ripped-up lettuce tumble out onto the floor.

"You girls are so critical all the time!" She looks at the washed veggies, now scattered across the room like confetti, and I see instant regret in her eyes. All that chopping for nothing. But then she turns to face us, and the regret disappears. "Make your own goddamn salad!" And then she storms out of the kitchen so fast, it takes me a few seconds to realize she's crying.

"PMS." The wrinkles are gone from Chloe's nose, so I know she feels bad, but she's still joking around. "Big-time PMS."

"You shouldn't set her off like that," I scold, almost without thinking.

Chloe turns to me, and her earbud falls out of her other ear. "You always tell me not to make waves. But *come on*! Because I drink Sprite instead of vitamin water? Because I like my own music? Because I express myself through my clothes? Because I joke around?" She shoves her Sprite into my hand, still cold with condensation on the outside, but about half empty. She turns to leave but then swivels back.

"Those things wouldn't even be waves if you weren't dodging every conflict like it's a freaking tsunami. I make waves because *you* don't. So how about you give me a break and make some waves of your own?" And with that she snatches the Sprite back out of my hands. "You wouldn't drink it anyway."

I grab the drink right back and chug it. All the way down. I don't think about sugar or calories or preservatives or backwash. I don't think about the carbonation. I just guzzle it. Then I crumple the empty can in my hand and shove it back at her. "Maybe you don't know me as well as you think."

I love the look in her eyes. And I love that she doesn't say anything. Maybe doesn't know what to say. At first I hate that she starts laughing. But then I'm laughing too. Hysterically. And crying. Both at the same time.

We collect all the chopped vegetables in the salad bowl. "Should we rewash these?" Chloe asks.

"Probably." The tomatoes are making my hands all sticky. The little seeds have leaked out everywhere. "But let's not, how 'bout it?"

"Right on. I support you in your rebellion. Next let's dye your hair bright pink."

I sock her arm. Hard.

For the next three hours, I have the worst case of carbonation burps ever known to man. And it's totally worth it.

* * *

The LGBTQ Club and the Red Ribbon/Suicide Prevention Committee are battling it out. The anniversary of Jo Moon's suicide is coming up in a week, and they both want to host a moment of silence. It's a PR thing really. Not like anyone in either of those groups ever knew Jo Moon, but it's popular to pretend they did.

Because let's face it, Jo was sort of a closeted lesbian, so she wasn't a member of the LGBTQ Club. And she most definitely was not on the Red Ribbon/Suicide Prevention Committee, because they didn't start up until last year. Besides, Jo Moon being on a suicide prevention committee would have been kind of hypocritical. Although I suppose she didn't know she was going to kill herself until she actually did it.

This thought catches in my brain for a moment. It's kind of uncomfortable, like a hangnail stuck on a piece of fabric. Because I wonder how it works. Is suicide one of those things people think through over and over again before they build up the guts to pull it off? Is it a decision they edge closer and closer to, or is it more like quicksand? Something they stumble into, get stuck in, and rapidly sink into, unable to crawl out.

And what about homicide? This bomber guy seems like he's got it all planned out. All calculated, mathematical, not emotional. Is he a ball gathering speed, faster and faster down the hill, unable to be stopped? Is he carefully edging closer and closer to a decision, waiting for the final straw to push him over the edge? Or is he hoping someone will stop him? Figure him out and stand in his way?

I walk down the main quad, where each group has a fold-up table out, recruiting membership and petition votes to try to get a moment of silence approved by administration. I guess they both figure whichever one brings the largest number of petition votes to admin will get to host. Not being a member of either group, I want to point out to them that they can cohost the moment of silence.

But that's not the way my school works—not with the clubs, factions, and cliques parked in nooks and crannies. Everyone scrambling to find a space to fit in. Like a game of musical chairs, everyone knowing there won't be enough seats when the music stops. It makes me admire Chloe, kind of. Because her group is not about fitting in. In fact *none* of them fit in.

I remember, for a moment, Jo's memorial. In my life I had maybe exchanged ten words with Jo Moon. I didn't know her. I didn't particularly like her. Although I didn't hate her either. She was just sort of not in my league. I know that sounds awful and conceited, but I don't mean it to be. I just mean it to be real. Because people are like magnets. And we attract people who are sort of in the same category.

Jo Moon had that laugh-at-me hillbilly thing going on. Stringy hair and stringy limbs, none of her clothes ever looking clean. She laughed way too loud in a hyena way that sounded so bizarre that it sucked other people into laughing too—but more in an "at her" kind of way. Someone should've taped her laugh, because I bet she had no idea how ridiculous she sounded. I had only one class with her. P.E.

So why did I go to her memorial? To honor this girl I didn't even like? I went because I laughed. I heard what those cheerleaders did to her, and I laughed. The meanness of it didn't register in my mind until after she died.

So when I heard, no one had to explain why she did it. I knew. And the knowing made me sick to my stomach.

At the memorial, I wondered how many people were there out of guilt. Like me. The auditorium was packed. Maybe everyone just wanted to get out of class. Or maybe it was morbid curiosity. I craned my neck to see her parents. They were stiff, like their bones had been frozen and hadn't yet completely thawed. Her mother leaned forward in that brittle way, curling in on herself. Her head tipped forward toward her chest, her hands balled, her stomach concave and turned in on itself. All I kept thinking was that she wanted to disappear.

At least two thirds of the students sat, body to body, sweaty. The air too thick to really breathe. Some people cried. At first I felt irritated that anyone dared to cry. No one had a right to cry for her except her family and her scrawny sidekick. But then I felt my own tears creeping up my throat and welling up at the bridge of my nose. I swallowed hard.

The tears were pushy though, backing up my nose and forcing themselves through the ducts in my eyes. I couldn't hold them in. I tried to hide it at first, dabbing at the corners of my eyes and swiping my sleeve across my nose. Guilty thoughts nipped at my mind. *Oh, well*. I thought. *Too late*. And that just made me cry harder.

After that day, I tried to forget. Maybe we all did.

Stranger's Manifesto
Entry 16

You probably think I don't have feelings,
That any asshole who could do something like this
Must be totally devoid of feelings.
So I'll tell you—
I don't cry. I forgot how.
I bet you'd say it's one of those things you never forget.
Like riding a bike.
But I can't do it.

Corny as it sounds, I want to cry.
I feel it building inside me like a wave. I feel the pain of it,
The way it burns the back of my throat and pinches my nose,
But there is nowhere for it to go.

I didn't cry when I broke my arm in P.E.
I didn't cry when my neighbor backed up over my dog.
I didn't cry when I found Jo hanging like a goddamn marionette.
The last time I cried was when my mom left. I cried hard then.
I wanted her to twist in her seat, stare out the back window,
And wave until I couldn't see her anymore.
But she didn't wave long enough.
Just turned back around and started talking to the driver.
I waved until my hand nearly fell off.
I cried until my eyes were so swollen I could barely see.
But then it all dried up and my tear ducts shriveled,
And I haven't cried since.

27

"Who picked this movie? It's gonna be stupid," Mel complains from the backseat of my car. I glance in the rearview mirror, and Chloe bugs her eyes out at me. I know she's thinking I'm getting what I deserve for trying to be all peer counselor-ish about Mel. She kept telling me that Mel was a good "group friend," not a good one-on-one friend. I'm beginning to understand why.

Janae is in the front seat, her legs pulled up to her chest and her head resting on them. She is along for moral support although she doesn't know why. I can't tell anyone I recognized Mel's voice on that line, but I also can't shake this feeling of responsibility.

"I thought a comedy might be fun."

Mel makes her sarcastic *mmhmm*. Truth is, I knew a slapstick comedy wouldn't be Eeyore's style, but I wasn't about to sit through a tearjerker when my goal is to pull Mel from marinating in self-pity.

It's gonna be a long night. My parents are out of town, so Mel and Janae are sleeping over. And I can tell just by looking at Janae's hunched shoulders that she is so done with anything Eeyore.

At least there will be no talking during the movie.

* * *

Miguel slips his hand into mine, and the butter on his fingers makes them soft. He and Garth met us here at the movie, and we are all split up in different sections of the theater. Chloe and Mel are sitting up front in the fifth row. Janae and Garth in the very back, for optimal make-out potential, and Miguel and I are off to the right side.

We are actually trying to watch the movie. Only the way he's rubbing his thumb across the outside of my hand is distracting me. It's making me want to crawl right into his lap and pepper his neck with kisses.

I think I might be distracting him too. He's all but forgotten about the popcorn bucket that he set down on the floor in between us. He's wrapped his ankle around mine, and it's a little awkward but who cares. Everyone in the audience laughs, and it startles me. I missed whatever was funny. Miguel shifts in his seat and leans in toward me.

Okay, so never mind. We are no longer going to watch the movie. We are going to make out. And I'm going to wish we'd sat in the back like Janae and Garth. He kisses me softly, and he tastes so different that I almost feel like I'm kissing someone else. All salty and buttery, his tongue icy cold from the soda he's been sipping. The stubble on his upper lip and chin rubs across my lips. I lose myself in it.

Miguel leaves the movie to use the restroom, and I sit in the darkness, tasting him in my mouth and contemplating whether I love him. I have never felt like this in my life. I could sit here in a dark theater and kiss him forever. If I move to Washington, DC, for college, I'll have to leave him behind, and I may never find someone like him again.

When he comes back in, it's awkward at first, like maybe we

forgot where we left off. I don't want to act like I expect him to make out with me the entire movie, so I face forward and put my eyes on the screen. He goes back to rubbing my hand, and then I relax. I nuzzle my head against his shoulder. He plays with my hair, running his fingers through the length of it.

I peek up at his round, dark eyes and lean in. Bold, like I haven't been before. His hands are full of my hair. The sounds of laughter blur into the background, and I am floating.

I leave the movie having no idea what it was supposed to be about. And I don't care one bit.

* * *

After the movie, we say good-bye to the boys and then walk out into the bright sunshine. I squint, feeling disoriented. I click my car doors unlocked and notice that there is an advertisement face-down and stuck under my windshield wiper. It's rectangular and white. Probably an advertisement for a furniture sale.

Janae, Chloe, and Mel walk around to their respective car doors. I pull out the ad and start to crumple it, but it's thicker than paper. I flip it over in my hand. *Shit.* A playing card. Written on with Sharpie like all the others. But this one has no words. No veiled threats. Just a queen with little heart bubbles floating out of her chest.

Who is watching me?

I whirl around, scanning the parking lot. I see nothing out of the ordinary.

Or is one of my friends pranking me with these cards?

They're all climbing into their seats, not looking at me.

I shove it deep in the pocket of my sweatshirt. I'll deal with it later.

Stranger's Manifesto
Entry 17

Why playing cards, do you ask?
Besides their durable nature?
And how easily they slip through the slats of a locker?
Or under a windshield wiper?

Because they're a metaphor, you dumb ass!
Don't get it? No big surprise.
Let me spell it out for you.
There are Winners and there are Losers—
Just like Life.
BIG cards trump the puny ones,
And Top Dog takes all, a true popularity contest.
Just like Life.
Or they're grouped by suits,
Segregation at its finest.
Because if you think those hoity-toity Hearts would be caught dead
Hanging out with them stupefied Spades…
You got another thing coming.
Solitaire's my game
For obvious reasons.

Janae's backpack clunks as she sets it down. And when she goes to the bathroom ten minutes later, I do something so totally sneaky. I unzip her backpack and peek inside.

I immediately wish I hadn't. Because her backpack is stuffed with empty alcohol bottles. *Oh my god*. She's back to being a drunk. And it's all because I took her to that stupid party.

I zip it back up real fast. Should I confront her? Tell her dad? Tell my parents? But then they'll never let me hang out with her again. *Crap*.

She comes back in the room slowly, watching me. I hope she can't read the expression on my face. I try to smile, but I've never been a good faker.

"What's wrong, Gabi?" she asks.

"I, uh…I'm wondering how you're doing."

She laughs, and it feels so out of place that I almost fall over. "You can't lie to save your life, can you?"

"What?"

"You look totally tortured. I don't want to be *that* mean. This is your prank. To make you think I'm drinking again."

"What?" I'm confused.

"You looked in my backpack, didn't you?"

Then it dawns on me. She planted those bottles, knowing I'd look when I heard them clanking and she acted all secretive.

"That's *mean*."

"I know. Garth's idea."

"You told him?"

"Yeah, I told him. You were right. He doesn't care that I went to rehab and that I can't drink anymore."

"I don't know whether to attack you or hug you." I cross my arms.

"Oh, hug. I totally vote for hug."

*　*　*

An hour and a bag of pretzels later, I'm lying on my bed. "Do you ever wonder who you can trust?" I ask Janae. She's plucking my eyebrows. Chloe and Mel are downstairs.

"Uh, Gabi? You better trust me. I've got your life in my hands. Do you have any idea how bad botched eyebrows look? A hundred times worse than the most god-awful haircut you've ever had." She pauses with the tweezers midair. "Why do you ask about trust?"

I take a deep breath. "This is ultra, ultra, ultra confidential. I might have even committed a crime."

"Seriously?" She sets down the tweezers and I sit up. "This is the most exciting part of my day."

"So when my dad is working on a case, sometimes he brings home copies of evidence to mull over. He keeps it locked up."

"No way!" Janae's eyes are wide. "You're breaking into his files?"

I sort of shrug, and she goes on, "Shit. Why're you telling me? I don't want to be an accomplice."

"You said I could trust you," I remind her. She nods, her face hesitant. "I keep finding these playing cards in strange places, like someone's leaving them for me." I pull out the queen with the hearts floating.

"Funky." She reaches for it.

"I found photocopies of cards just like this with different messages, threatening ones, in my dad's lockbox. It's got to be the bomber guy."

Janae flips her hair out of her eyes. "What makes you so sure it's a guy? You still thinking about that one caller who freaked you out so bad?"

I nod.

She scoots up close and examines my forehead. "Okay, so it's possible. But we've had so many crank callers. How could you know what's real and what's fake? You know all the crazies get off on copycat shit. All someone has to do is want to freak you out. It doesn't mean it's the real dude."

"I don't know. I just have a feeling." I touch my eyebrow. The skin underneath stings. "Did you know Jo Moon?"

She pulls back and considers me. "I knew *of* her. Did anyone really know her? She's practically an urban legend. Besides, what does that have to do with anything?"

"I think it has everything to do with this bomber."

Janae laughs. "What? Is she a ghost coming back to haunt us by bombing the school? Did she fake her own death and she's really lurking around, ready to punish us all?"

"No—listen. One of these cards, a queen, was drawn to look like her, with a noose around her neck." I don't mention that I saw this one in my sister's hands. "Maybe the bomber was a friend of hers."

"Hello?" Janae knocks on my head. "Anyone home? Jo Moon didn't have any friends. That was part of the problem."

"I remember there being this one guy. This scrawny little guy, no color, like he's made of milk."

"I don't remember a guy."

"Are you sure? Think hard. Because I remember him being there, sitting with her at P.E., maybe eating lunch with her under the far tree in the quad."

"What's his name?"

"That's the problem. I don't know his name, and when I see him in my mind, he has no face. My guess is that he's someone we just don't notice. Someone who flies under the radar. Maybe that whole bomb thing was for revenge."

"Yeah, but it's over. Bomb disassembled. End of story."

"Maybe not. The cards are like threats."

"Why would someone leave them for you?"

I run my fingertip over my raw eyebrow skin. "I don't know. I haven't figured that out yet. Maybe because my dad is the cop investigating all this?" I have another thought that I don't want to say out loud. *Maybe because it's someone who thinks I can figure it out?*

"Maybe. Still don't get the link with Jo Moon though. I don't see why someone would want to blow us all up because of her. That whole mess wasn't our fault. None of us tied that noose for her." Janae flips the ring in her lip around. "The only ones to blame are those irritating cheerleaders."

"Yeah, but we all knew it was happening and nobody stood up for her. Nobody tried to be her friend." My voice sounds intense even to my own ears. "What did she die for? To make a point?"

"Maybe. But her point to make."

"Here's the thing. Her point didn't stick. We all thought about her and cried about her for a week or two, right? And now it's as if she never existed."

"That's because none of us ever knew her." Janae speaks louder and slower, like I'm hard of hearing. "We only knew her when we saw that video and when we read about her hanging from that tree. What did we have to remember?"

"So I think her friend, whoever he is, is trying to make her point again. And this time make an impact people won't forget."

"By *bombing* the school?" Janae says this like it's the craziest thing in the world, and of course it is.

"Maybe. I think he did that whole bomb threat to scare us. To put us on alert. To make us realize we better start being nicer to the underdog."

"Twisted." Janae is quiet for a moment. "So he's like an activist? He never really intended to bomb the school?"

"Maybe. But I also think he's sending these playing cards to the cops, and maybe to other people besides me, as some kind of warning."

"Of what?"

"I think he's going to try again. Maybe he thinks the only way to make people really care is to make them hurt." Saying it out loud makes me shiver.

"You're scaring me."

"I'm scaring myself too," I admit. "I have to figure out who he is so we can stop him."

"Or maybe we should just leave it to your dad. We're talking serious shit here, Gabi. Life-and-death shit. No offense, but you are not qualified."

"Maybe," I say. But inside I'm thinking that the cops are doing everything they can. It can't hurt to have another pair of eyes on this.

Janae spins her lip ring round and round, and she must be thinking along the same lines, because finally she says, "Can I see all the cards? Maybe the wording or the handwriting will help us figure him out."

I run down, unlock Dad's safe, and grab the cards. Chloe and Mel are watching music videos. Then I jam back up the stairs.

Now Janae is cross-legged on my bed and all intense. "I'm surprised the cops haven't found a way to trace these cards," she says after a while. "Like, you'd think the guy would leave fingerprints or have analyzable handwriting or something."

"He's too smart for that." I go up to the mirror and examine my eyebrows. The skin is bright red and raw around where she plucked. I pull out the tweezers to clean up the hairs she missed.

"Creepy. They're all the people cards. The jack, the queen, the king, the joker. He's the joker, right? And the rest are us." She's quiet for a moment. "Huh. Most card games are games of strategy."

"And some luck, in whatever card you draw."

"Right. But mostly strategy. I wonder what significance these cards have? Is this a game to him?" She stops and stares at my reflection. "Are you crying, or did you tweeze a nerve?"

"Very funny." I stick out my tongue at her reflection. "So how do we find him? Go through the yearbook and circle every senior we don't know?"

"And then what? Stalk them? Listen to their voices so we can figure out if they're your mystery caller?"

"We could try to send him a message." I tweeze out the last stray hair. "And then trap him in some way."

"Uh, Gabs? This is a kid who might blow us up into little pieces. Who hasn't been caught by the police. This wacko is probably smarter than both of us combined."

"He's also a kid who doesn't feel heard. Or noticed." I turn to face her. "Maybe we can figure out who to watch if we can somehow set up a forum for him to be heard."

"Like what? A peer counseling helpline?"

"Very funny. You don't think he's one of us, do you?"

"Not until I just heard you say that," Janae says. "We do have a couple weirdos among us. Whoever handpicked our team picked out people from just about every clique. Even the ones who are their own clique because they aren't a clique." She stops suddenly. "Like what about Eric?"

"People know him—he's not invisible."

"I'm just brainstorming here. But it's interesting, because what if they created this helpline to watch *us*? The listeners. Like what if their main suspects are on the Line?"

"Are you saying you and I are suspects?"

"No. Who could suspect us of anything?" She bats her eyelids all innocent. "At least you, anyway. They'd have to have regular kids too. Otherwise it would be obvious."

"This is like major conspiracy theory."

"Maybe. Do you remember Eric from freshman and sophomore year? Do you remember who he hung out with?"

"No," I say slowly.

"Here, grab your yearbook from freshman year. Let's check him out." We flip through freshman year's yearbook. I find his picture on page thirty-three. He looks like himself, only scrawnier. With his washed-out face and shaggy dirt-colored hair.

"Is this the guy you remember? The guy who hung with Jo Moon?"

I stare at the picture so hard it changes shape. "I'm not sure," I admit. "But it's possible."

If it is Eric, I've got to stop him. Before he ruins his own life and everyone else's.

29

The gun is gone.

When I go back to put the cards away, I see that the safe door has swung wide open under Mom's desk, open like a dark, gaping mouth. I stick my head nearly inside the safe to make sure I'm not missing something. The smell of metal is so strong it makes me dizzy. I try to remember. Did I lock the safe after I came down to get the cards for Janae?

I don't know. But the gun is gone. And so is my stomach. It has dropped completely out of my body and disintegrated onto the floor.

I run back to the living room. The television is still blaring. I see legs. Covered in jeans. Hanging over the edge of the couch in front of the TV. Not moving. I can't tell whether they are Chloe's or Mel's. Even the thought of Mel in all her Eeyorish gloom makes the little hairs on my arms stand on end.

I stumble forward, trying to see what is attached to those legs. Blame it on too many horror movies, but my brain keeps flashing images of bloody bodies. I almost turn away, but then I remind myself that I have heard no gunshots. There is still hope.

Once I get close enough to see the hair, I know it's Chloe. She's either dead or asleep. I watch, trying not to shake uncontrollably and failing miserably. I hold on to the back of the couch and force myself to watch her chest. I am too scared to touch her hand.

It's moving. Her chest. So she's sleeping. I spin around, scanning the room for Mel. If Chloe's asleep, Mel must have taken that chance to go poke around in Dad's office. Possibly looking for the gun?

My eyes have gone all superhero on me. Maybe it's the adrenaline, but I can practically see through walls. I'm twisting the knob on the door to the downstairs bathroom. It's locked. I shake the handle.

"Mel, are you in there?" My voice sounds like it's coming from somewhere else. I press my ear up against the door, but everything sounds muted. I bang on the door again. "Melissa! Open the door!"

I feel someone come up behind me and I whirl, ready to block. The irony hits me. Ready to block a bullet? This superhero thing has gone to my head.

It's Chloe though, and I lock in on her eyes. She's got her hands up, like "What the hell are you doing, talking to my friend that way?" But my eyes must tell her something too, because she pulls away from that stance and her own eyes widen and change from irritated to alarmed. Somehow she knows to whisper, "What's wrong?"

I mouth back. "Dad's gun is gone. Safe is open."

She understands. Not at first, maybe, because she twists toward the office as if she's going to go back there to check, to verify that the gun is really gone. But then she stops, looks at the closed bathroom door, and she gets it. She moves toward the door and raps her knuckles against it. Twice.

"Hey, Mel, you in there?"

No answer.

Chloe dips her head toward mine and whispers, "Remember what Mom used to do when we locked ourselves in there?"

I do. We used to eat candy in the shower. As part of her healthy-eating-for-our-whole-family philosophy, Mom confiscated our candy from Valentine's Day, Halloween, and any birthday-party piñatas. As soon as we got home, we had to turn it over. If we gave her puppy-dog eyes, she'd let us each eat one piece before she stashed it away.

Of course it didn't take us long to figure out we could hide some of the candy in our pockets before we turned it in. We found all kinds of creative places to stash it, and then we'd stand in the shower eating piece after piece, knowing we could wash any telltale crumbs down the drain. The wrappers were a problem though. If we dumped them in the trash, Mom might find them. So we balled them up and stuffed them in our backpacks until we could dump them.

We got away with it at least four times before Mom figured us out. She sat us down and explained that she'd set up the household nutrition for our own good. It all had the flavor of a great, big pep talk. That's probably why we tried it again.

She caught us one more time after that. We'd locked ourselves in the bathroom, and we could hear her rattling the door. Chloe and I stood, cramming sweets in our mouths like starving street kids. Mom shouted ultimatums through the door. We both sank down on the shower floor, holding hands and panting, and I could smell our breath, mine chocolate peanut-buttery, hers sweet-and-sour sugary. Maybe it was the smell or maybe it was the thousands of calories I'd just consumed, but I felt like I might puke.

We stayed there, sticky hands entwined, until Mom got the door unlocked with a tiny screwdriver.

She separated us and grounded us from any party where there might be candy, which was every birthday party and school party for the next six months. Apparently grounding from social events was much more effective than the pep talk because we never did it again. Plus around then Chloe and I took separate sides. I went with the Perfect Daughter Program, followed the rules, and dove into academics full force. Chloe decided about that time that Mom was a complete lunatic, that she didn't care about Mom's rules, and in fact she'd defy them as often as possible.

Chloe bangs one more time on the door, bringing me back to the present. "Mel?" she asks, and the unsaid question in her word hangs over my head. She spins around and dashes for the kitchen. I can hear her rummaging around in our miscellaneous drawer next to the silverware one, searching for that baby screwdriver.

She must have found it, because the rummaging stops and suddenly she is by my side again. I hear another voice behind me and I jump at least a foot.

"What's up?" It's Janae. I put my finger to my lips.

Chloe twists the screwdriver in the side of the doorknob, trying to find that secret button that pops the lock undone. And suddenly I realize what complete imbeciles we are. We're about to barge into a bathroom with a deranged, depressed teenager who's probably holding a gun.

I reach for Chloe's shoulder to stop her, to tell her, *Wait, let's call Dad. We should let the professionals handle this.* But just as I reach, I hear the pop of the lock, and she's already pushing through the door. I follow, wanting to be first at the very least, not wanting Chloe to beat me, but I'm swimming upstream, and I can't seem to move past her.

Until she halts.

Then I bump into her and Janae bumps into me from behind.

Mel is sitting on top of the toilet cover, her head bowed forward like she's praying, a black metal object square on her lap. She is not touching it.

"Goddamn it," she snaps. "Can't you give me a tiny bit of privacy?"

I think we are all a bit out of breath and certainly shocked, and so it takes us a few moments to gather our words. I'm the first to speak. "Well, not if that privacy involves blowing your brains out."

Mel cocks an eye open, and I see that her mascara has bled around her eyes. She looks like a monster. "You do realize there are no bullets in this gun, don't you?"

I hadn't. Well, I mean I knew my dad didn't keep the bullets with the gun. Come to think of it, I don't know where he keeps the bullets, but all this happened too fast to do much thinking at all.

"What are we supposed to think?" I try not to sound too accusing. "You locked yourself in the bathroom with a gun!"

Mel opens her other eye. "First of all, I wasn't going to really do it. I was going to *think* about doing it. But then I look at this gun and there are no bullets. I feel royally gypped. In fact, I've been sitting here cursing my luck."

I look back at Chloe and at Janae, who both seem to have lost the ability to speak. "You need some professional help."

"Gee, thanks."

"No, really. I don't care whether you were really planning to do it or not, this is totally not cool. You need help either way."

"Yeah, well, I've been telling my parents that for the last three years, and you know how many counselors they've taken me to?" Mel glares at me, as if this whole thing is my fault.

I don't know. But I have a feeling she wants to say.

"Zero. They come from the school of figure-it-out-your-damn-self, don't lie down on some couch and share your soul."

Janae finally speaks. Quietly. "You don't actually have to lie down on a couch, you know. A lot of counselors don't even have couches in their offices."

"And how would *you* know?" Mel snaps her voice and her head, pointing her darkened eyes at Janae.

"How do you *think* I know?" Janae retorts, her cadence and tone mirroring Mel's. This seems to work, because Mel goes all quiet. "And you don't need parent permission, by the way."

"Really?" This comes from Chloe.

"I've gone by myself before. In California, there's some law that says if you're over twelve, you can consent for counseling on your own. There's a free clinic run by Central University. They staff it with counselors in training, so they're mostly pretty young, but that's not so bad. Sometimes the young ones are the best."

"Really," Mel says. The word is a statement, not a question. With attitude. But I watch her face, watch how she lets the idea sink in. And then she says the word again, slower, and it's a question. "Really?"

"Sure. I'll take you there."

* * *

Actually we all take her there. Because even though she says she wouldn't have pulled the trigger if there were bullets, I am not convinced. Janae walks with her, arm in arm. I'm glad for this, because now my superhero eyes have turned paranoid. I see every potential danger. I see how fast the cars barrel down the street, how they swerve around the corners, and how easy it would be for Mel to dive beneath their wheels. I see the rusty pocketknife in the gutter. I see everything.

Chloe and I walk about ten steps behind to give them a little privacy. I am tempted to link my arm in hers the way Janae has linked arms with Mel, but I worry that she'll pull away. We haven't walked like that since we were kids.

But she surprises me, because she's the one to grab on to my arm. I accept it, grateful for something to hold on to, realizing now how shaky I am. Holding on to her settles me.

"So do we tell Dad?" Chloe asks.

"If we tell Dad, he'll know I was in his safe without permission."

Chloe fake-gasps. "Oh no! The golden child will fall from honor!" She laughs. "They probably wouldn't believe it was you anyway. Somehow I'd get blamed for it." I search for bitterness in her voice, but it must be down deep somewhere because I don't hear it. "Why were you in there, anyway?"

I walk ten steps without answering. Then I take a deep breath and I tell her. I tell her everything I know (except for the part where I spied on her).

"Holy batshit," she says softly. "I got a card like that too."

I know this, but I don't say.

"I found it in my locker. It was a queen with a noose around her neck. I didn't realize it was related to any of the bombing crap. I just thought it was from one of the guys I dumped."

"Did it look like that card you found in Dad's wallet? The one with the 'tick-tock' written on it?"

She pauses for a moment. "Yeah," she says. "I guess it did."

"Why would you think one of your ex-boyfriends would have sent you something that awful?"

"I don't know." She scuffs her feet.

"And who was the queen supposed to be?"

"I thought it was me." She says this to her feet.

"Seriously?" I stop walking. "Who the hell have you been dating?"

She runs her fingers through her hair, probably trying to decide how much to share with me. "Scum. Guys who know just how to make you feel special and beautiful and important, then after they play around a bit, know just how to make you feel as insignificant as an ant."

"Why?" I am incredulous, and I just want to repeat the word over and over again. "Why?"

She narrows her eyes. "No comment."

I know I should tone it down, not sound so big sisterly, but I can't seem to do it. "No way—you don't get off that easy. You always do that. You have to talk to me."

"Well, I'm single *now*," she retorts, "if that makes you happy. Not all of us can date Latin hotties, you know." She starts walking again, fast, and I struggle to keep up. "Besides, you study-dated that brainiac, and he's a weirdo too."

Thinking of Eric makes my stomach twist.

"So are you gonna tell Dad?" Chloe takes advantage of my silence.

"I think I have to."

"Why? Mel doesn't have the combo. Dad's been getting the same cards that we have. If he could've figured out who the asshole is already, he would have. Just because a few of the cards have come directly to us doesn't really give us any new info."

"You think?" I ask, trying to reassure myself.

Chloe grabs my arm again. "If Mom finds out some sicko is targeting us directly, we'll be homeschooled so fast we'll get whiplash."

She has a point.

* * *

An hour and a half later, Janae walks out of the Central University clinic. Mel isn't with her. "Where is she?" I ask at the exact moment Chloe says, "What happened?"

"They kept her. Psychiatric hold."

"A what?" Something deep in my gut twists.

"She talked to the counselor in private for a long time, and then the counselor came out and said Mel wanted me to come in. The counselor brought in her supervisor too and asked a whole boatload of questions. They basically said Mel was a danger to herself and others, and they had to keep her in a hospital for a few days to make sure she was stable."

"Her parents are going to shit bricks."

Janae smiled. "They pretty much already have. Mel called them, once she figured out she wasn't going home today. This is going to sound crazy, but I swear Mel was happy. Someone is finally taking her seriously."

I think I feel better.

30
MID-FEBRUARY

"Dad, I need to know something." I corner Dad at breakfast. I keep thinking back to my conversation with Janae, that maybe the school set up the helpline to watch us. That maybe some of *us* are the suspects. That maybe Eric is the guy behind all this. I wonder if they're tapping the phone lines or bugging the room.

"Shoot." Interesting choice of words. He's sprinkling salt and pepper, and it looks like an egg-bound snowstorm.

"As a part of the investigation of the school bombing suspect, are you tapping any lines?"

"Haven't we had this discussion before?" he asks with his mouth full. He shifts the food in his mouth from one side to another, like the eggs are way too hot and he hadn't waited for them to cool.

"Maybe." My voice sounds as testy as I feel. Dad looks up sharply, like he's only just noticing how serious I am.

"You know I can't discuss cases with my family."

"What's more important, Dad, work or family?" My skin prickles.

"Oh come on, Gabi." He shovels in a bite of eggs. "My job is based on confidentiality. It doesn't mean I'm picking it over you if I follow the basic guidelines of my profession."

I've got the playing cards in my back pocket, and they are so hot I think they may burn a hole in my jeans. I have to tell him. "What if one of your cases has something to do with me?"

"Gabriella, I have no idea what you are talking about. The only link between you and a case of mine is where you go to school." He says this all final, like the conversation is over. And it is for a moment, until Dad looks up and adds, "For now, anyway."

"What's that supposed to mean?"

"It means Mom and I are putting some serious thought into pulling you and Chloe out of Central."

I am sure my jaw has hit the ground. Chloe was right. Homeschool is lurking around the corner.

"It's not a decision I would make lightly. I've always pushed for you to be educated on a public campus. But we haven't been able to close the bombing case." He says nothing about the notes in his safe. "I'm just not sure Central is a safe place to be right now."

"Those sound like Mom's words, not yours."

He takes a monstrous bite of scrambled eggs, and I think he's buying time. "We're both worried about it."

I translate for him. "So Mom's freaking out, and you, Chloe, and I have to go along with it to appease her. What about what the rest of us want? Or are we just all her puppets?"

Dad doesn't answer. Just takes another bite of his eggs and chews.

Decision made—those cards will stay in my pocket for now.

* * *

If it's Eric, I need to know.

If it's Eric, I probably messed him up big time with that incident at Cruz's party.

If it's Eric, maybe I can stop him.

I wait by his locker, watching the swirl of people around me bumping into each other, teasing, and pushing their way down the hall. A bunch of football players are messing with this shrimpy freshman, threatening to shove him in a locker. He looks like he's about to wet his pants.

I throw an apple at one of the football players, a good shot too, because I smack him square in the neck. He turns toward me, slapping his neck like he just got stung by a bee. I pretend to be twisting the combination on Eric's locker. The guy looks around, wondering where it came from. The warning bell rings and the football players all meander off, leaving the shrimp alone. He saw my shot apparently, and he offers me a mini smile of relief, then turns and books it in the other direction.

"You're in my way." Eric elbows past me. His elbow bumps into my boob, but I think that's by accident. "Oh. Sorry." He half meets my eyes.

"It's okay." I edge back in front of his locker. "Eric, I want to talk to you."

"Well, that's a problem, because I don't want to talk to you."

He's not gonna make this easy. "Come on, Eric. I don't want you to think you're alone."

"I'd have to be an imbecile to think I'm alone." He tips his head toward the swarm of kids all heading to their classes. He snorts, and his eyes are hard. I realize this might be the first time in my life that I've really felt like someone hates me.

"That's not what I mean, and you know it." I'm about to say more, but someone tugs on my hair from behind.

I whirl.

Miguel. He has horrible timing. But I wonder if maybe his timing was on purpose, because I see the way he is watching Eric. "*Vámanos*, Gabi. You're gonna be late."

I turn back to Eric, and his face is dark. "Go, Gabi. Just go."

Miguel tugs on my arm and leads me toward first period. "I don't like you talking to that guy," he whispers in my ear.

"Well, you're not in charge of me, now are you?" I snap.

He turns me around a corner and pulls me to face him. "Look, Gabi. I'm not trying to be controlling. I'm just trying to look out for you."

"Not to diss your machismo, but that's not your job. I can look out for myself." I leave him standing there and slide into my seat a fraction of a second before the tardy bell.

That sure went well.

❋　❋　❋

When I get home I see that Mom has left a note for Lucia on the kitchen counter, next to a check. "Work on the grout in the master bathroom. Spend extra time on the guest room, guest bath, and windows." Her handwriting loops around in perfect circles. Next to the note is a check.

Apparently Lucia being Miguel's mom hasn't made her any easier to talk to. Mom's right back to avoiding as much interaction as possible. It's not like she can stop using Lucia to clean the house just because she's the mother of my boyfriend. But on the other hand, it *is* pretty awkward to have her keep scrubbing our toilets. *Sheesh*.

I briefly consider writing this note to her: "Dear Mom, I've been accepted to the school of your dreams. But I'm turning it down because I'm in love with the house cleaner's son." I think she might go into cardiac arrest on the spot. Maybe I should tell her personally so I can dial 911 when she collapses.

So I search for her in the house, the Georgetown acceptance letter in my hand. Lucia's vacuuming upstairs, so that means

Mom will be as far away from her as possible. I find her in her downstairs office, typing on her computer.

"Mom?" I ask, creasing and re-creasing the letter with my fingernails. "Do you have a minute?"

She stops typing and swivels toward me on her chair. She looks over her glasses at me. "What's up?"

I almost change my mind. I almost go back to Plan B, leaving a note for her on the kitchen counter. The vacuum stops upstairs. "It's about school."

Furrows immediately appear on her forehead.

She takes off her glasses and carefully folds them up. She starts to speak, and then puts a finger to her mouth and seems to think for a moment. "Senior year is academically intense, sweetie. You need to drop a volunteer activity?"

"Mom, I'm tired of doing everything to make someone else happy. I'm ready to think about what *I* want. What makes *me* happy."

Suddenly a glimmer of recognition shines in her eyes. "Oh. I understand." She glances at the folded papers in my hands. "You're discouraged. Did you hear back from one of the universities?"

I feel frustration building up behind my eyes, and I hope it doesn't explode into tears. I don't want to cry right now. Maybe I should have written this all down. She isn't hearing me. "I got in to Georgetown," I say softly. "Early action." I watch her eyes light up, brighten with anticipation. "But I'm not going."

I turn on my heel and walk out of the room.

31

Ping! We're midway through our shift, and the Line is hopping with activity. The new text reads, **Maybe I finally found a winner.**

I can tell immediately that this is from my "man problems" texter, because the computer links the previous texts to the current one. That helps for continuity. Mostly the repeat texters have been in communication with other shifts, so I can read what they wrote as well.

Right on! How do you feel about it?

Good. Mostly. Pause. Afraid to be burned, of course. But good.

Thanks for letting us know. What makes him a winner?

He's more mature. Not into playing games.

That all sounds good.

Yeah. Treats me good. For now anyway. That can change.

What will you do if that changes?

Run like the wind.

Sounds like you really thought this through.

Yep!

I crunch an apple while I scroll back into this texter's previous conversations. She's texted about five different times, all with relationship issues. I don't want her to get dependent on us—she should be talking to someone who knows her. So I text again.

Is there anyone you trust that you can talk to about these kinds of things?

Maybe. My sister is princess perfect, but it looks like she's loosening up. Maybe she won't judge me the way I thought she would.

Do you think you'll try talking to her?

Maybe.

Good luck!

I don't have time to think about it much longer, because the phone rings. Man, we're busy. *Riiiiing. Riiiiing.* "Helpline, this is Grace."

I know it's him before he speaks. I can tell by the hesitation in his voice and the way he clears his throat. "Funny, you sound a helluva lot like the Gina I spoke to the other night. You sure have a lot of girls working this line with *G* names."

"Cut the crap." Out of my peripheral vision, I can see Janae, Miguel, and Garth snap their heads up. They edge closer to me.

"Well, that's not very supportive."

"Look, I don't know who you are, but…"

"Are you sure?" he asks.

I close my eyes as I listen to his voice, trying to place it. It doesn't sound like Eric, not unless he can change his voice quality. He's playing games with me now. I say again. "No, I don't know who you are, but I want to help you."

"Well, that's a crock of shit." The voice laughs, and the laugh grates on my ears in a familiar way. I do know that laugh, but I can't place it. Listening to the voice without the face makes me feel like I'm finding my way in the dark. "You're slow on the uptake, aren't you?"

"What do you mean?"

"Nobody cares, that's what I mean. I've given plenty of people the opportunity to step up, and no one has."

"I don't understand."

"You're no different. Are you?"

I must hesitate too long in my answer, because he clicks off.

Miguel spins my swivel chair toward him. "Gabi?" he asks, touching my shoulders. I can't meet his eyes. He knows me too well now. "Gabi, what was that?"

I look at Janae. Maybe it's okay to tell? The bomber couldn't be anyone in this room. Right? Unless there are several people working together to pull off this whole thing. Like maybe it's too big for one mastermind, but a few people working together can pull it off? But that sounds so conspiracy theory. That doesn't happen in real life.

So I spill. I spill about the playing cards. I spill about the caller. I spill about the connection to Jo Moon, and I spill about my theory. That he's coming back to finish the job. Because he thinks we didn't get the message.

"His message is be nice to people?" Garth sounds angry. "And he's trying to get this message across by terrorizing a school?"

"I'm not saying it makes sense."

"Remind me again why we aren't going to the cops." This comes from Miguel, who doesn't usually have a whole lot of faith in cops.

"What would I tell them, for one? All I have are theories, not facts. Plus I read confidential material that I wasn't supposed to see. That's probably a prosecutable offense like tampering with evidence or interfering with an investigation. And if Dad knows this guy's sending cards directly to me, he'll pull me out of school." Why do I feel like I'm defending myself? "But if we get any real proof, we'll go straight to the cops. I promise."

"Gabi?" Miguel touches my arm. "I'm all for you going to this school, but if someone is targeting you directly, your dad needs to know."

Riiiiiing. Riiiiiing. We all stare at each other. "Helpline, this is George." Garth picks up the phone.

The voice is so loud I can hear it from sitting next to him. It sounds like the caller has his mouth pressed up against the receiver. "I'm watching you."

"What?" Garth stiffens.

"I'm watching you."

"Who is this?" Garth demands.

"I'm watching you."

Garth slams the phone down so hard my ears throb. "What the hell is this?" he asks me, as if I know. "None of us signed up for this. We're here to help people, not field threatening phone calls."

"That was a different voice. He was talking so loud I could hear him," I tell Garth. "That's not the bomber."

"Well, maybe he has a partner." Hmm. Conspiracy theory anyone?

Riiiiiing. Riiiiiing.

We all jump. This time it's RAPP. A fellow helpliner calling in to chat. Garth puts the phone to his ear. We all watch as his face loses color. He doesn't say a word, just holds the phone out for us to hear. "I'm watching you." The same voice. Whoever-the-hell-it-is knows the number to our private line. Whoever-the-hell-it-is might know the location of our secret office too. We are sitting ducks. I think immediately of the playing cards with the duck bottoms.

Garth slowly hangs the phone up. "Uh, Gabi? Now might be a good time to call the cops."

32

Two hours later we're sitting in an interrogation room drinking soda and eating pumpernickel pretzels. Dad pushes through the heavy door and then grabs a chair, flipping it around so he can sit facing us with his chin on the backrest. I watch his eyebrows. They're all bunchy and stern, which is not a particularly good sign.

When we called him from the helpline office, I made my friends promise on their lives not to tell that I'd read the cards in his safe. All we were reporting was that we'd been threatened and that we thought we'd spoken to the bomber. If Dad knew I sneaked into his safe, he'd never trust me again.

Of course I was completely exposing our roles on the helpline, but at that point we didn't care. We'd thought about just dialing 911, but we didn't know how that would play out. Cops invading the darkened campus? Totally exposing all the privacy the Line had worked so hard to create? We decided it made the most sense just to call my dad. We gave him directions to the helpline office, and he came to pick us up, along with three plainclothes detectives from the squad.

"We were able to obtain the phone records from the incoming

calls tonight." Dad spreads a piece of paper out on the table. "You were right about the caller being the same. The last call on the helpline and the call on the back line were from the same number." He clears his throat and looks mostly at me. "This was not a sophisticated caller. He called from his own cell phone."

Garth lets out a heavy breath, like he's got all this pent-up energy inside and now it is deflating. "Well, that's good, right? Now we can catch the guy."

Dad considers him. He drums his fingers on the table. "We'll bring this guy in and assess the situation. Certainly he made a threatening call. But does anyone see an inconsistency here?"

"I do," I volunteer. "That caller is not the bomber."

"How do you know?"

"Because our bomber is sophisticated. He doesn't want to get caught. This caller phoned from his own cell phone. That shows zero planning and zero sophistication."

Dad doesn't exactly smile, but I see his eyebrows shift position and I know he is proud of what I just said. *Cop-in-training*, he probably thinks. "Exactly."

"Can you identify the caller from the second-to-last call on the helpline number?" I ask.

Dad looks down at the sheet. "The one that came in at 7:57?"

I think back. "What time did the final call come in?"

"At 8:05."

"Yeah. The one at 7:57."

Dad taps the paper with his finger. "Huh." He looks up at me. "Why do you want to know?"

"Because I think *he's* the real bomber."

Dad clears his throat. "That one came in from the pay phone directly in front of the school."

"He was there," Janae whispers. "He might have even still been there when we left, watching us."

* * *

Some people use car rides to talk. But not my dad. He switches on National Public Radio the second he starts the engine. If you try to ask him a question, like *how much longer*, or *can we make a pit stop*, he holds up his hand like he's a crossing guard. I learned long ago not to try to make conversation in the car.

So it surprises me when he doesn't turn on the radio. Instead we drive in silence for a few blocks until he finally says, "What do you make of tonight? Of us bringing that kid in?"

"He was scared to death. I believe him—he didn't mean any harm." I picture Eric, sitting there at the interrogation table, all white and shaky. He confessed immediately that it'd been a bad joke. That he wanted to join in our prank war (and repay a certain someone for publicly rejecting and humiliating him—although this went unsaid) and thought it'd be funny to call the Line and give us a scare. That he'd called back fifteen minutes later to tell us he was just kidding, but that no one had picked up. This is because we'd already had our mini freak-outs and were then on the way to the police station. Eric swore up and down he didn't make any earlier calls tonight. He made both calls from his cell phone in his bedroom and hadn't left the house until being brought in.

"That's my sense too." Dad clears his throat. "What I'd like to know is what makes you so sure that the caller before him was the real bomber."

This feels like a trick question. This feels like him trying to get me to confess that I've been breaking into his safe. I roll down the window, partly because I suddenly feel hot and partly because I need to buy time. "It's a gut feeling, Dad."

"Okay. I have those all the time. Tell me more."

I search for my words very carefully so that I don't accidentally give myself away. "This guy is brilliant, right?"

"It appears so, especially if it's a kid." Dad rolls the window back up. "I believe it was no accident that the initial bomb did not deploy."

"Right. It was a warning." I lean my forehead against the cool glass.

"But a warning for what?"

"I think he'll try again. I don't think he wants to hurt anyone, I really don't. But he may feel he has to up the ante."

"Gabi." Dad puts his hand on my shoulder. "You're a bright girl. I think you're on to something. I'm also quite concerned that there may be another incident. So concerned, in fact, that I'm unsure whether you should continue to attend Central High."

"I have to stay at Central," I say, moving his hand off me. He places it back on the wheel. "Look, Dad. It would be total hypocrisy to tell the world Central is a safe school and then to pull your own kids out. If something goes down, people will accuse you of knowing something. Do you know something?"

"I know a lot of things. And I have a helluva gut instinct on this one. But I don't know anything I can do something preventive with. And I have no idea who this kid is."

I speak softly, not sure I really want to say this. I do anyway. "I think he knows who I am."

"What?" Dad stops driving in the middle of the road. Just takes his foot off the pedal and looks at me.

I point to the road. "Keep driving. I'll explain but keep driving." His eyes linger on me, but he does turn back to the road. I decide on a half-truth. "I think he knows who I am, and I think he'll try to contact me. He's left me a couple messages."

"What kind of messages?"

"Do you remember those playing cards I gave you? The ones with the writing in Sharpie?"

His head snaps toward me and the car veers. I think maybe my chances of dying in the car with him trump my chances of being blown to smithereens.

"Eyes on the road," I remind him.

"Yes," he says, his voice tense. "I wasn't able to pull any prints from those, except for yours."

"Well, I'm pretty sure they were left for me to find." He looks at me again, and the car wheels cross the divider.

"Dad!" I scold him. "Watch where you're going!"

He straightens out the wheel. My mind is spinning, and I'm trying to think as fast as possible. In this moment, I decide not to tell him about the one with the queen and the hearts. That would be my ticket to homeschooling. I sneak a peek at Dad. His brow is bunched.

"Listen, Dad, I'm pretty sure he called tonight. I told him on the phone that I want to help him. That I want to help him find a way out."

"Gabriella." Dad says this in a tone that makes me feel five again. "I'm going to assign an undercover officer to follow you." He turns the wheel quickly. "And one for your sister too."

"No way."

"Yes, way. You're my children, and there is no way I'm going to allow you to be in harm's way for the sake of an investigation. No way in hell."

"He's smart, Dad. He'll know if you have someone following me."

Dad is quiet, driving. He doesn't speak for at least three minutes. When he does, his voice is tight. "Gabriella. You have to promise me that if he contacts you again, you'll tell me right away."

"I promise," I say immediately, but I think I might be lying. I'm not sure why. "Give me a week. If I can talk to him or reach out to him in some way, I think I can stop this."

Dad shakes his head, harder than he should while he's driving. "God damn it. Where did you get your superhero complex?"

"Uh…that'd be from you."

Stranger's Manifesto
Entry 18

I have to admit
That it's fun
To watch everyone scramble.
It reminds me of when I was a kid
And I'd drip water into a
Stream of scurrying ants.
Drip.
Scramble.
Drip.
Scramble.
Watching someone else's frenzy
Is way more entertaining than
The crap they have on TV.

I feel sorta like Clark Kent must feel.
Because he has to
Fake being normal
So much of the time.
Listening to people make small talk about Superman
And inside he's got this big old secret
He's probably bursting to tell.

Only—
I am definitely not Superman.
I like to think of myself

More as Robin Hood.
But I bet the world will think of me
As something supremely sinister.
The Joker? Count Dracula? A Death Eater?

I wonder what people will think
When they read this journal.
I have a feeling my explanations
Will fall on deaf ears.
No surprise, really.
It's pretty damn clear that
I have no voice.

33

"How serious are you about this guy?" Chloe asks. We're having Miguel and his mom over for dinner tonight, but this time I'm cooking. Penne Arrabbiata. And we'll eat on the back patio so nobody has to clean.

"I don't know," I tell her. "I like him."

"A lot? A little?" Chloe rummages through the cabinet for the bottle of olive oil.

"I don't know. He's my first real boyfriend. I don't have anything to compare it to. But I've never felt this way about a guy before." Chloe and I have been hanging out more ever since the Mel incident. Mel's come over a couple times since she got out of the hospital. She seems different. Better.

"How about you?" I place the colander in the sink and carry the steaming pot of noodles over to it. "You into anyone?"

She ducks her head. "Maybe."

"Someone I'd like?"

She laughs. "Thank you, Mom. Yes, I think you'd give your vote of approval for this one." She chews her lip. "Not sure if he likes me yet though. He's different from the other guys I've been with. Kind of shy."

"That's okay," I reassure her. "Shy is good."

The doorbell rings. They're early. Miguel carries a casserole dish with tamales layered across. He holds it with a towel and does a fake curtsey, holding the pan up so that the tamales don't go sliding out. *What an idiot.* I kiss him, a quick peck but enough to breathe in his Downey freshness.

A lot, I decide. *I like him a lot.*

*　*　*

I spin the combination to open my locker, lunch bag in hand. There's a playing card taped onto my math book. This means he has my combination. It's one thing to slip cards through the slats, but taping a card onto my math book takes this to a whole new level.

I whirl around, eyes scanning the kids around me, wondering if he's watching. He'd have to be, wouldn't he? Don't guys like him get off on watching someone else's panic? Does it make him feel powerful?

There is one dude watching me. I've never seen him before. Sort of preppy looking, like he shops out of a teen magazine. He's off in the corner, earbuds in, nodding his head to the music. As soon as I make eye contact, he looks away.

I hold my locker partially closed, so I can examine the card without anyone else seeing it. A joker. Drawn over in black Sharpie to look like a burnt-up skeleton. Remnants of a bomb on the ground. Those same block letters around the edges. *Would anyone care? Granted, I'm a jaded piece of shit, but I sure as hell wouldn't.*

I look back for that preppy kid, but he's gone.

*　*　*

Dad gets home late. I've been waiting up to show him this card. Apparently I'm not the only one. Mom corners him the moment he walks through the door. I stand on the top step of the stairs and listen.

"I've got it all set up," Mom says softly. "The girls don't know yet."

Dad sets down his stuff with a thud. "Okay, hon." He sighs. "Change is hard. Let's hold off on telling them for a couple days, okay?"

Shit. I slink back upstairs. *Private school, here we come.*

Maybe I won't tell Dad about the skeleton card just yet.

Stranger's Manifesto
Entry 19

Ever play the game of hearts?
Nope? No big surprise.
Neither have most kids with even a freaking *shred* of a life.
So let me enlighten you.

Two strategies to win.
One—play keep-away from those nasty hearts,
Like they got the raunchiest B.O. ever
And ditch that Dirty Dora.
Shouldn't be too big of a stretch for some of you.
Two—snatch up all those hearts like the greedy bastards you are.
But do it on the sly, sticky-finger style.

Either way, there's one key to success.
Bluff.
Hide your cards. Disguise your strategy.
Plaster that poker face on, then go for the kill.
Just like Life.
Just like *my* game.
I've dealt the cards…
Only difference is that this time,
I *want* someone to call my bluff.

34

The school is ramping up for the moment of silence. Only the "moment" of silence has morphed into a memorial. The LGBTQ Club and the Red Ribbon/Suicide Prevention Committee have called a truce and will both be hosting the event. Did I call that, or what? They're both plastering the halls with their fliers and making announcements on the loudspeaker after the Pledge of Allegiance. Reminding everyone to come to the memorial, guilting us all if we don't, hyping up the importance of accepting everyone for who they are. *Yada, yada, yada.*

I see that preppy boy everywhere now, and I wonder if it's *him.* He definitely seems to be watching me, but trying to look like he's not. He looks old—he's got to be a senior, but someone I haven't noticed before. Wrestler-like, built rock solid with clean-cut hair. There's something big brotherly about him, so he doesn't scare me as much as he should. Still, I'm careful. I don't approach him. That'd be too risky.

Every time I open my locker I expect to see a new card. My heart catches as the combination catches, and I hold my breath. But all I see are books and crumpled papers. The bomber's getting trickier. Sneakier. Maybe he knows I'm trying to watch out for him. I find a card, face up, in my lunch bag.

A plain joker with a question-mark bubble coming out of his head. No words.

What does that mean? That he's questioning himself? That he's changing his mind?

I find another one stuck in my passenger-side car door. Same thing. A joker, no words, but a telephone stuck to his ear.

He wants me to know that he will be calling.

Soon.

* * *

Riiiiing. Riiiiing. "You're up," Janae tells me. "He wants to talk to you anyway."

She's right, I know. We've had three hang-ups tonight. Each ten minutes apart. I'm the only one who hasn't picked up the phone. I know it's the bomber and I know he's waiting for me.

I sit down in the swivel chair. "Helpline, this is Tina."

Pause. At least it's not a hang-up. "Is that you?" he asks, and I hear the anticipation in his voice. I'm not sure if I feel flattered or sick.

At first I want to play it off, like I don't know that he's been waiting for me. But come on, he's been planting playing cards in my locker and on my car. He knows who I am. What good does it do to play games with a madman? Especially one who's holding all the cards? So I say quietly, "Let's talk."

"I've been calling all night. Waiting for you." His voice is thicker than usual. I try to match his voice to that preppy wrestler boy's body. Maybe. I'd think that guy's voice would be huskier than this one's, but who knows.

"So we're talking." I hear an edge in my own voice. "What do you want to talk about?"

"I want to talk about why you've got a cop guarding my favorite pay phone."

My heart stops for a moment. It figures that Dad would station a plainclothes policeman in an unmarked car by the pay phone, to see if the bomber came back. But wouldn't Dad know that this kid wouldn't be fooled by that? "I'm not sure what you're talking about."

"I guess I'm not too surprised." He goes on like I haven't said anything. "But it makes me wonder how much you're telling Daddy Dearest."

Ridiculous, but I feel like I've betrayed him for a moment. Like I have some loyalty to this nutcase? I ignore the twinge and pick up a pencil to doodle on my note-taking paper. I'm not making anything meaningful, just a series of tiny circles. Around and around and around.

"Did I insult you?" he asks after not too long in this strange, eager sort of way that makes me remember he probably doesn't have any real friends. I might be the closest thing this kid has to a friend.

"Look. You're putting me in a tough position here," I tell him, and it's honest. "I don't know what to do. But I do want to help you find a way out of this mess."

"What makes you think I want help?" he asks softly.

"I can tell." I match his tone. "I don't want anyone to get hurt. I don't think you do either."

I can hear him breathing. "How do I know I can trust you?"

"You don't." I blacken in a circle so there's not a speck of white. "How do I know you're not going to blow up this building right now with me in it?"

"I wouldn't hurt you." He says quickly, and it feels real.

"Thank you." The politeness makes it seem like we're setting up a movie date. "You've got to give me something to work with here. How can I help you?"

"I put something in your locker."

"Yeah?" My heart catches.

"I want you to share it with the rest of the school. Will you do it?"

"What does it say?" Now my heart is pumping again, but at double speed.

"Doesn't matter, does it? If it will get me to call this game off?"

"*Will* you call it off?" I grip the phone with both hands.

"Take a freaking look." There is an edge to his voice again.

And before I can ask another question, he clicks off. I realize then that I've ripped the note-taking paper to shreds. My friends are staring at me like I've lost my mind.

Janae stands in front of me, gathering my hands in hers. "You've got to have your dad trace that call."

"No. I think he trusts me. I can stop him."

"Are you completely *insane*?" Janae's voice is shrill enough to shatter glass. "You were just talking to a terrorist. You *have* to trace that call."

"No." I say, standing up. "I've got to get something out of my locker."

Janae blocks my path. "More than two thousand students go to this school. We're all at risk. You might think you're big shit because your dad's a cop, but you don't get to call all the shots."

I move toward the door. "I need to get something out of my locker," I say again.

Miguel grabs my arm, hard. "You aren't going alone." And what might have once felt protective now feels intrusive. "I'm going with you."

I ignore him, as much as a girl can ignore a boy twice her size gripping her arm. I push out the door into the darkened hallway. As the door clicks shut behind us, I hear Janae whispering loudly, "Its official. She's losing it."

* * *

Except for playing cards, my locker is completely empty.

The bomber took everything out. All my books. All my scraps of paper and notes and crumpled-up lunch bags.

Instead, the walls are covered with playing cards. I tug one and realize they have been taped to the sides of the locker. They're arranged in an orderly fashion, in neat little rows. Like they're watching a show. And all queens, kings, and jacks. There's got to be at least forty of them, staring at me.

"Holy shit," Miguel curses from behind me.

I scan the cards, looking for some clue, some explanation. My eyes catch on one. A joker. The solitary joker in the bunch. Crossed out with a big, fat X. This bomber dude is getting too creepy for me.

I rip the cards off the walls of the locker, in a hurry. Miguel's breath puffs against the back of my neck. "What the hell?" he whispers.

I notice black envelopes scattered all over the bottom of the locker. In the darkness they sort of blend in. There must be twenty of them. I gather them up in my arms and shove the playing cards in my sweatshirt pockets.

"Here. Help me carry them," I hiss. I wonder if the bomber is here watching us, feeling betrayed that I brought someone with me. "We can't look through them here."

"This is crazy, Gabi. Did that guy put all this crap in your locker? Then he's been watching you. Watching us!"

217

"Shut up," I tell him, harsher than I mean to. I touch his arm to soften it, because I see the sting on his face. "We can't talk now. We can't, okay?"

He nods and helps me carry the envelopes back to the office.

* * *

Riiiiing. Riiiiing.

"It's him again," I tell Miguel. I am sure he is calling to chew me out for letting Miguel see the envelopes.

I'm only half right.

"Helpline—"

"*Back-stabbing bitch!*" He cuts me off, and I hear pain.

"Excuse me?"

"You traced my call?" His voice is shaking, probably with anger. "I thought you were different. I thought you cared. But no—you're just like everyone else."

I glare at Janae. She must've called my dad when I was searching my locker. Note to self: he was not watching me at the locker. He's somewhere else, and he saw the cops show up. He hasn't been captured.

He speaks again, and his voice is still shaking, but the quality has changed. It sounds tight, as though his throat has constricted, like maybe he is crying. "I thought you wanted to help me."

"I do," I protest, feeling desperate, as if he's slipping away from me.

"Bullshit."

35

There is no way to open the envelopes in private. Miguel is breathing down my neck like a gorilla bodyguard. He's got his arms all crossed and huffy. I'm crouched in my bedroom, with the envelopes surrounding me.

The police traced the bomber's calls to a cell phone discarded in a trash can at the library. The bomber had stolen it, used it, then dumped it. Dad texted my cell and informed us that he'd send a plainclothes officer to the helpline office to escort us to our cars. We were all going home early.

I drove Miguel home, only we made a detour—to my house. Dad was still at work, Mom was asleep. Now it's ten thirty and there's a boy in my room. Unsupervised. If Chloe was awake, she'd be proud of me.

"How do you know there isn't anthrax on these envelopes?" Miguel is too close.

"I *know*." I fight the urge to push him away from me.

"How do you know there isn't some kind of bomb you're going to trigger?" Too bad this particular boy is annoying the crap out of me.

"Look, Miguel. I *know*. If you're worried about it, you don't have to watch."

"You don't get it, do you? I can't let you do something that might hurt yourself. I love you. I'm staying." He pulls my desk chair up to my bed and sits down.

I freeze for a moment when I hear him drop the L word. I peek up at him, at the way his eyebrows bunch together when he's worried. Then I get back to work, slipping my finger through the slit in the first envelope and ripping it open. A picture falls out. Black and white. I hold it by the edges and lay it right side up on the rug. It's an action photo. A picture of a scrawny freshman, arms flailing and hair wet with sweat, being shoved into a trash can. The photographer blurred the freshman's face somehow, swirling the image where his face should be, leaving an unsettling, haunted mirror-like face. The faces attached to the hands shoving him in the trash can, however, are crystal clear. I can even see a zit on one of their noses.

I open the next envelope. Same thing. A circle of girls laughing as another walks by, their faces screwed up with something ugly. The photo is taken directly in front of the girl who's walking, and it captures how she hunches forward, how she holds her books to her chest, but her face is swirled, leaving her mostly unrecognizable. I gasp when I see my own face in the background, looking irritated and biting my lower lip. I seriously don't even remember being there. How many times have I watched people be rude to other people and just minded my own business?

I pick up the next one. Kids snickering as a boy points and gestures. Even though the gesturing kid is swirled out, I can tell by his backpack and his stance that it's Petey Plumber, our resident tattletale.

The next one looks oddly familiar. It's from the other day, when I waited at Eric's locker. When I saw those football types picking on a scrawny freshman. The photo must have been taken moments before I threw that apple. The scrawny kid's face is swirled out, but I can see the boxy faces of the football players as they loom behind him.

It's photo after photo of this. All black and white. All with the victim's faces swirled, and all with the other faces in clear view.

Miguel sits next to me, picking up the photos by the edges. "This makes our school look really bad. Like nobody cares about anyone else."

"Yeah, but think about it." I touch one of the swirled faces with my fingertip. "Do any one of these pictures surprise you?"

"No one single shot surprises me. Seeing them all together surprises me. I guess I didn't realize how often people do shitty things."

"Wait a sec." I feel like the pieces of the puzzle are coming together for me.

I spread out all the taped-up cards from my locker. I place the crossed-out joker in the center, where he'd placed himself before.

"What does this look like?" I ask Miguel.

He snorts. "Like somebody built a house of cards and it crumbled."

"No, be serious. If this kid is trying to recreate a scene to give me a clue, what does it look like?" I pause while Miguel thinks. "Here, imagine them the way they were in my locker, with some of them placed above each other in rows. Where in our school would kids be sitting in rows like that?"

"The football bleachers or the school theater?"

My thoughts exactly. "Maybe he's at a school assembly."

He repeats that slowly, the words rolling off his tongue. "A school assembly?" He turns to me, his eyes wide. He curses in Spanish with words I don't recognize.

"And maybe the joker's dead," I add. "But no one else appears to be. He'd have x'd out everyone else if he intended to hurt everyone. Right?" I say this partly to reassure myself.

I think back to all the other cards he's planted. I'm pretty sure the joker has always represented him…leaving the queens and kings to represent others. All the joker cards held threats, saying things like *I hold a thousand lives in my hands. I am invisible. I can obliterate an entire school. Comprende, amigo?* The joker drawn to look dead. Like a skeleton. *Would anyone care? Granted, I'm a jaded piece of shit, but I sure as hell wouldn't.*

Everything's pointing to the moment of silence. Something will happen then. I'm sure of it. That means I have two days to figure this out.

The bomber, this joker, he asked me to help him. To share the photos. I play back his words in my mind: "Doesn't matter, does it? If it will get me to call this game off?" I know he's pissed that his call got traced. But can I earn his trust back?

I have the power to stop this.

If I play by his rules.

If I gain his trust.

I can save everyone.

Including him.

Stranger's Manifesto
Entry 20

Enough with hearts.
Enough with rummy, spades, and even pathetic pinochle.
Enough with goddamn solitaire.
I say it's about time for some freaking 52 pickup!
Just watch the cards scatter...
Watch the imbeciles scramble to pick them up.
Watch me bring this school to its goddamn knees.
Teach it a lesson.
Trust me...I will leave lives changed forever.

This moment of silence
Is like putting a Band-Aid
On a gushing wound.
Everyone's rushing around
Trying to get that Band-Aid to stick
When what they really need
Is a tourniquet.

36

Eric is sitting on my front steps when I pull up to the curb after sneaking back out to take Miguel home. Normally I park in the driveway if there's a space, but I don't want to take the chance of waking Mom up. The porch light is on, but I'm still a tiny bit creeped out. Like, why couldn't Eric wait until morning to come say whatever he has to say? It's got to be at least eleven thirty.

I sit in the car for a moment, engine off, deciding what to say. I know why he's here.

It turns out I don't have to say much.

"Gabi." He stands up. His face is tight and I know he is at least ten times more uncomfortable than I am. "I want to apologize."

"It's okay," I tell him.

"No, it's not." His voice comes back strong, and I step back. "But it's also not cool to lie to me."

Big lump in throat.

"If you're not into someone, you should just tell them that."

He's in my way. I want to walk around him, but that would be rude. "I didn't want to hurt your feelings."

"I gave you lots of opportunities to tell me. But you didn't and I wound up looking like an idiot in front of half the school.

Thank you for that."

"I didn't want to hurt your feelings," I say again.

"Well, if that was your goal, you failed royally." His tone is hard, and I'm tempted to cover my ears, like if I don't hear it, he's not saying it.

I close my eyes, listening to his voice and pretending it's on the other end of a phone receiver. He sounds nothing like my mystery caller.

"I'm sorry too. I didn't mean for it to play out that way," I tell him, and I mean it. But I'm not sure he cares.

* * *

"Mom's been acting weird all day." Chloe is lying on the floor of my bedroom with her butt against my closet door and her feet in the air. I'd thought she was already asleep, but I guess not.

"Apparently she's not the only one." I step over her, thankful for two things. One, that Eric turned away and walked home. Two, that I piled up those pictures and hid them in my underwear drawer before I left to take Miguel home. "What are you doing in here? It's late. You should be asleep."

"It's got to be the end of the world." Chloe taps her feet against the closet door, and the whole thing shakes.

"Nice. That's just what I wanted to hear." I fling myself on my bed and consider falling asleep right here, fully clothed. "What's she doing that's so strange?"

"I don't know. Asking me to order in for dinner because she's too busy to cook. Or order it herself, apparently." Chloe flexes her feet.

"Whoa." I unsnap my bra. I hate sleeping with my bra on. "She's really letting loose."

"I'm serious. I ordered fried chicken, mashed potatoes, and about a gallon of Mountain Dew. She didn't say a word."

"Maybe it's Alzheimer's, and she's forgotten that fried food and high-fructose corn syrup will make you fat." I pull my arms through the straps and slip the bra off one arm at a time, leaving my shirt on. I'm talented that way.

Just then Mom pokes her head into my room. "Oh good. You're both here." Now I feel supremely lucky that Mom didn't see me bringing Miguel up to my room. I'd assumed she was asleep.

Chloe's right. It *is* the end of the world. Mom hasn't sat us down together for a girl talk in years. And it's nearly midnight. Maybe they're getting a divorce. But wouldn't they tell us that together? Maybe she's got cancer or something. Maybe she's having an affair and wants us to know. Maybe she's decided to ship us off to a boarding school in England.

Mom must be anxious because she starts to drop the bomb before she even gets all the way into the room. "I have something important to tell you." I look at Chloe, lying on her back on the carpet, and I can see her stiffening. Bracing herself.

Mom takes a deep breath. "I'm going back to school. I've only got a few classes to finish up my bachelor's degree, but then I have a graduate program I'm considering."

That's it?

"I know you guys like having me home to support you…" she starts, not seeming to notice that Chloe's trying not to laugh. "But I've decided that I put my own life on hold for the last seventeen years, and now it's time for me to refocus on my education and career."

"That's good, Mom," I tell her. "We'll be okay."

But it's as if she doesn't hear me. She keeps talking. "I'm sorry if I've been trying to sculpt you into perfect little people. I'm sorry if I've been living vicariously through you. I just wanted you to have good lives." Her voice cracks. "Your dad's been telling me for years to loosen the leash, to let you make your own mistakes, but I just couldn't let go." She taps her finger against the door frame. "I guess I imagined you to be an extension of me. I didn't count on you two being your own people. I'm sorry for not allowing you to be whoever you are."

Neither of us says anything at first. What are we supposed to do, say, "Apology accepted?" Finally Chloe bursts out, "So does this mean you're cutting us loose? We can eat ice cream for breakfast and tattoo our tongues if we want?"

"Very funny." Mom snorts, and somehow this is reassuring. "It means I'm giving you my word that I'm going to back off. I'll be too busy to micromanage your lives. You might be on your own for dinner a couple nights a week, but you're responsible girls. I know you can handle it."

When Mom finally leaves, I lean over the side of my bed and stare at Chloe on the floor. "What the hell just happened?"

"It's all because of you," Chloe tells me like it's a compliment. "You standing up to her about Georgetown. Dating the maid's son." I make a face at that. "You coming home in a cop car, and with new friends with crazy hair and piercings. You're rocking her world."

"All I know is this day could not get any stranger." I kick off my shoes. "Why are you lying on my floor, by the way?"

"I'm decorating. You know you're going to have to redo this room so it matches your updated identity." She turns her attention to the walls. "I can brainstorm better from this angle."

"Enjoy." I can't even see straight anymore. I want to tell Chloe all about the cards and pictures in my locker, but I can't even keep my eyes open. "I'm going to bed right this minute. I'm not even going to get up to brush my teeth."

"Gross. Now I know we're in a twilight zone."

I'm not sure if I even smile at that one. All I know is I feel the heaviness of sleep sucking at me, pulling me down, down, down. I don't have the energy to fight it.

Stranger's Manifesto
Entry 21

When I say I'm watching her,
Leaving things for her,
I'm not trying to be a creep. Honest.
When you're invisible like me,
A dust parachute,
A particle in the sky,
You're watching all the time.
She just happened to catch my eye.
But things happen for a reason. At least that's what people say.
Granted, I've *made* a reason,
Because now she's an integral part of my plan.
Of course, she helped matters a bit
By being one of those people who types her locker combo
Into her cell phone
Just in case she forgets.

The thing that bugs me
Is my parents.
You know they'll blame them after it's over.
They'll say they screwed me up
Because it's way easier than seeing the truth.
But you know what they say—
When you point a finger at someone else,
There are four more fingers pointing back at you.

37

I let Chloe and Janae walk ahead. Are we being cruel to bother these people after all this time? Miguel is by my side, half a step ahead, but he keeps slowing down to match my pace. The yard is overgrown. The grass has grown in all directions, sprouting left and right, and it's at least as tall as my knees. The trees are dropping fruit that lies rotting on the ground. The flies buzz around, diving in and out, having a feast.

Janae is the first up the steps. Pressing her finger on the doorbell, ringing it once, twice. I cringe. What exactly are we going to say? Chloe looks back at me now, and I see a glimmer of what I'm feeling in her face. Miguel moves closer to me, protective-like, as if he can sense my hesitation.

A woman lumbers up to the door, her steps heavy on the floor, making it creak and groan in anticipation. I want to leave. I don't recognize her at first. Her hair is greasy, thinning on top, and her body is bloated, like what's inside her has swollen up and stretched out her skin. She pushes her face up to the screen door, and I can see her irritation.

"Don't you all see the sign here?" She points her thick finger at the "No solicitation" sign by the doorbell. "I don't want to be disturbed."

"Oh, we're not soliciting," Janae promises. "We just came to talk."

Now the woman's face darkens, and her lips tighten. "You kids never change. Always want to come around here on the anniversary, poking your fingers at our pain."

"No, ma'am," Chloe begins, and I realize I have never in my life heard her use the word "ma'am" before.

"Don't you 'no, ma'am' me. We all get our just desserts here on this earth. So did my daughter. She got her punishment for her own sins. And so will you if you keep messing with people's pain."

This is not going well. I step forward, hoping my voice won't shake as much as it feels like it will. "Mrs. Moon, I'm trying to find your daughter's friend."

This catches her attention. She wags her finger at me. "She didn't have no friends. She was a loner. Never interested in the activities the other kids did. No Girls Scouts for her. No soccer or piano."

"I remember her. I remember your daughter." Dust curls around my shoes as I edge closer.

"So does everyone."

"No—not in that way. I really remember her. I remember who she sat with at P.E. I remember all the times I could have reached out to her and I didn't." I stumble through my words, awkward. "I'm sorry for that." Miguel touches my hand, his skin soft, reassuring.

Her eyes get all watery now, and she pushes her face closer to the screen door.

"The school is holding a memorial for her this year," I say because I have to say something.

"I heard." There are dead bugs stuck in the screen door. Now she's close enough for me to see how dry her lips are. They're all cracked in the corners.

"And I want to make sure we reach out to her friend. This has to be a hard time for him too."

Mrs. Moon pulls back. "I don't know who you're talking about. She never brought any friends around."

Miguel clears his throat. "You don't remember her talking about anyone?"

"She didn't talk much. Not to me."

"Oh." *Bummer.* What else can we say? "Well, thank you for your time."

As we turn to walk away, she pushes the screen door open. I see her in plain light for the first time. Her skin is gray. Flaky. Like she hasn't showered in a long time. "That neighborhood kid hung around a bit. The quiet one. We used to call him the Stray."

"The Stray?" I try to act all casual, but I know immediately that this is who I'm looking for.

"Yeah. Like he didn't have a home. No place to be. Only saw him a couple of times. Scrawny kid. Looked like a stray puppy. He hung around the yard, picking fruit. Sometimes him and Jo'd talk a bit. Play some chess out in the yard. He'd beat her every time. I don't know if they hung out at school though."

"Do you remember his name?" Chloe asks, standing behind me.

"Nah. Don't know if I ever knew it. Just called him the Stray." Mrs. Moon moves forward.

Janae asks, "Would you recognize his picture in a yearbook?"

"Doubt it."

"Would you be willing to try?"

"If it'll get rid of you all, I will. I'm missing my favorite program." As Mrs. Moon steps out onto the porch, I see she still curves forward into herself. Stooped over like she's protecting something, as if her insides will spill onto the floor if she dares to stand tall.

I hand her my yearbook from tenth grade. I flip to the sophomore section. Mrs. Moon runs her finger down each page, looking at every face. "Don't recognize none of them."

"Are you sure?"

"I'm sure. Never did get to know that kid too well, you know. Maybe I wouldn't recognize him if he was standing in front of me. But none of those pictures there ring a bell."

We thank her for her help. She nods. Her eyes have glazed over, and I'm not even sure she knows we've gone.

* * *

I leave a message for the bomber in the only way I know how. I stand in front of my locker for a good ten minutes, hoping he's watching me. I carefully post my own playing card in my locker. One of a queen with the words, "You can trust me. I will help you get your message out. Be patient."

My locker is still bare bones empty.

I have a feeling he will look in there.

As I click my locker shut, I see the preppy wrestler guy getting a drink from the water fountain. A likely excuse. Just a reason to stand near my locker. As I walk past him, I drop my water bottle by his feet. It rolls into his sneakers. He bends to pick it up, and he avoids my eyes.

"Thanks." I say, my voice cool.

He nods his head. *Rats.* I wanted him to talk so I could hear his voice.

"I haven't seen you around before," I add. "What's your name?"

He hesitates. My internal alarm is blaring. *This has to be him!*

I can end this here and now. Maybe I don't have to wait until the moment of silence. Maybe I can scream bloody murder and get campus security over here, and leap on his back and get him in a choke hold.

He does speak though, and it stops me. "I'm a friend of Al's." His voice is quiet. He looks at me directly when he says "Al," like it's some kind of cloak-and-dagger message. He hands me my water bottle. "Just visiting for a while."

Crap. Al is my father.

This preppy wrestling boy is watching me because he's my bodyguard. An undercover cop trying to fit in at high school. Trailing behind me everywhere I go on campus. Just in case.

I should've known Dad was being way too chill about this whole thing.

Nice. So now I've figured out my mysterious stalker.

I just hope the bomber hasn't figured it out too.

* * *

Student government decides we need a pep rally. The moment of silence turned memorial will now be a pep rally. First they'll plug the two clubs (LGBTQ and Suicide Prevention), then we'll have the appropriately somber moment of silence-memorial, and finally we'll end with the spirit-building pep rally.

Chloe and her new boy-toy Jason (who looks surprisingly normal) have joined the Red Ribbon Committee. They seem to be sucking face more than they're working, but hey, it's the thought that counts.

Nobody seems to realize the hypocrisy of having the cheerleaders perform right after honoring the life-death of a girl tormented by cheerleaders.

I'm too tired to point this out.

* * *

I ditch school for the first day in my life. I convince Chloe to ditch too. Miguel, Janae, and Garth want to tag along, but I need their eyes on campus. I really just don't want too many people involved.

This is Mom's first week of classes, so she's out of our hair. I've already fielded the calls home from the school, reporting our absences. Except for my friends, nobody knows we're home.

We have very little time. The memorial is set to take place at 2 p.m. I need Chloe's help with the pictures. I've got them spread around my room. She'll scan them all, using Dad's scanner, hooked up to her laptop. For each picture, we will save two versions. One version will be exactly as the bomber left them for me. We will save this set, make copies from it, and hand deliver them to all the people we recognize from each picture so they get this as a warning.

Then we'll make a second version, a collage of the photos, only this time we'll disguise everyone's faces. When the jerks see our second version, even though their faces will not show, they'll know who they are. At first we think about doing it without disguising anyone's faces, but then we realize that kind of public humiliation makes us no different than them. It would be reverse bullying, and that's not cool. In the center of the second version, we glue Jo Moon's sophomore-year school picture. We add the following words in black, block letters: *Is it worth it?*

We do a quickie run to the FedEx store and make massive copies of the second version.

We'll pass it around today at the memorial.

* * *

As I'm stacking up the copies, I am struck by a thought. I wonder when and how the bomber got all these pictures. Did people know they were being photographed? Did he sneak around campus? Or was he someone with permission to take pictures? Someone on staff for the school yearbook or newspaper? Someone who could walk around campus with a camera around his neck all the time?

I grab last year's yearbook and flip over to the club section, poring over the yearbook and newspaper staff pages. *Oh. My. God.*

There he is staring back at me in black and white, unsmiling.

I know who the bomber is. I. Know. Who. He. Is.

It hits me so hard I'm sure I'll bruise. *Shit.*

I have to make sure I'm right.

And I have to stop him.

Stranger's Manifesto
Entry 22

I know it seems weird
To snap pictures of people
When they don't know you're looking.
But isn't that the only real Truth?
People do all kinds of crap
When they don't think anyone is watching.
It's only when they think they're anonymous
That the real claws come out.
Unless they want the audience.
Unless they get off on it.
Then they're even worse. And isn't *that* weird?

Besides, photos don't lie.
I doubt that girl
Will know what the hell
To do with them.
She keeps disappointing me,
Which is no big surprise.
Sadly.

38

I am running. My hair is flying loose behind me, tangling in my wake, and there's a blister working its way up on my heel. I have to power through it because I can't stop. I can't stop.

I parked on the street in front of the house and now I'm jamming down the driveway. I hold my yearbook under my arm. I have no idea if Mrs. Moon will be there again, but something tells me she doesn't get out much.

We showed her the wrong set of pictures.

She needed to see the freshman pictures from Jo's sophomore year. Because I know who he is. I *think* I know who he is. So brilliant he takes AP physics with the seniors even though he's only a junior. So bright he's hacked the teachers' computers and has access to the answers before the exams. So bright he skipped at least one grade. But quirky bright. The kind of kid who doesn't fit in. Who walks around campus with a camera, snapping pictures of random people. The kind of kid who is invisible. So invisible he stopped caring a long, long time ago.

Mrs. Moon is irritated. And maybe a little drunk. She smells like she bathed in cheap wine, and even that can't cover up the smell from not showering. But it doesn't matter. Because the second I show her the page with his picture, I see her eyes narrow in.

She does not hesitate. She points her finger at him. The name under it says Simon Blackwell. The geeky kid who gave me the answers to the physics test a couple months ago. I hadn't even known his name for sure.

"That's him," she says. "That's the Stray."

* * *

I am late. The trip to Mrs. Moon's cost me precious time. But I had to know for sure. I'm driving illegally, trying to dial my cell phone en route. I call Dad directly.

I have never hated voice mail so much in my life. I hear his message start immediately, which means he doesn't even have the cell turned on. I slam my phone down. I screech into a parking place in the student lot and start running again. Running, running toward the school. The sun shines its angry rays down on me, beating against the top of my head.

I scan the parking lot frantically. *Where is an undercover bodyguard when you need him, damn it!* No sign of my preppy wrestler dude. *Shit.*

I call again. Maybe Dad will pick up this time. *Damn. No luck.* I leave a message though, all out of breath and panting. I probably sound like I'm dying. "Dad! I know who it is. I think I know who it is. Meet me at the school. Call me on my cell."

I don't even think to call the station until I'm nearing the side gate. I don't know the number by heart, so I punch in the number for information. "Central Police Department." I am practically wheezing. The automated responder can't recognize what I'm trying to say, because I'm so out of breath and not able to enunciate. I press zero to speak to a live attendant.

"Information, can I help you?"

"Yes. The number for Central Police Department."

"Is this an emergency?"

"No."

Short pause that tells me she doesn't believe me. I must sound like a crazy woman. "I can connect you to 911 if you like."

"It's not an emergency. I just want the office number." I don't want the emergency responders out here. They'll barrel in with sirens screaming, and the bomber will feel totally betrayed. He might even blow up the school out of spite. No, I have to do this covertly. I have to talk to Dad directly.

She makes a *tsk-tsk* sound, which is totally unprofessional, and I'm just about to get pissed when she connects me to the number.

"Central Police Department, can I help you?"

I stop running. I stand with my hands on my knees, hunched over and panting. "Hi, is Officer Mallory in?"

"Hold on just a moment, please. I will check for you." Brief pause, while I hyperventilate. I try to slow my breathing. "No, ma'am. It looks like he's in the field. Can I take a message for you?"

I start to say no but then I change my mind. "Sure. Please tell him to call his daughter on her cell."

"Is this an emergency?"

I take a deep breath. How to answer this one? "Yeah, it's pretty urgent."

"All right. We'll get the message over to him ASAP. Thank you."

I race onto campus, flashing my school ID as I enter through the office. I shove my cell into the back pocket of my jeans. Hopefully Chloe is already here, slipping the personalized copies of photos into the appropriate lockers.

The best term to describe the school atmosphere is "organized chaos." Students are being herded into the stadium stands for the memorial. This is where we hold all campus-wide events, because the gymnasium isn't big enough. The halls are clogged with students, and despite my best efforts to push through the masses, I'm totally stuck.

As I'm being pushed along with the current of bodies, I realize we're passing my locker. On a whim, I edge over to the side and step out of the massive wave of students. My hands are shaking so badly as I spin the combo that it doesn't even work the first time. I try again. When I fling it open, I gasp. All my books are back inside. My scraps of paper and crumpled-up lunch bags are back too, but folded neatly.

There is a single rose and one playing card attached to it. A thorn pokes through the card, right in the center of the joker's chest. Black Sharpie blood drips down, and his eyes are crossed out, making him look dead. There are other black marks on his chest, like someone pushed the Sharpie in hard. They look like bullet holes. *Isn't sacrificing yourself for a cause the highest kind of honor? Or is that just the crap they feed suicide bombers?*

And this is when my heart stops.

* * *

I lose at least five minutes. I blame panic. I find myself sitting against my locker, my knees drawn into my chest and the joker in my hand. I have no idea how to stop this train wreck. I can already hear the squealing of the train's brakes. And I know, on some level, that no matter how hard I try, I won't be able to stop it. It's already in motion and I'm not strong enough. The best that can happen is that I'll witness it.

Why did he want me to pass out the photos? Why didn't he do it himself? I look at the card. *Isn't sacrificing yourself for a cause the highest kind of honor?* What is his cause? Anti-bullying? Be nice to the underdog? Step in and stand up—don't be a silent bystander? And why did he send me all those cards? Call me on the Line? Did he think I could stop him?

I am comforted by the thought that if he put that new note in my locker, then he must have gotten mine. My note that he could trust me, asking him to give me time. I scan the lockers for Chloe. I wonder how far she's gotten in distributing the fliers.

The halls are still packed, but there's more air space between each person. Most of the students are probably already in the stands. I realize, stupidly, that the student body is all together in one spot. If Simon were to set off a bomb at this moment, we will have played right into his hands. Now everyone is in one place. The casualties will be massive.

I read the card again. I find a single strand of hope. To me, it looks like the joker has been shot multiple times. If he was really planning on blowing himself up like a true suicide bomber, he'd be a mess of black scribbles. He'd have put other playing cards in the locker—queens and kings—and they'd all be dead too. Maybe Simon just wants to make us *think* he's gonna blow up the school. To have the power, to be in charge, to make us scared. That was basically what he did with the bomb threat earlier in the year. Maybe fear is his goal, not actual casualties.

I run my finger over the card. I touch the dark blotches on his chest and the hole where the thorn held it to the rose. Why would he be shot multiple times? If he shot himself, it would be a bullet hole to the head. If he has multiple shots to his body, then someone else would have to shoot him. But how would he *know* someone was going to shoot him?

Does he have accomplices? I've wondered that for a long time.

This has been an elaborate plot—even for a genius brainiac. Maybe he has partners (one or two or more) and maybe those partners will shoot him today. Like a staged event. But who could they be? And isn't he a loner? How in the world would he rope in someone to help him? Unless *he* was the one roped in.

And if he doesn't have a partner, then who else would shoot him? How would he *know* for sure someone else would shoot him? The only way he could know is if he set up a scenario for the police to shoot him. They'd blast him away in a heartbeat if they thought they were saving innocent lives. I take a moment to catch my breath. Maybe this is an elaborate set up for a suicide by cop.

"Gabi?" I recognize Bruce's voice before I look up. He and Katie are standing over me, their backpacks strapped over both shoulders.

I scramble to my feet. How much time have I wasted? *Got to move!*

"Go home, Bruce. Take Katie with you."

Bruce looks at his watch. "Not time yet. See?"

I grab one of each of their hands in mine. "Go to the office. *Please*. Sit with the nurse. Tell her you feel sick." Assuming the whole school is not blown to smithereens in the next ten minutes, Simon Blackwell will be gunned down in front of the entire school population. Bruce doesn't need to see that.

"Lookie here, a little reunion of the lunch bunch." Beth's tone is playful teasing and I whirl to face her. I must look a mess, because she says, "Gabi? Oh my god. What's *wrong*?"

"Beth." I grab at her shirt, frantic. "Take Bruce and Katie to the office."

"Did someone die or something?" Her eyes widen.

Not just yet. But maybe soon. I shove their hands in hers.

"Please. If our friendship means anything to you, do this for me. Trust me."

I see the meaning of my words sink in. "Okay," she whispers.

And then I can't waste another second. I turn in the other direction and force my way through the crowd. I check my phone, hoping to see a missed call from my dad. Nothing. So instead I text Chloe, Miguel, Janae, and Garth. On a whim I add Eric. **Important. Can anyone put their eyes on Simon Blackwell?** The only reason I know his last name is from looking at his yearbook picture. **Scrawny kid, junior, school-issued camera. Text me if you find him. Don't approach him, just text me.** And then I text Dad. Just Simon's name and these words. **Suicide by cop.** I hope he knows what I mean. I hope he has his cell phone on. And most importantly, I hope I'm on the right track.

* * *

I get three texts back at once.

From Janae and Eric. **Simon Blackwell? Who's that?**

From Garth. **That puny kid from calculus?**

To him I respond. **Yes. Him. Do you see him?**

No. But I'll look.

I turn around, and the world blurs. I feel sluggish, like I'm underwater and my limbs are heavy. I'm trying to push through people, scan the crowd, but my eyes fail me.

When I spot him, everything sharpens. He's wearing a bulky backpack that looks stuffed with books. But maybe it's stuffed with enough explosives to create a crater in the earth. He walks like it's heavy, like it's weighing him down.

I don't want to take my eyes off him, but I have to. I scan the crowd for our campus police officers. I feel like I'm playing *Where's Waldo?* Because they're all in uniform. They should be easy to spot. But they blend in, disappear. Until the crowd moves, shifts through space, and I do see one. No, two. I see two uniformed officers. One in the stands, looking outward. One on the field, looking at the stands. One of the officers twists toward me and I see his face. Officer Murphy. The jerk who drove me home from Cruz's party. Great. Just who I want protecting my school. The cop with a chip on his shoulder, according to Dad.

I shift my eyes back to Simon and his backpack. He has moved. He's quick, and it takes me a moment for my eyes to settle on him. I realize I'm holding my breath. Once I grab him with my eyes again, I start to breathe. But only for a moment. Because he's looking directly back at me. His face grim and determined. Like he knows what's coming next won't be fun, but he feels compelled do to it anyway.

He nods at me. Slightly. An acknowledgment that we both know what's happening. And the game is officially on.

Stranger's Manifesto
Entry 23

All along I knew
It would come to this.
That's why I've been writing these
Ridiculous wannabe journal entries.
Because I knew it would end this way.
And I knew I'd want to tell the world why.

Stupid me
For thinking the
School administrators or campus supervisors
Might be sufficiently suspicious
To search me.
Or whip the metal detector out
And use it.
For once.

Stupid me
For entertaining the thought
That someone would care enough
To stop me.
Apparently, no one can.
Because I still float,
Invisible as dust.
Lost.
Forever.

39

The sound of Chloe's cell phone interrupts my panic. She has different rings for each of us. This one's the theme song from the Winnie the Pooh movie. At first I feel irritated with her. She knows better than to take her phone off vibrate at school. It's going to get confiscated.

And then the meaning of the ringtone sinks in. It's the tone that means Dad is calling her. Why is he calling *her*? Why not *me*? Suddenly I realize that when I left the message at Dad's office, I didn't identify myself. I just said I was his daughter. Maybe his cell is still off. Maybe the officer at the department called him on the intercom in his car. Maybe he hasn't seen my text yet.

The music continues. People turn to look, chuckling at the song choice.

I see her suddenly in the crowd, fumbling in her pockets to try to find the cell, to silence it. She's wearing her bright red "Yes, they are real" shirt with big white letters across her boobs. She's maybe twenty feet from Simon.

"Hi, Dad!" she answers, and I can hear her from here. I flick my eyes over to Simon. He is watching me. "No, I didn't call you. Maybe it was Gabi."

Simon's eyes narrow. His skin deepens in color.

I push through the crowd, moving closer to Chloe.

He does too.

Simon gets there first. I watch as he slips his arm through hers, gripping it, and speaks in her ear. Her shoulders droop, and she drops her phone. Leaves it there on the ground to be stepped on. Simon whispers again in her ear, turning his head to look at me. His eyes are pointed, and I know exactly what they're saying. They say, *Stay away. Don't get too close.*

Chloe is his hostage.

* * *

The phone in my pocket vibrates. I glance at it as I move, hoping it's a text from Dad.

It's Garth. I see him. He's with your sister. What do you want me to do?

It's hard to text and walk and keep my eyes on Simon and my sister at the same time. But I do. I text blindly, hoping I'm hitting the right keys.

Tell the others where he is. Get close, but not too close.

I edge forward. My senses are on overdrive. I see every slight movement in the crowd. I hear the sounds of people chatting, moving forward, the sounds of the band warming up, getting ready to play a song.

I see my preppy wrestler bodyguard in the corner, eyes on me, and I want to scream at him. What good is he? He's too far away for me to reach him, and it's too risky to yell, so I just gesture with my arm for him to follow me. I hope he has a gun.

Simon and Chloe walk stiffly, like their bodies are connected and they have no joints. He leads her to the stadium, to a spot on the side. His positioning is genius. There is no one behind him.

Everyone is in front of him. He can see the stands. He can see the stage. He's driving this train wreck.

* * *

Students settle into their seats. The band is playing strains of Elton John's "Candle in the Wind."

I see Chloe's face. Her eyes must be filling up, because her mascara is beginning to drip. Her whole body is shaking uncontrollably. She says something to Simon. Gestures to her backpack. He seems to be listening. Gripping her arm still, but listening. He slips her backpack off her shoulders. Unzips it for her. Pulls out our photocopies of the pictures. Looks at them. Nods.

He turns to me, his eyes pointed, but the anger is gone. He nods his head again. I know he is trying to say something to me. But I don't know what. I want to scream, *What? What?* But I don't.

Text from Miguel. Garth and I are close enough to tackle him. We can totally take him. You tell us when.

I search the crowd and see Miguel and Garth, as close as they can be without alarming Simon. They are both wearing sunglasses, looking like Secret Service men, their eyes hidden. I text back, **K.** But I don't know when to say "when." I don't know what Simon has in that backpack. My sense is that he's got some kind of explosives. Probably fake ones meant to look real, but who the hell knows? I can't make that judgment call. If they tackle him, we might all go down.

Another text from Miguel. I love you.

I realize something. I love him back. On some level I didn't totally trust him until now. Like maybe he had some part in this bomber mess. It's such a huge relief that he's not involved. I promise myself that if I live through today, I'll tell him that I love him.

No wait—what if either one of us doesn't live through today? I text him now, even though I know I'm wasting precious time. **I love you too.**

The president of the LGBTQ Club is speaking. About remembering Jo and giving her a moment of silence. And plugging his club. Not to be outdone, the chair of the Suicide Prevention Committee steps up and talks too. He says something almost identical and then plugs his committee. The band will play one more song; we will all have a moment of silence to remember Jo; and then the cheerleaders will perform.

Simon turns Chloe, all stiff, to face me and whispers in her ear. She and I lock eyes. Hers are a mess. Mine might be too, for all I know. But whatever he said must have been reassuring. Because her face has relaxed. She looks the way she used to as a kid, when she knew she was going to get a shot at the doctor's office. She'd lie on her stomach, butt bare, waiting for the poke.

At first she'd cry, but then I'd hold her hand and help her count the cars in the parking lot. "How many red cars do you see, Chloe? How many blue? Here, let's link pinkies. We won't let go until it's over. It won't hurt, Chloe, if we count the cars. It won't hurt much."

We must be on the same wavelength, because she moves her left hand slightly, like she's linking pinkies with an invisible someone. I know it's a message to me.

* * *

The moment of silence must be the longest minute in the history of man. Three uniformed officers are in the crowd, moving down slowly, edging toward Simon. I wonder if he sees them. Dad must have gotten my text. I see other movement. Four adults I don't recognize, in plain clothing, positioning themselves around the stadium. Sharpshooters?

I text Dad again, hoping he got my original text, even though he never responded. **He's got Chloe. He wants you to kill him. Suicide by cop.**

People are taking the moment of silence pretty seriously. This surprises me a little, because normally we get the half-swallowed giggles, the whispers, the jackasses who make fun of it. Even the cheerleaders have stopped stretching for a moment. They stand hand in hand, their heads bowed.

I inch forward. Simon is angled away from me and cannot see my movement. This is my chance. I have to get closer. I can't give Miguel and Garth the go-ahead, but I can't stand being so far from them. So I inch. And inch. And inch. Until I'm five or six steps away from Chloe.

The moment the band starts playing again, there's movement. The cheerleaders drop their hands and come out on stage for their performance. And Simon moves. He whispers one more time in my sister's ear, and then he whips out a gun. And places it against her temple.

Stranger's Manifesto
Entry 24

Remember Jo's game?
What's the best way to die?
She never said hanging, remember?
There's another one she never said.
Suicide by cop.
All you gotta do is get them to think you're a threat
And think you're armed.
And then you don't have to do a goddamn thing.
And your parents don't ever have to know that
You *wanted* to die.
Better they think you're a criminal
Than that you want out.
Out early.

I'm not sure people would have noticed right away if it hadn't been for me. Because the people in the stands are busy watching the cheerleaders, and the music is loud. But I scream. The kind of bloodcurdling scream you'd hear in a horror movie. Both Miguel and Garth move instinctively forward, like this is the time to tackle the guy, but then they both freeze. Probably because of the gun pointed directly at my sister's brain.

The officers all draw their guns in unison, but I can tell they are too far for a good shot. The sharpshooters draw their guns too. I can see the bugs in their ears and their mouths moving as they position themselves.

Simon is going to die.

Chloe is not going to die, I tell myself. She's *not*. I won't let her.

But maybe we're all gonna die. If he has a bomb in his backpack, it will go off when he hits the ground.

I'm no longer using my brain. I'm just reacting. My body's in motion, and it's barreling toward my sister. I realize this is stupid—that I'm making the sharpshooters' job way harder. Dad will probably ground me for life. I realize this on some removed level, like this whole thing is happening to someone else and I'm watching a movie. But I can't stop.

Someone shouts, "This is the police. Drop your weapon!"

Simon's stance does not falter. Chloe's eyes are closed. Her arms hang down, her pinky still curled like we are linked together.

I am running-leaping-lunging toward my sister. As I pass him, I feel Miguel's hands reaching for me, trying to hold me back, but I am slippery and I am Superwoman. Nothing can stop me. Not even a bullet. As I leap toward my sister, Simon turns his head slightly. Our eyes connect.

Right before the first blast, I see Simon smile.

* * *

Time has turned all choppy. I get bits and pieces of input, but I'm not sure it's in order and I can't stop screaming.

Me, Simon, and my sister falling backward together like we're in one big group hug. Probably from the force of the blast. Sharpshooters don't miss, do they?

The sounds of mass chaos. People running in all directions. Screaming. Panicking. Me squished to the ground, stuck, unable to move.

There is blood now. I smell it before I see it. I feel it next. Warm and sticky. Somebody is bleeding.

* * *

Miguel scoops his arms through mine and pulls me backward, away from the pile. The screaming is fainter now, losing strength. I watch as Miguel examines me—my head, my chest, my arms, my torso, my legs, my feet. He must be looking for the source of the blood.

"I think you're okay," he whispers, and I bury my head in his chest. I breathe him in, all the way in, as if his fabric-softener scent could clean my mind.

The screaming stops. It was all coming from me. I stay there in the safety of his arms while the police and emergency personnel intervene. He won't let me get up, but I'm glad. Because if I'm okay, that means the blood is coming from Simon. Or my sister. And I don't want to see.

Miguel pulls me gingerly to standing. I hold my face to his chest.

A moment later Chloe joins my Miguel huddle. She wraps herself in with us, her body still shaking, and I hold on to her like I never have before.

I hear Miguel sniffling and I know he's crying too. He stays there, holding us together, keeping us from seeing the blood or the mess.

And then I see Dad's shoes. He folds into us as well. I feel Miguel pull back, pull away, like he doesn't want to intrude on a family moment. But my dad holds him there. Miguel relaxes into us.

I don't know how long we stand there. I just know that when we move from that spot, there is no sight of Simon and my pinky is sore from having been linked with Chloe's for so long.

Stranger's Manifesto
Entry 25

Pain.
It hurts.
I *hurt*.
From the center of my soul.
I'm a piece of shit.
A disgusting piece of shit.
There's a blackness leaking through my veins,
Infecting every part of me,
Pumping through my body
Like my heart is some kind of evil machine.
And it hurts.
I can't make it go away. The pain.
Nothing helps.
I can't survive like this much longer.
I'll do *anything* to make it go away.

41

EARLY MARCH

Simon is alive.

He held my sister hostage, the lunatic. He deserves to be dead.

But he also whispered in her ear. He told her he wouldn't hurt her. That she should close her eyes and she wouldn't see anything. That he was sorry, but this is what he had to do. That he didn't see any other way.

Sharpshooters are trained to kill.

But Dad is the boss. He got my text, and he'd been compiling and analyzing Simon's profile since day one. His gut feeling told him that I was right. This was Simon's very public attempt at a suicide by cop. But it was *his* daughter up there with a gun to her head. Could he take a chance that he was wrong?

Simon was shot four times within two seconds. One shot to each hand, one shot to each kneecap. Zero shots to the heart, brain, or stomach.

So he's alive. Probably wishes he's dead. But he's alive.

* * *

When they search his room, they find a package on his neatly made bed. It's wrapped up with a bow. At first the bomb squad is called in to open it. But it's just a bunch of papers. Titled

"Stranger's Manifesto (As If You Care)." It's a whole bunch of journal entries he'd written like free-form poems. Based on what Dad tells me about them, I think they were Simon's attempt to explain himself. The newspapers are saying he had a God complex. They interview some top psychologists who talk about sociopathology and narcissism and the desperation of our youth.

I collect everything. I read it once, and then I put it away in my own little box at the back of my closet. I know my parents will think I'm obsessed if they see it. But I don't ever want to forget what happened. I figure if I keep these things in a box, then I can look at them when I want to remember and allow myself to forget about it the rest of the time.

Dad brings home a copy of the last journal entry in the Manifesto. It pisses me off.

I've read all the stories, you know.
Same as you.
About school shootings and school violence.
And it makes me want to puke my guts out.
Same as you.
I am not *that* guy. I hate that guy. I want that guy to rot in hell.
That guy is the worst piece of shit bully there is.
I just wanted to catch your attention,
And I did, didn't I?
But no one would have ever been hurt
By my hand.   -
I promise.

By the time you read this I will be dead.
I don't apologize for scaring everyone.

No offense.
It was the only way to make people sit up
And notice.

I take offense. I take a lot of offense.

I feel sorry for Simon and I'm glad he's not dead, but I take a hell of a lot of offense about the whole thing. He deserves to be locked up for a long time. Maybe forever. The district attorney just announced he plans to try him as an adult.

Because Simon, for all his earth-shattering IQ scores, is a complete idiot. There are a hundred million better ways to make a change in school culture besides terrorizing everyone. Or trying to get your brains blown out in front of a thousand people. Now he's going to spend his life in jail, instead of trying to make a difference in a way that might really matter.

What a waste.

42
APRIL

Our helpline is expanding. Paisley wrote a grant, and we got funding to buy equipment for satellite "texters." Those of us who are graduating this year can continue to support the Line in this way…from our homes and dorm rooms. Next year we'll be able to extend our hours. Janae and I are working on a "policies and procedures" manual to pass on to next year's recruits. Meanwhile, I'm enjoying the shifts. This one's almost over.

Ping! It's my 8:55 friend. **Are you still there?**

I'm here.

Nothing.

Next year we'll extend our hours, but for now we're here every night from four to nine.

Nothing.

If you like to chat late, I bet there are people you can reach out to. In previous texts you said you thought you were losing your best friend. Why don't you text her right now? Maybe you can reconnect.

Nothing.

A few minutes later I'm walking out after my shift, and my cell phone buzzes in my pocket. I take a peek. I knew it. **Hey Gabi! Are you there?**

Beth! I'm so glad you messaged me. I've been missing you. Physics is kicking my butt. I need a study partner.

Me too. Want to come over on Thursday to cram for the test?

Sure.

* * *

"Dad?" I'm waiting up for him when he gets home.

"Yeah," he answers, making a beeline for the chips and salsa.

I've got to come clean. Deep breath. "I know the combination to your safe."

He rips open the bag with his teeth and barely looks up. "I know."

"You do?"

His mouth is full. "Yeah."

"Oh." I run this over in my head for a while, and I wonder if Dad left those playing cards there on purpose for me to read. I must look totally confused, because he shoves another chip in his mouth and gives me a big wink.

43

"At least it's within driving distance," I tell Miguel. We're sitting on the sand at the beach, hip to hip, and I'm burying my feet under the warm grains.

Miguel nods, but he keeps his face forward, looking at the waves rolling in, one after another, crashing on the shore.

"And you can transfer there after you get your AA if you want," I point out for the tenth time. I got in to UCLA, early admission. I posted my acceptance letter in the center of my ceiling, so I can look at it while I fall asleep. Mom has been surprisingly supportive.

He nods again. "You've mentioned that." He keeps his eyes away from mine, and it worries me.

I am so ready to be done with high school. And to move out of my house. And move on to college.

I am so *not* ready to leave Miguel. Or Chloe.

I watch the waves for a while, loving how the rushing of the waves fills our ears and makes it easier to sit without talking. I'll start at UCLA as an undeclared, but I'm thinking of majoring in social psychology. Something about psychology tugs on me. I want to understand people. Why people do what they do. Plus I hear UCLA runs its own crisis phone line. I just might apply.

I lean into Miguel, resting my head on his collarbone. "Are you sad?"

"Why would I be *sad*?" There's a challenging tone to his voice. "You're going to college. It's what you want." He sounds mad, almost.

I lift my head up. "Are you pissed?"

"Pissed?" And suddenly I can hear humor creep into his voice, way down, like he's trying to swallow it. He answers me with a thick accent. "I am not familiar with that term. I do not need to take a piss."

I sock him in the arm, hard. "You're too much."

"Too much? I am too much man for you?" He wraps his arm around my shoulder. "No such thing as too much." And then he drops the accent. He says softly. "I'm just enough." When he turns toward me, I see that his eyes are moist. He lowers me onto my back and kisses me. The grains of sand settle in around me, and I try not to think about how much of the beach I will take home in my hair. The sun beats down on us, but in a nice way, like a blanket.

He pulls away so that we're nose to nose. "And you are just enough. I love every inch of you."

He kisses me again, deep and long, and suddenly I don't care about the sand in my hair. All I want is for this moment to last forever. His sweet taste in my mouth, his solid body pressed against mine, him wanting me. Loving me.

We'll stay together, I promise myself. I know people say that all the time and don't stick with it.

But we will.

* * *

"Come here," Chloe whispers when I walk up to the house. She's got that secretive I'm up-to-no-good look I know so well.

I brush the beach sand from in between my toes. "I've had enough trouble to last me ten years. Stay where you are."

"I'm celebrating. I've been single for a whole month, and I'm loving it. Help me celebrate. It'll be fun," she promises.

I love that she's single. It's so good for her.

"I hate fun," I tell her, trying not to laugh at her shirt. It reads "Eff Ewe See Kay Owe Eff Eff."

"It involves chocolate."

"Now you've got me."

She pulls me into the bathroom by the hand. "Feel like some secret chocolate consumption for old times' sake?"

"What the hell. I've broken just about every other rule in the book."

"Can we agree this was a stupid rule?"

"Totally idiotic."

She pulls out two hard See's Candies lollipops.

"I love these!" I squeal. "They last forever."

"Exactly. Let's park it in the shower and suck down a lollipop."

"Why not? The shower is the perfect place for a secret indulgence."

We sit and suck, sharing ideas for my room decoration. The walls have been blank now for weeks, but I don't mind. It feels clean. Fresh. When inspiration hits, I'll recognize it. Then we sit and devour our lollipops, not really talking, but that's okay. Because the quiet lets me listen to all the sounds the house makes. The sounds that are comforting and familiar and all around us. The drip of the bathroom sink, the one Mom has been after Dad to replace forever. The shushing of water in the pipes, meaning Mom has a load of laundry running. The ticking of the clock in the hall. And footsteps. Footsteps coming closer.

Out of old habit, my heart rate accelerates. I hear the hand on the doorknob, the turning. Chloe and I freeze, our lollipops stuck in our mouths, our cheeks bulging.

"Girls? You in here?"

Chloe brings her finger to her lips in an exaggerated *shh*, but because her bulging cheek makes her look like she's got a tumor, I burst out laughing.

"We're here, Mom. Come on in," I call, but the words come out all warbled because of the lollipop.

She pokes her head in, and I watch her face register what is happening here. And then she climbs in with us.

"Can I come in?" she asks, but she's already halfway in. "You don't have another one, do you?"

"Just so happens I do." Chloe reaches into her back pocket and pulls out two more.

Mom accepts one and unwraps it slowly. Her knees are drawn up to her chest and suddenly she looks young, like her years have magically vanished. "I feel like we're sneaking a smoke."

"A smoke?" Chloe clutches her heart all dramatic-like. "Mom, you never smoked!"

"Of course not." Mom pulls the lollipop out of her mouth and stares at it. "And I never had sex either."

It takes us a moment to get over the shock of her talking about sex, because aside from the save-yourself-for-marriage lecture she gave us in middle school, she never says that word. And then the ridiculousness of her statement hits us, and we laugh like we haven't laughed in years. So loud, in fact, that Dad comes into the bathroom and pokes his head in the shower. "Looks like I'm missing a party in here. Girls only?"

We invite him in, Chloe hands him the remaining lollipop, and we sit there sucking our lollipops, squished and uncomfortable with our legs folded in and up, but somehow it doesn't matter a bit.

ACKNOWLEDGMENTS

Thank you to the real Line, a crisis hotline where I worked as a "Listener" throughout college. I can't acknowledge my fellow Listeners by name due to our mutual pact to maintain confidentiality, but they know who they are. (You know who you are!) However, I'm not sure they're aware of what an impact they had on my life. Sure, I joined the Line to help other people. But the friendships, feeling of connection, and sense of purpose the Line gave me probably helped me at least as much as we helped our callers. I had spent the first year of college looking for my people, my family away from home. When I joined the Line, I knew I'd found them.

I'm no longer on a helpline, but I have my own personal Line—people who are there for me every day. My family. My husband, Rob, whom I love more every day. My kids, who make me laugh and cry and bring meaning to my life. My parents, in-laws, siblings. My wonderful circle of friends. (You know who you are!)

I would like to give a huge shout-out to all the unsung heroes working to make a difference in our schools and communities every day. You're largely under-recognized (and underpaid), but you shouldn't be! A special shout-out for the Hornets, Wolverines,

Panthers, Comets...and for all the good work you're doing for your students! Thank you to the staff at VCOE, SELPA, VCBH, CLU Community Counseling Center, Casa Pacifica, Interface, Clinicas, Apiranet, and United Parents.

Thank you to the folks who helped bring this book from an idea to a reality—Wendy, Diane, Danielle, and Kristin for whipping this book into shape; Jordan and Ellen for making it visually appealing; Mike and Annette for your marketing manpower; and Deborah, Julie, and Lisa for helping to get this project off the ground.

RESOURCES

If you (or someone you know) are having thoughts of harming yourself or someone else, help is out there. You are not alone. See below for some resources:

National Suicide Prevention Lifeline Provides free, 24-hour assistance. 1-800-273-TALK (8255).

National Hopeline Network Toll-free telephone number offering 24-hour suicide crisis support. 1-800-SUICIDE (784-2433).

The Trevor Project Crisis intervention and suicide prevention services for lesbian, gay, bisexual, transgender, and questioning (LGBTQ) youth. Includes a 24-hour hotline at 1-866-488-7386.

The "It Gets Better" Project Resources and support for LGBTQ youth. www.itgetsbetter.org

Crisis Text Line Free, 24-hour support for teens via text message. Website also includes listings for live chat support with other support organizations. www.crisistextline.org

Everyone needs support sometimes. Reach out and talk to someone. Remember…it gets better!

DISCUSSION QUESTIONS

1. Which character in the book do you most relate to and why?

2. How does Gabi's relationship with her sister, Chloe, change over the course of the book? Discuss how you relate to this changing relationship.

3. How does Gabi's role in her family change?

4. As you read the story, who do you suspect Stranger is? Why?

5. If Stranger was someone you knew, what would you have done?

6. What are Stranger's motives and rationale for his actions? What life experience influenced who he became?

7. Explain the function of Stranger's Manifesto.

8. If you were the author, would you have picked the same character to be Stranger? Select a different character to be Stranger in the story and explain why he/she would be so angry.

9. Compare and contrast Gabi's relationship with Janae and Beth.

10. Select part of the story that you find both funny and sad. Explain why the passage elicits both feelings.

11. Describe how a helpline that doesn't give advice (just listens and supports) is helpful. Are there any drawbacks to having a peer helpline in a high school? Would you use one if it were available in your school? Why or why not?

12. What would you have done if Stranger had left messages for you?

13. How much of Gabi's involvement do you think her father was aware of? Why do you think he chose not to say anything?

14. What main themes run through the story? What messages do you believe the author was trying to relay?

15. Project one year into the future. Where do you think the main characters are now?

*I'm writing to say good-bye...
please don't hate me for doing this.*

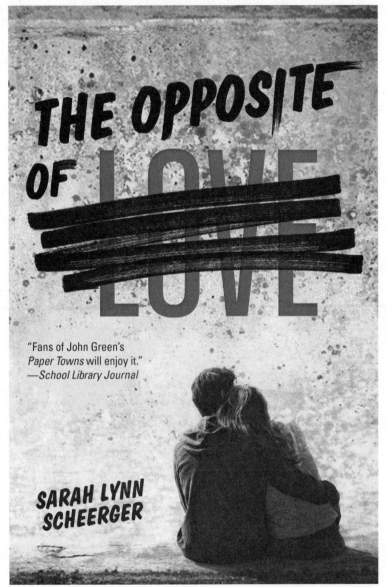

THE OPPOSITE OF ~~LOVE~~

"Fans of John Green's
Paper Towns will enjoy it."
—*School Library Journal*

SARAH LYNN
SCHEERGER

PB 978-0-8075-6131-7 $9.99

READ ON FOR A SPECIAL PREVIEW!

CHASE

CHASE'S CELL PHONE VIBRATES on his dresser. It sounds like a swarm of mosquitoes. He sits up straight in bed, slapping his hand down on the phone. *Hard*. The text message glows in the dark, and he squints while his eyes adjust.

Check your email ASAP. Then call me.—D.S.

Whatever Daniel Stein wants to tell him in the middle of the night had better be important. Bordering on earth shattering.

He groans. He considers ignoring it, but curiosity and goddamn loyalty get the best of him.

He drags himself out of bed, across his room, and down to the apartment's tiny kitchen/dining room/living room to flip on the computer. The computer warms up, humming to itself. Everything in his mother's apartment seems so much smaller than it was when he left nearly eight months ago. Still, it feels good to be home. Home for Christmas. In some ways it seems like he's never been gone, and in others it feels like a lifetime.

The cell phone vibrates again, muffled between his fingers. The cell is an early Christmas present from his dad, Walter. His first cell phone ever. Chase flips it open. Another text. Hurry, bro. Urgent.

Chase types in the user name and password for his email account. Three new messages. But when he opens his inbox, only one message jumps out at him. Untitled, but from his old girlfriend, Rose. He hasn't heard a word from her since he left. Maybe now that he's back in town, she'll want to reconnect. His heart catches.

He clicks on the message, opening it. Addressed to Daniel, Becca, and himself. Short and sweet.

> I'm writing to say good-bye. Becca, you can have anything you want from my room. Chase, I saved you a bunch of sketches. Thanks for being my friends. Please don't hate me for doing this. Love, Rose.

His mouth dries. What does that mean? *What the hell does that mean?* He stares at Rose's artwork, tacked to his wall, especially his favorite— that black-and-white chalk drawing of two hands connecting. It looks like her hand is reaching for him, as though he can hold on to her or save her or something.

Chase dials Daniel's number before he can sort out his thoughts. Daniel picks it up after half a ring. "Did you see it?"

"What the hell does it mean?"

"She's gonna kill herself! That's what it means. She's giving away her things. She's saying good-bye. Becca's freaking out over here." "Freaking out" sounds about right for Daniel's sister.

Chase tries to breathe. "I know it sounds like that. But I don't think Rose is the killing-yourself kind of girl."

"We gotta call nine-one-one," Becca's voice breaks through on the phone, like she just grabbed it from her brother's hands.

"I'm going over there," Chase decides. "Maybe I can talk her out of it."

"Shit, Chase, it might be too late." Daniel's voice pops back on.

"Or we might be wrong. Maybe she's running away. If we call the cops, we'll give her up. We both know her parents have kept her a prisoner in that house. Maybe she's finally had enough."

"I don't know..." Daniel breaks off. Chase can't remember another time he's ever heard Daniel speechless.

"Here, look. She sent the email ten minutes ago. There's time for me to get over there."

"Unless she has a gun."

"She doesn't have a gun." Chase sounds more confident than he feels. "I'll keep my cell phone on me. And I'll run."

BEFORE

CHASE

CRASHING AT DANIEL STEIN'S HOUSE had undeniable perks. The biggest perk was the sister factor. Younger sisters have hot friends, especially when they're only a year behind you in school and they just got their braces off. The second biggest perk, and the one that most often led him to stay over, was avoiding his own mom and the brewing of World War III on the home front.

Chase didn't bother to knock, just let himself right in like always. He found Daniel lounging in the living room, his earbuds tucked into his ears. Chase flicked a dangling blue-and-silver foil menorah and looked pointedly at Daniel. "Chanukah decorations?"

"It's been November for a whole freaking week, bro," Daniel said, taking the earbuds out. "Besides, you know my mom." He gestured to an overflowing box of Halloween skeletons and bats, decorations that had been up three days ago.

"I know your mom." Chase flopped onto the taupe suede couch—the kind of couch you could sink into. Everything about the Stein house felt like home. Well, not like *his* home. But the way he always imagined home *should* feel. "Is she cooking tonight?"

"Are you inviting yourself over *again?*"

"There a problem with that?" Chase grinned.

"Not as long as there's enough food for me." Daniel patted his belly. For such a compact guy, he sure could put away a lot of latkes and roast. "Besides, you're not the only one. Becca's got a friend staying over too."

"Seriously?" Chase had been hoping that.

"Yeah, that Rose girl. The one who looks like an exotic porn star."

Chase knew who she was right way. "She's hot," he agreed. Suddenly, he wished he'd taken the time to pull on a clean T-shirt or comb his hair. He leaned over to catch a look at himself in the long, oval hallway mirror. His brown hair hung all messy and half covering his eyes, like it always did, even when he *had* combed it.

Daniel grinned. "I thought that'd cheer you up."

"Cheer me up? I'm a goddamn pillar of sunshine. What're you talking about? I don't need cheering up!"

Daniel ignored this, leaping up and tackling Chase on the couch. He rubbed his knuckles in Chase's hair. "What, your mom bring home some guy again?"

"Don't want to talk about it." Chase grabbed on and held both of Daniel's wrists in one of his hands, keeping him an arm's distance away. Chase nearly doubled Daniel's size, so Daniel twisted and squirmed, trying to wrench a hand free.

Chase loosened his hold and Daniel scrambled away, back to a safe distance on the couch. "Your dad's not back, is he?"

"I don't want to talk about it," Chase repeated. For all Daniel's self-piercings and pen-doodled tattoos, he was a good kid with one of those normal cookie-cutter lives. Not like Chase.

"Okay, okay." Daniel grinned. "Go visit the girls. That'll cheer you up."

Chase ran his fingers through his curls and took a deep breath.

"Right on, bro. I like the way you think. I'm gonna wander over there like I'm looking for you. Sound believable?" Chase didn't wait for an answer, just turned and headed that way.

ABOUT THE AUTHOR

Sarah Lynn Scheerger is the author of *The Opposite of Love* and several books for younger readers. *Are You Still There* was inspired in part by her time volunteering for a helpline in college, an experience that led to her career as a clinical social worker. Today Sarah runs counseling groups for at-risk teens on middle and high school campuses. She lives and writes in Southern California with her family. Visit her online at www.sarahlynnbooks.com.